Cam's Quest

The Continuing Story

of

Princess Nevermore

and the

Wizard's Apprentice

Cam's Quest

The Continuing Story

of

Princess Nevermore

and the

Wizard's Apprentice

∾

by Dian Curtis Regan

Cataloging-in-Publication

Regan, Dian Curtis.
Cam's Quest : the continuing story of Princess Nevermore and the
wizard's apprentice / by Dian Curtis Regan.
    p. ; cm.
ISBN-13: 978-1-58196-056-3
ISBN-10: 1-58196-056-5
Sequel to: Princess Nevermore.—Summary: Cam stood by while
Princess Quinn ventured from Mandria to Outer Earth last year.
Now, his world has changed completely, and it's his turn to travel to
Outer Earth to find his identity while Princess Quinn waits in
Mandria.
1. Apprentices—Juvenile fiction. 2. Princesses—Juvenile fiction. 3.
Identity (Psychology)—Juvenile fiction. 4. Quests (Expeditions)—
Juvenile fiction. [1. Apprentices—Fiction. 2. Princesses—Fiction. 3.
Identity—Fiction. 4. Quests (Expeditions)—Fiction. 5. Fantasy.] I.
Title.
PZ7.R25854 Cam 2006
[Fic] dc22
OCLC: 70696309

Published by Darby Creek Publishing,
A division of Oxford Resources, Inc.
7858 Industrial Parkway
Plain City, OH 43064
www.darbycreekpublishing.com

Printed in the United States of America

1 2 3 4 5 6 7 8 9

For Jane Kurtz,
Joanne Stanbridge,
Nancy Werlin,
and
Deborah Wiles,
who know how to make magic
with words and pictures

ACKNOWLEDGEMENTS

Special thanks to Ginger Knowlton, Tanya Dean,
Debra Seely, Clare Vanderpool, Lois Ruby,
Lee Wardlaw, and Sally Hefley.

Contents

1

Melikar's True Apprentice

"She won't eat, Sire."

Cam hushed his voice even though the comment begged to be shouted as he hastened into the uppermost chamber of the underground castle that sprawled beneath the Mandrian River.

But the topic was a dangerous one. He feared he'd say the wrong words and Princess Quinn would be lost to him forever.

Melikar, a wizard known in the world above the river as well as in the world below, sat in a chair by the fire. Lifting his concerned gaze, he fixed it on his young apprentice. "It is almost time for the princess's sixteenth year to begin."

Cam knew what the wizard's comment meant. He needn't respond since there was no good answer to the dilemma. If Quinn did not choose one of the many suitors swarming the kingdom of Mandria like cats swarm the Marnie tunnels, King Marit would choose for her. A suitor for his daughter to marry.

Cam shuddered just thinking about it.

Bad enough to watch a handsome parade of knights and noblemen presented nightly at one ball or another, but the thought of the princess choosing one who caught her fancy was more than Cam could bear.

He'd tried to foil the hopeful lads' efforts by calling up every bit of the weak magic he possessed. When the arrogant knight from Tenningham danced an estampie with Quinn, Cam whispered a simple spell that cursed the knave with clammy hands.

A mumbled chant was all it took to make the noble twit from Pelling stomp on the princess's jeweled Mandrian slippers every third note of the pavane. And for the King of Wick's haughty eldest son? The one who'd ordered Cam to stable his horse as if he were a lowly manservant? Well, a malodorous spell worked better than he'd foreseen.

Cam had to step behind a marble pillar to hide his delight as he watched maidens in fancy gowns flee from the Prince of Wick, holding kerchiefs to their dainty noses until the prince stomped angrily from the Great Hall.

As much as he enjoyed the mild curses, Cam's most urgently needed charm was an enchantment to make Quinn realize her prince had been here in the kingdom all along. Her childmate. Her confidant. The one who adored her.

But fate had rolled two boulders onto his path, blocking his way.

First, he was the Un-noble Cam of Mandria, born not of nobility, but of mystery, dashing him out of the race before he could compete.

Certainly his heritage was a puzzle, but he doubted he would one day wake to discover he was the long-lost prince of one of the underground kingdoms, batted on the head as a child and left abandoned for Melikar to raise, not knowing of his royal lineage.

As much as Cam would love it to be true, that faery tale would never become a Mandrian truth. He knew his age—seventeen—but did not even know the day of his birth.

The second boulder in his path was Adam Dover, a lad Quinn met during her sojourn to Outer Earth almost a year ago. *I was meant to accompany her,* Cam thought. *It was my duty to watch over the princess and keep her safe.*

I failed.

Sighing, the apprentice recalled the boggled spell that'd sent the princess into the other world, completely unescorted. But this is what he feared most: Adam, the Outer-Earth lad who'd captured her heart, must be reckoned with before the princess could choose her future.

An insistent rapping at the portal drew Cam's attention.

"Enter!" Melikar ordered, seeming annoyed by another interruption.

Cam opened the door. There stood a snip of a lad, no bigger than a full-grown Marnie. The top of his head barely reached Cam's waist. Puzzled, Cam asked, "May I assist you?"

The lad strode into the chamber as if he'd been invited, drew off his cloak, and dropped a worn satchel onto the floor. "I am Baywin of Cocklethorn, and I'm seven years old," he declared, as if announcing the king himself.

Cam laughed at the boldness of such a tiny fellow. "And you've come to court the princess?" he asked in jest.

"Of course not," Baywin answered, staring up at Cam in scorn. "I have come to be Melikar's true apprentice."

"Apprentice?" Cam repeated, then guffawed at the sprite's mistake. "I am sorry but Melikar already *has* an apprentice, and there's not much room for—"

"Welcome," came the wizard's voice.

Cam whirled to gape at his usually gruff master, not expecting him to respond with such kindness.

"I have been expecting you," Melikar added.

Cam turned back to the lad. "Who are you again?"

The boy simply grinned, dropping his voice to a whisper so Melikar would not hear. "You have a hideous rat on your shoulder."

"I do not!"

"Then, pray, what is this?" Baywin flicked his hand toward Cam, and when he pulled it away, a scruffy gray rat hunched in his palm, nose twitching.

"I—I—" Cam began, whirling again to see if Melikar had witnessed the improper use of magic and would thereby scold the imp. But the wizard was putting on a cloak to depart.

"Please prepare a cot for Baywin," Melikar said, "and make him feel welcome. I must go speak to the princess." Pausing to stroke his beard in a thoughtful manner, he added, "I must see if there is anything I can do."

"Do?" Cam repeated. *As in—hasten her choice of a husband?* "Sire, please do not—"

The wizard's glance silenced him. One did not question an elder's decision. It was a Mandrian truth, and Mandrian truths could not be argued.

Melikar disappeared down the spiral rock stairway, amber cloak trailing behind.

Cam's heart skittered as he closed the heavy oak door. The matter was out of his hands. His magic was not strong enough to cause further delays. In fact, he wondered if his selfishness had already sent Quinn undue pain. For that, he was truly sorry.

A sharp kick in the shins reminded Cam of the uninvited guest.

"Ow!" he cried, turning to face the lad. But the boy was not behind him. "How did you—?"

Cam's gaze was drawn to the center of the chamber where the lad, still holding the rat, stood in the circle of light, staring up through the underside of the wishing pool. The pool served as Mandria's always-clear window to the outer world. Always clear because of a spell Melikar cast long ago to keep the water from splashing down into his chamber.

"So this is it," Baywin whispered in a voice filled with awe.

The lad's fascination reminded Cam that the existence of the pool was mostly a child's tale whispered among lads and lasses. They did not know if the stories were true or fanciful rumors—unless one of their kin happened to see it, and few had reason to find their way to Melikar's chamber.

Cam watched the air around the lad shimmer in the muted light, the same way it glimmered when Melikar stepped into the circle.

Baywin's words came back to him: "I have come to be Melikar's true apprentice." *True*, because he, himself, had been only a substitute—a *poor* substitute with not enough magic to cause any sort of shimmer around himself—or even to make a rodent appear with such ease.

Baywin obviously belonged here with Melikar. He did not.

So, Cam thought. *The princess will marry, and this whip of a lad shall follow in the great wizard's footsteps.*

And me?

There is no place for me. I am an imposter. I came from nowhere—and nowhere shall certainly become my ultimate destination.

2

Searching for a Future: Quinn

$\sim$

Princess Quinn fanned herself as she waited in the stifling chamber, deep below Mandria's wide tunneled avenues. She was in the Marnie village, watching old Grizzle fashion a lump of gold into a ring.

His fur almost matched the gold of the band, yet was shaggy with age. Quinn figured he must be more than three hundred years old—ancient, but not as old as Melikar, who was ageless.

Lifting the gold band with tongs, Grizzle held it over the flames. In spite of his thick fur, the top of his head was bald—and almost as shiny as the metal in the firelight.

Quinn backed away from the heat but did not take her eyes off the glistening gold. How ironic to watch the making of a marriage band. Everyone in the kingdom had paused their lives, waiting for their princess to announce her intention to marry, yet the ring Grizzle crafted with care would not be worn by her. It would belong to Ameka.

My beloved tutor and my cousin, Dagon, in love, Quinn thought. *I could not have imagined a more perfect match. If only I could find the same.*

The princess heaved such a heavy sigh, Grizzle cocked a curious brow and studied her.

Quinn avoided his gaze, even though she knew he would never ask any questions. Marnies were care-takers of the underground kingdoms, so it certainly wasn't Grizzle's role to offer opinions to the future queen of Mandria.

After the ring cooled and the fancy-lettered inscription—*Hearts Embraced Forever*—passed the Marnie's scrutiny, he dropped the band into a leather pouch and gave it to the princess.

Quinn was eager to leave the Marnie tunnels. They were narrower and dimmer than those above, and so full of cats, it was difficult to walk without stepping on a tail here or a paw there. The Marnies' soft, padded hooves were not a threat to the cats.

When she reached the wide, airy tunnels of upper Mandria, Quinn pulled a hood over her head to hide her identity as she dodged a horse and carriage. Usually Cam or Ameka accompanied her about the kingdom for safety, but this quick errand she preferred to do alone.

She did not want to be recognized because every-one seemed to have an opinion about whom she should marry. "That knight from Bootle is quite the handsome one, Your Highness!" Mrs. Cantor, the baker's wife, had called earlier.

Hiding was easier than answering, yet in this case, her answer would be: "And all the knight from Bootle talks about is becoming the future king of Mandria—by marrying me."

With a stinging heart, the princess remembered a lad who saw only her—not who she was or who she might become. And he loved her.

Quinn hurried down the lane that led to the tiny cottage where Ameka lived alone, now that both parents were gone. Rapping on the door, she tried not to daydream about the Outer-Earth lad, but stifling her memories was difficult.

Adam.

Remembering him was an old wound that never stopped aching. How could she marry another after the way he'd once gazed at her? Was true love nothing more than a jester's tale?

The door swung open, and an excited Ameka drew Quinn inside. The usually plain cottage burst with spring blossoms, grown in the Marnie grotto. Pots of pennyroyal, wild succory, and red heather bloomed on every windowsill, stool, and table. Bergamot, sweet laurel, and candleberry circled the floor like faery rings. Tansy and freesia decorated the hearth.

Quinn gasped as she took it all in.

"I cannot stop smiling!" Ameka exclaimed.

The princess laughed with her former tutor, who was only three years older. Ameka's lengths of chestnut hair matched her plain gown. *What a shame to cut her beautiful locks before the wedding,* Quinn thought, but such was the law in Mandria.

"Tell me how my cousin proposed," Quinn said, winding her way through the colorful blossoms.

Ameka removed a pot of lady's bedstraw from a stool so the princess could sit. "A small army of Marnies carried in the bouquets, then Dagon arrived, kneeled in my cottage garden, and asked for my hand in marriage."

Quinn folded both hands over her heart. "I am so happy for you. And now we shall be family! I just wish . . ."

"You wish there were more time?" Ameka asked. "Ay, we do have to marry and leave for Pendrog Manor as soon as the marriage celebration is over."

"Yes," Quinn agreed. "Were it not for the war in Twickingham, my cousin could tarry, like he used to when his father came to visit."

Ameka nodded in sympathy as she perched on a stool next to the princess. "Did you obtain it?"

"Oh, the ring!" Quinn pulled the leather pouch from the pocket of her cloak and withdrew the band for Ameka to examine.

"It's lovely," Ameka said, handling it gingerly. "You will stand with me at the ceremony, won't you? And see that Cam remembers to come?"

"Of course, I'll stand with you. And I'll make sure Cam is dressed nicely, and his hair is combed for once."

Ameka laughed. "Darling Cam, raised by an old wizard without a mother to tell him to straighten his tunic and smooth his hair."

"Well, I think he turned out quite fine," Quinn said. "And handsome as well." Not one of the arriving nobles had been near as amusing as Cam, nor as deliciously wicked at just the right moment.

Bother, she thought, hating to even think about the long line of suitors and their pretentious attempts at cleverness as they tried to win her favor. They were not charming; they were boring.

"Go on," the princess said, urging Ameka to tell her more so she would not have to think of what awaited her tonight in the Great Hall.

"The wedding will be in Albans Chapel," Ameka told her. "Lord Derry shall preside."

Quinn watched Ameka's eyes flash with joy. "I shall miss you so," the princess told her.

"I shall miss you, too," Ameka said. "But I promise to return for *your* wedding. If passage is safe, I mean. Dagon says the Bromlians have invaded south of Ashford."

Quinn stopped listening after the words "your wedding."

"Oh, wise tutor, tell me what to do," she said. "My time is running out, and not even turning away food has persuaded my father to allow me another half year to find the one with whom I want to share my life and future kingdom."

"Are you still thinking about . . . ?"

Quinn nodded. "I know it is foolish to consider, but I wish I could make one last visit to Outer Earth just to see him again."

Ameka faltered at the princess's words. "The king does not know about your *first* visit, and he would *never* allow—"

"But I long to know if Adam still wants us to be together. If he does not, then I can go down the path I must tread here in Mandria. Not knowing is a curse."

A knock sounded on the door. Before Ameka could rise, it flew open. "Melikar!" she cried. "What brings you to my humble cottage?"

The wizard greeted Ameka, taking in the flowered surroundings without reacting, as if he already knew. Turning his gaze to the princess, he spoke. "Is that what it would take? For the Outer-Earth lad and you to come face to face once more?"

Quinn did not question how Melikar came to be at Ameka's door or how he knew the words she had just spoken. He was a most powerful wizard.

"Is it possible? Oh, Melikar, is it?"

Tilting his head, he studied her. "I believe, dear child, you may have picked the best solution."

Ameka looked from one to the other in confusion. Yet the wizard's words made hope spin into Quinn's heart.

"When can we do this?" she asked.

"There is not much time. The king will soon choose your prince, and I believe you would rather make that choice?"

Before Quinn could answer, Melikar began to speak once more, yet this time, what he said did not make sense. The strange words filled the cottage as full as the blossoms, until the room tilted precariously.

Grabbing Ameka's hands, the princess held on in fear and awe.

Blue fog swirled inside the cottage, blocking the light. The icy air made Quinn shiver. When the fog cleared, all three were standing in Melikar's chamber.

The princess let go of Ameka's hands, pivoting to view her surroundings as she realized what had just happened. There was Cam, standing beneath the wishing pool, looking quite startled. A lad she'd never seen before stood next to him. A rat wiggled in the boy's hand, but with a subtle flick of the lad's head, the rat disappeared. It happened so quickly, Quinn was not sure she had seen it at all.

Melikar gathered everyone around and told them of his plan. "I am certain the princess would prefer not to have spectators, so, Ameka, please take Baywin on a tour of the castle."

Agreeing, Ameka offered her hand to the lad, but he acted miffed at not being allowed to stay. Urging him from the chamber with the promise of sweets, she turned back to Quinn, giving an earnest nod, which, the princess assumed, was for luck.

"Cam," Melikar said. "You may stay, if you choose."

But Cam was backing toward the portal with such a despondent look on his face Quinn's breath caught in her throat. In two steps he was gone, leaving the princess to wonder why his sudden departure so deeply troubled her heart.

3

Face to Face

The princess trembled as she waited in the shadows of the wizard's chamber. She could scarcely breathe. Absently fidgeting with her lion-colored braid, it occurred to her that, before marrying, she, too, would be bound to cut her hair after growing it all of her life. *How odd it will be not to have the braid tumbling down my back.*

She watched Melikar pace from hearth to herb cabinet and back again, passing each time beneath the wishing pool, mumbling softly, motioning with his hands.

What kind of magic will it take to bring the lad from Outer Earth to Mandria? she wondered. *And what kind of shock will it be to the poor boy's heart?*

A rippling sound drew Quinn's attention to the water in the wishing pool. Water that was always as smooth as a looking glass was beginning to swirl.

It's happening, she thought. *The same way it happened when I stood beneath the pool and was drawn up into the outer world.*

The water swirled faster and faster until she became dizzy with the sensation. Then, before her eyes, a figure appeared, sprawled on the cobbled-rock floor in the circle of light. Leaping to his feet, the lad braced himself, as if ready to fight, yet not knowing who the enemy might be.

The person, who was completely dry, acted befuddled. When he realized there was no immediate threat, he unclenched his fists, turning one way, then the other, trying to decipher his surroundings.

But it wasn't Adam!

Quinn's heart shrank in disappointment. How could the wizard make such a mistake? How could he bring the wrong lad to Mandria? This wasn't a lad at all. This was a grown man. Taller than Adam, with broad shoulders and the shortest hair she'd ever seen. Hair almost completely shaved off.

He was dressed in garments the color of dry sand, with clunky boots like those worn by knights going off to battle.

"Welcome," Melikar said to the stunned visitor. Holding out his hand to Quinn, he urged her toward the circle. "Come, Princess."

The man followed Melikar's gaze. "Quinn!" he cried. "Is it really you?"

26

In two strides he crossed the chamber, grasping her hands to draw her into the light as if wanting to see her better. "It *is* you. You look exactly the same."

"Yes," Melikar put in quickly. "She looks the same because she *is* the same age as when last you saw her." He backed away into the shadows so the two could speak.

Quinn stared at the man's face, the eyes, the smile. "Adam? Ay, you do *not* look the same."

He laughed. Wrinkles she did not remember crinkled his eyes. Taking in the entire chamber, he shook his head, as if finding himself in the middle of a storybook he'd once read. "I must be in your kingdom," he said. "Mandria, is it? How did I—? Why am I—?"

Quinn glanced at the wizard, and he nodded. She knew he was giving her freedom to say what she wanted. But now that she finally stood face to face with Adam, words deserted her. The person before her was not the one she had spent hours dreaming about. He looked like a stranger.

She waited while Adam peered at the curved rock walls, the cabinets of tinctures and herbs, the simple oak furnishings. Then he turned his gaze to her with the same intensity. "Answers are coming to me even though no one has spoken. I cannot tell you how many hours I thought about you during the year you came into my life. And the next year, and the next."

"Ay, the time difference," Quinn said in a hushed voice. She knew Outer-Earth folk aged faster than

Mandrians, yet she had refused to apply it to herself and Adam.

Adam's smile faded, and his eyes turned serious. "I look older because I *am* older, and you are not. I didn't know about the time difference until after you left. I wondered if that's what you'd started to tell me the last time we spoke."

She nodded, remembering their last moments together on the night of the Halloween ball.

"Mondo explained it to me," he added.

"Mondo," Quinn repeated. "How is your grandfather?" she asked, thinking about the Mandrian who had defied Melikar and chosen to live on Outer Earth with the maiden he loved. Mondo was still in the world of his beloved's, yet old age had taken Hannah, his Outer-Earth wife, generations ago.

"He is ailing, Quinn. Not good. Even though a Mandrian ages only one year while the rest of us age more than three, their life in either world must eventually come to an end, yes?"

She nodded. The news of Mondo's ill health saddened her. She had cared about him even while resisting his wish for her not to spend time with Adam—all because he knew how much pain the time difference would bring them.

Quinn shook it from her mind and focused on the person standing before her. Somewhere inside him lived the young lad she once knew and loved. Where was he? If she stood here long enough, would she glimpse what used to take her breath away?

Or had she spent all this time dreaming of a person who no longer existed? *Stop*, she told herself. *Talk to him now that you have the chance. Ask all the questions you have longed to ask.*

"What of your sister?" the princess said. "How does she fare?"

"Sarah is married now—to Scott—and has a child."

"True?" Quinn tried to imagine the young maiden whose chamber she had once shared at the Dover home now a wife and mother, and it made her smile. She remembered Scott, too, the shy red-haired lad who adored Sarah.

"And you?" Quinn added. "What of your life?"

"I graduated early from the university and joined the Army." He hesitated, as if watching to see if she understood. "Surely you have armies in Mandria?"

"Of course," Quinn said, suddenly alarmed by the idea of Adam riding off into battle.

"I just arrived home on leave, due to Mondo's condition. Before I had time to change out of my uniform, I suddenly ended up here." He glanced about, still seeming awestruck by his surroundings.

"I never thought I'd see you again," he added. Emotion hushed his words. "I've avoided marriage in hopes of someday finding you, and here I have. You're just as beautiful as you always were, but I am shocked that you are still the young girl I knew in high school. My life has moved so far away from those years."

Quinn nodded, understanding his shock because she was feeling it, too. Not that she couldn't fall in love with him again, but the distress washing over her was something more. This is what Mondo so desperately tried to warn her about. Now she could see the inevitable with her own eyes. The time difference was real. It had brought Mondo and Hannah terrible unhappiness. When the two met and fell in love, they were close to the same age, yet when Hannah became an old woman and died, Mondo was only in his forties.

The same fate would befall her and Adam. When he turned thirty, she would just be turning nineteen.

Thinking about this when she'd first met him had not seemed so awful, but looking at him now made it all too real. The sadness in his eyes told her he realized it as well.

Not even Melikar could cast a spell to alter the inevitable. It was a Mandrian truth.

Reaching out, Quinn touched Adam's arm—a forbidden gesture beneath the river, but she knew it was acceptable in the outer world—touching a person when you had something important to say. "This can never be," were the only words that came to her. She watched for his reaction, wanting his acknowledgement that she was seeing things clearly.

Adam paused a long time before answering, and in those uncertain moments, she finally glimpsed him—the vulnerable lad she once knew. Something in his intense gaze shifted. This was the way he'd looked at her long ago after realizing she might not remain with him in his

world. This was the loving gaze she had carried in her
heart ever since.

"No, Quinn," he finally answered. "There can never
be anything more between us." A telltale quiver softened
his words. "I see that now, and I know you do, too."

Quinn felt the need to say more, but the words
became vipers on her tongue. "Do you . . . Will you . . . ?"

He grasped her arms as if knowing what she was
trying to ask and wanting to help. "I think this meeting
has set us both free. Free to build lives in our own
worlds, where we each are meant to remain."

He was right, of course. She could not ask him to
stay in Mandria, giving up his entire life in his own
world. Besides, he would never be accepted by the
royal family or by Mandrian folk. Likewise, he could
not ask her to deny her royal heritage and return to the
outer world with him.

Adam smiled at her with a heart-breaking gentle-
ness, as if reading her thoughts. "You are only fifteen.
In my world, you're not old enough to marry without
your parents' permission. And my friends would think
it quite odd of me to marry a teenager."

Teenager? Quinn had forgotten that word, but now
that he'd said it, she remembered hearing it in his world.

Adam faced the wizard. "Sir, I thank you for this
incredible gift. I would have spent my entire life wondering 'what if?' Now I can see with my own eyes how
that scenario would play out."

Melikar gave a slight bow. Quinn could see relief on

the wizard's face and knew he must be feeling immense satisfaction. He had brought to a close the final chapter of a story that was never meant to be written.

The princess shared his feelings of relief. Ignoring royal protocol, she slipped her arms around Adam's neck. He returned the hug warmly and with great tenderness. "Be happy and safe," he whispered into her hair.

"And you," she whispered back. "Thank you for releasing my heart so I can search for my future."

"And I say the same to you."

Quinn let him go, stepping back into the shadows to watch his departure.

Melikar moved toward Adam and spoke softly to him, which scratched Quinn's curiosity. Stepping out of the circle of light, the wizard began to spin his magic from the hearth. Mumbling a chant, he stirred the cauldron with a ladle. In seconds, the water in the wishing pool began to swirl.

While the princess watched, Adam, the lad she once believed was her heart's desire, was drawn up into the pool and out of her life for the final time.

Rushing to the circle, she gazed up at the outer world. The rushing water slowly settled back into stillness. Now she could see the footbridge arching over the river, a fringe of spring leaves bursting from branches, and sunshine lighting a blue sky.

Adam remained on the footbridge, gazing into the pool for a long moment. Taking a coin from his pocket, he kissed it and tossed it into the pool. The coin, unaffected by the wizard's spell, fell through the pool and *plinged* onto the cobbled rock floor of the chamber.

Quinn's breath faltered as she picked it up. It wasn't a coin at all, but rather, the magic ring Cam had made on that long-ago day. The ring that accidentally traveled to the other world with her. Adam was returning it.

Clasping the ring in her hand, Quinn gazed through the now-clear window of the pool, watching Adam stride down the curve of the bridge and off into the rest of his life.

"Melikar?" she asked. "What was it you said to him before he departed?"

The wizard joined the princess in the circle of light. "I told him to tell Mondo, if he so desires, he may come home to Mandria to die."

4

Touring
the Castle

Cam trailed along a stone corridor behind Ameka and
Baywin, dragging his feet and feeling lower than a pebble in
the deepest pool of the grotto.

The thing he feared most was happening this
moment, up in Melikar's chamber. Quinn and the lad
from the other world were being reunited. Could things
turn any worse? As unworthy as her suitors had been,
at least if she married someone beneath the river, she
would stay in his world. Wasn't that better than his
princess going off to a place where he would never see
her again?

Cam did not know a heart could ache so sorely.

Up ahead, Ameka stopped to call back to him. "I want
to show Baywin the kitchen. Come with us?"

Shrugging, Cam followed the two down a winding

stairway to the lowest level of the castle. The air warmed as they grew closer to the cooking area, reminding him of the Marnie chambers.

The kitchen was massive. Fires crackled in all four corners and were kept roaring most of the day and night. Plucked chickens dangled from the ceiling. Pheasants lay in a pile on a chunky wooden table. Baby goats hung across the far wall beside bunches of herbs, drying in the stifling heat.

Marged, the head cook, barely noticed the arrival of the threesome as she bustled about, calling orders to the kitchen maidens. Some, about the age of Baywin, were stirring pots, pounding grains, or mixing great vats of flour and lard for meat pies.

Three pages entered from a tunnel that came from the stable. They carried the carcass of a doe, brought in from the hunting chambers. Gesturing with a skillet, Marged looked as if she were conducting the choir at Albans Chapel as she directed the pages toward an alcove where fresh kill was skinned.

Cam listened while Ameka told Baywin how busy the kitchen had been all week, preparing nightly feasts for the visiting suitors. Cam did not fail to see the look of endearment on Baywin's face as he attentively watched and listened to Ameka.

"She has won him over in a matter of moments," Cam mumbled beneath his breath, "but me, he looks at with scorn."

Can he tell I'm an imposter, not worthy to sweep

dust from the cobbled stones of Melikar's chamber?

Still, Cam thought. *The lad could be kinder to me.*

With a bit of commotion, the princess burst into the kitchen, pulled by Scrabit, her tiny pet dragon, on his leash. She laughed at her unroyal entrance. "I told Scrabit to find Cam, and find you he did."

"Get that creature out of my kitchen!" Marged barked. Her expression switched from anger to remorse as she recognized the person she'd screamed at. Dropping to one knee, she exclaimed, "Forgive me, Your Highness, I did not realize it was you."

"Arise, Marged," Quinn said. "Foolish of me to bring him in here."

Scrabit was determined to nab a Cornish game hen fleeing for its life among the table legs. The princess yanked on the dragon's leash, pulling him out into the corridor. In his haste to follow, Cam almost collided with a maid lugging a sack of sugar.

"I have something to show you," the princess said, presenting one hand to him.

The ring on her middle finger looked familiar, but it took him a moment to place it. "Ah, the token I made the day you—" He stopped abruptly, as if that was the intended end of his comment. He avoided talking about her adventures in the other world. As curious as he was, the conversation always turned to the lad she'd met, and he would rather not listen to her speak of him.

"How did you . . . ?" The answer came to him before she could explain it.

"Adam gave it to me. He tossed it into the wishing pool, and it fell through the spell the way coins do."

"So he did not come through himself?" Cam asked, hope filling his heart that she hadn't actually talked to the lad.

"Oh, yes, he did."

Quinn's expression darkened as her thoughts turned inward.

The next question was so difficult for Cam to ask that he could barely form the words. "Are you coming here to tell me good-bye?"

"Pardon? Oh, no, of course not."

"You are not going to the other world to be with him?"

"Ay, no. I could not. My life is here."

Cam's poor brain felt taxed as he tried to determine what the princess was telling him. "Is he staying in Mandria then?"

"No, Cam, you do not understand. My life is not with him—neither here nor there. Alas, my life is still a mystery, but I shall remain in our world."

Relief made Cam want to grasp her shoulders with joy. But he restrained himself, more from shyness than royal protocol.

"I wanted you to have your ring back," Quinn said. Slipping it off her finger, she carefully handed it to him. "I think the magic may have faded since the token was out of our world for so long."

Cam refrained from telling her that the magic was never strong to begin with. But, he recalled, it *had* been strong enough to put her into grave danger in the other world.

He slid the ring onto his finger, thinking how odd it was to have it back after believing it was lost forever. "Shall we take Scrabit for a run in the outer tunnels?" he asked, willing his voice to be light and playful. They'd previously talked of riding to Oxbury Falls to see how strong the underground currents had become as a result of spring rains in the outer world.

The princess answered with a groan. "I would love to, but it is time for my ladies to start their pinching and pulling and other agonies they put me through to get me ready for the evening's festivities."

Cam nodded as though it mattered little to him when, in truth, her words tightened his chest until he could barely breathe. Could this be the night the princess would meet the one who pleased her most?

"Oh, I almost forgot," Quinn added. "Melikar needs you to return to his chamber at once."

"Princess!" Baywin called. "Come watch what I can make!"

Cam opened the door to the kitchen. Baywin and Ameka were elbow-deep in batter, helping a maiden shape lemon cakes with poppy seeds.

"Coming!" Quinn called.

Cam noticed that he, himself, was not included in Bay's invitation.

Quinn offered the dragon's leash to Cam. "Would you mind taking Scrabit back to my ladies on your way to Melikar's chamber?"

Cam grasped the leash, urging the dragon to come with him. Averting his eyes from Quinn's, he started off down the corridor. If his master hadn't needed him at this moment, he might have tarried in the kitchen with the others, rolling up his sleeves and helping to divide batter into tea cakes.

Perhaps he might discover that he possessed a knack for making cakes instead of making magic. He could move his apprenticeship duties from Melikar's chamber to Marged's kitchen.

Cam sighed at his depressing thoughts, yet finding *some* sort of talent might brighten a future that looked rather dim and hopeless at the present time.

5

Free
to Seek

In the inner courtyard of the castle, outside the royal tower where the princess lived with her parents, King Marit and Queen Leah, Cam ran into Jalla, Quinn's former nanny. She was chatting with a castle guard about the war in Twickingham and the heroic deeds of Dagon, son of Lord Ryswick. The lord's departed wife had been King Marit's sister.

As Cam handed Scrabit's leash to Jalla, twinges of envy twisted his heart. Dagon. Heroic deeds. Battles in Twickingham. *And here am I, watching over a pet dragon, tending Melikar's fire, and sweeping the hearth. What a noble calling.*

In truth, Cam liked Dagon—who was now betrothed to Ameka. The lad used to join Quinn and him on adventures in the hidden tunnels when they all were very young.

The twinge made him question his feelings. How could he feel envious of a kingdom under attack by the cruel Bromlians?

No, it was not envy for the war, but envy that Dagon knew his purpose. Not only was he the son of a wealthy nobleman and a Knight of the First Order, but his days were filled with strategies of battle, matching wits with the enemy, and one exciting adventure after another. Or so Cam imagined.

Add to that, taking home a bride, who happened to be one he chose and truly loved. Cam had seen the way he and Ameka gazed at each other once they got past the age of chasing and teasing.

After the wedding celebration, Dagon and Ameka would ride off to Twickingham, where Ameka would become the new Lady Ryswick of Pendrog Manor.

Cam sighed. Perhaps the new bride and new home were more the cause of his envy. As for the invading Bromlians, Cam was not the only one who did not understand why King Marit refused to send the mighty Mandrian army to push them back to their own kingdom. Under ill advice from Lord Blakely, his advisor, the king had decided that Mandria had seen too many wars to become involved in this one.

As he hurried up the spiral stone steps to Melikar's chamber, Cam shook off the depressing thoughts and gladly focused on the newest Mandrian truth: The princess and the lad from the other world had parted ways for good.

This news lifted his spirits so much, he began to hum. How long had he worried about it? Now, the dreadful topic flew out of his mind quicker than a red-feathered trega skimming the tops of wych elms along the avenues of Mandria.

Entering the wizard's chamber, Cam stopped humming. On the floor sat his knapsack and a small trunk he'd never seen. On its curved lid, blue paint was peeling off the image of a horse.

"What is this?" he asked, certain it had something to do with the arrival of the impudent Baywin from Cocklethorn, who was presently charming the princess and Ameka in the castle kitchen.

"Cam of Mandria," Melikar began. "You have been a loyal apprentice for all of your stay with me."

Cam's blood ran cold as he listened to his master's words. Was Melikar sending him away? Where was he to go?

"Are you dismissing me from service?" Cam blurted. "Merely because someone better has come to assist you?"

Momentary confusion touched the wizard's face. "No, lad, you do not understand. I have known about Baywin since his birth—nay, before his birth. I knew he would possess a special gift for enchantments. It is rare, but it happens as it happened to me. Baywin's mother traveled to Mandria after his birth to seek advice. Thus it was determined years ago that the lad would come to me for proper training. Bay's life and future here have nothing to do with you."

Melikar's words calmed Cam—but not much.

"You, my faithful follower, have a higher calling."

This news perked Cam up immensely. "Higher calling?" he repeated.

"It is time you learn of your past in order to travel toward your destiny."

Cam had waited years to hear the story of his life. He was eager to settle in by the fire and listen. "Are you finally going to tell me?"

Melikar busied himself over a concoction he was mixing on his worktable. The bitter aroma of featherfoil scented the air. "Some things are best learned by oneself. You must unlock your own mysteries to better find the answers you seek."

That sounded far too difficult. "But how?" Cam asked.

"I am releasing you from your apprenticeship. You are free to go and seek your fortune. Your belongings are in the knapsack. The trunk contains everything that came with you when you were brought to me."

"I was *brought* to you? By whom? When? Why?"

The wizard shook his head. "You will find the answers on your own. Meanwhile, a small chamber has been prepared for you in the south wing of the castle. You will go there with your possessions and sit with them until it is clear what you must do."

Cam could find no words with which to answer. He felt as though he were being abandoned all over again, by the only "father" he had ever known.

"Do not think of it that way," Melikar said, and Cam

knew the wizard had read his thoughts. "Think of it as a new beginning. You are free to leave this world if that's where your searching takes you."

Cam pondered Melikar's words as he retrieved the knapsack and trunk. Nobly, he faced the wizard. "Thank you for this opportunity. And thank you for giving me a home for . . . for however many years I have been here."

"You were brought to me when you were three," the wizard told him. "And you've been here for fourteen years."

In the light from the wishing pool, Cam watched Melikar's face soften. He waited for the wizard to say more—perhaps a word or two of endearment. But that was not the wizard's way. Still, Cam was certain he saw sadness in Melikar's eyes.

"Go in the peace and grace of the High Spirit," the wizard said, then softly added, "Son."

And even though Cam's impulse was to beg the wizard to let him stay in the only home he'd ever known, he straightened his shoulders and carried his paltry belongings out the door before tears made him stumble on the narrow stone steps.

6

Reluctant Preparations

The princess sat as still as she could at her dressing table while her lady, Gwynell, fastened an unbearably long row of peach-colored pearl buttons down the front of her gown.

Her other lady, Cydlin, vigorously brushed the princess's hair, quite oblivious to any pain she might be inflicting.

"Ouch," Quinn muttered as the comb caught a snarl. *Maybe I will* prefer *having all my hair cut off when I'm betrothed. At least my ladies will not be able to torture me twice a day.*

After tonight, there would be a respite from her royal obligation to smile, say polite things, and, most of all, try to develop a fondness for one lad or another. They all seemed to blur into a hazy line of eager bumbleness.

Eager dull *bumbleness*, she thought, recalling the sameness of the questions asked by the noble lads:

"Will the king's land be given to build your own castle?" (Meaning theirs, too, if she chose them.)

"When will you announce your choice?" (This usually said with a wink, as if they knew for certain the name announced would be their own.)

Or, "Do you know the amount of the dowry?" (Greedy, greedy, greedy.) She felt disgusted with them all.

Then there was Lord Blakely of Kilmory Manor, her father's closest advisor. Quinn felt certain her father wouldn't be so urgent about following royal protocol if it were not for Lord Blakely nudging him to do so. She suspected the man found a bit too much enjoyment in the fact that the king listened to his nudges. Power-hungry, he was.

She'd never cared for him since the time, years ago, when he'd grabbed Cam by the collar, called him a lowly commoner who did not deserve the life he'd been given with the wizard, then ordered him never again to seek out the company of Mandria's princess.

Granted, she'd only been a child at the time, but she *did* have royal authority over Lord Blakely. She had always regretted not correcting him right then and there, making it clear to him that Cam would always be welcome in her presence. After that, Lord Blakely seemed determined to condemn Cam for one silly reason or another, simply because the lad disobeyed his order to stay away from the princess.

"Your Highness?" spoke Gwynell, her younger lady, who was not much older than Baywin.

Before Quinn could respond, her old nanny, Jalla, hoisting a platter, bustled into the royal chamber with Scrabit scuttle-flying ahead of her. "Yah do not need to announce me, lass. Methinks I am known in this part of the castle."

"Jalla!" Quinn cried, pleased for the interruption—especially by one who always made her smile. She gave Scrabit a delighted pat on his scaly head. "What have you got there?"

The woman set the platter on the princess's dressing table and pulled away the towel that covered it.

"Scones!" Quinn exclaimed.

"Ay, not just any scones. These are me lingonberries with sauce of the apple. Yah gobbled them up when yah was no bigger than an elf."

Quinn reached for one, then remembered her resolve not to eat until her father agreed to give her more time to make a decision.

You do not need more time, her conscience reminded her. *You've said a final good-bye to Adam. What would more time bring—other than anger from your father?*

Jalla lifted a scone and placed it in Quinn's palm. "I know of your plan to refuse food, child, but yah must eat. I've buried more young ones than I care to recall, from one malady or another, and all refused food at the end."

Quinn opened her mouth to explain her reasoning, but the nanny shook a finger to stifle her.

"Eat," she insisted.

And since it was Jalla, whom the princess had gladly obeyed as a child in return for affection she'd never known from her parents, Quinn bit into the scone. The tart berries were just as wonderful as she remembered. Finishing it off, she ate another two before she could help herself, even though she knew her ladies were hiding giggles behind cupped hands.

Protocol did not allow a royal to be touched, yet that is what Quinn loved about Jalla. She defied rules when it came to the care and feeding of the princess. Castle guards always looked the other way, as if they knew a child needed pats and hugs as much as she needed mashed fruit and muffins.

Jalla opened her arms. Quinn stepped into the warm embrace.

"If yah want to maintain the charade with the king at tonight's feast, then fine," Jalla said, brushing wisps of hair from Quinn's forehead. "But I shall be here with honey biscuits and jasmine tea before bedtime so our princess does not go to sleep hungry."

Quinn knew it was pointless to object. Thanking the nanny, she watched her depart, then sat again at the dressing table and braced herself for a final pampering and polishing from her ladies.

At least this was the last night of the "charade," as Jalla had called it. For now. The next three days would be filled with wedding festivities for Ameka and Dagon. Lots of gatherings at which Quinn could play the role of friend and cousin—and not feel obliged to appear as the kingdom's almost-betrothed princess.

Quinn thought about the upcoming feasts and knew she would partake. How could she resist? Tables would be laden with roasted quail, venison, goose, and a delicacy called kemble stew, made from the rare kemble fish, caught in the underground streams. According to legend, kembles brought vitality and health to all who consumed them, and, it was rumored, they had been known to return life to folk mere minutes from death's portal.

Platters of fruit from the Marnie orchards would likewise fill the tables: pomegranates, peaches, and plums, as well as sweets whipped into objects of art by Marged in the kitchen. Marged was at her best creating fancy dishes for Mandrian celebrations.

Afterward, the wedding party, Lord Ryswick, and a few elderly aunts would travel to Twickingham for another three days of wedding festivities at Pendrog Manor. Under normal conditions, Quinn and her parents would attend the faraway celebration, but the war had made travel between kingdoms unsafe. As it were, a small army of knights would escort the Twick relatives home.

Thinking of Ameka's wedding reminded Quinn that she had forgotten to mention the ceremony to Cam. The marriage plans had been made with such haste, he probably didn't know where or when to arrive, scrubbed and groomed. She must go tell him.

After one more hair-yanking session while her ladies strung peach pearls through her braid, Quinn decided to beg a break from her tormenters so she could deliver the message to Cam.

Hurrying upstairs to the highest chamber in the kingdom, she slipped through the door without being noticed. There was Melikar, hunched over his work-table in the midst of a lesson with his apprentice. This was a sight Quinn had witnessed dozens of times, but the fact that Baywin was the one perched upon the stool listening to the wizard instead of Cam seemed incredibly odd and unsettling.

She glanced about the quiet chamber. "Sorry for the intrusion, Sire. Where is Cam? I need to speak with him."

"He does not live here anymore," Baywin said, bursting out with the announcement as though it pleased him very much.

Befuddled, Quinn waited for Melikar to confirm the lad's news, which he did, giving her directions to Cam's new home, yet not offering any explanation for his departure.

As the princess hurried away, something inside her wanted desperately to turn back and re-enter the wizard's chamber. This time, Cam would be sitting with his master and all would be well.

What could have made Cam leave his home with Melikar?

No more changes, please, her mind begged the High Spirit. *I cannot bear to lose Cam as I am losing Ameka.*

7

An Abrupt Good-bye

The princess hurried along the corridors in the south wing—a part of the castle unfamiliar to her. Many of the chambers were seldom-used, left over from previous times when royal families were larger and required more cooks, pages, squires, and ladies-in-waiting.

When Quinn arrived at Cam's new chamber, she thought at first he wasn't there. The door was ajar. Inside was dark and quiet.

She knocked softly. Perhaps he was sleeping. "Cam?"

The door swung open, and a tousled Cam appeared.

"Did I wake you?" she asked, suddenly feeling as if she were intruding.

He gaped at her as though she were a ghost, but then he probably wondered why she'd be tarrying about a deserted part of the castle when she was supposed to be preparing for the evening gala.

"No, you did not wake me," he said after finding his tongue. "Come in." Opening the door wide, he hesitated, as if wondering whether or not it was proper to invite her into his chamber. Leaving the portal open, he lit a candle sconce on the wall with a burning twig from a small fire in a hearth hardly big enough to offer much warmth.

The sparse chamber, smaller than the princess's closet, contained a simple table, two stools, and a cot. In the middle of the table sat a small trunk, adorned with a painted blue horse.

Quinn wondered about the trunk as she quickly explained the reason for her errand. "What are you doing here? Why did you leave Melikar?"

Before he could answer, she added, "Did it have something to do with the arrival of the lad from Cocklethorn?"

Quinn saw him wince at her question, making her sorry she had asked.

Cam's response was a shrug. "I am supposed to sit here and ponder my life until something comes to me. Something that looks and sounds like a higher calling. But for now, it remains a puzzle. Perhaps my calling is only as high as a worm can see."

Quinn grimaced in sympathy. Her gaze fell upon the magic ring on his finger. Seeing him wearing it again gave her comfort.

She gestured toward the trunk. "What clues does it contain?"

Opening the lid to show her, Cam lifted out three

items and set them on the table. A worn ball, a frayed blanket, and a toy—a stuffed dragon of many colors, wings spread, with one pointed ear missing.

The princess sat at the table to study the items. Cam joined her. Picking up the bedraggled dragon, she straightened his wrinkled wings. "Does he have a name?"

"Mop," Cam answered, immediately rearing back on the stool as if he had startled himself. "Ay, where did that name come from? It must have been buried somewhere in my memory."

"Mop," Quinn repeated. "A good name for a dragon." Setting it down, she peered at the other items. "What comes to you when you touch these things and look at them?"

"Glimpses of my past," he answered, looking quite pained at having to say those words. Picking up the blanket, he absently held it to one cheek. "When I touch them, I remember things I had long forgotten."

"Tell me," she urged.

"I remember a softness that surely was my mother. I remember something white and cold falling from above. I remember an animal that was a pet, only it was not a dragon. I think it might have been a Marnie cat, yet I do not remember Marnies in this place."

Quinn drew up straight, shaken by his words. "Cam! You are not remembering your childhood in Mandria. You are having memories from Outer Earth. Snow falling. Cats. Yes, they have cats in the other world," she added, remembering the Dovers' kitten that had once startled her.

Quinn watched the former apprentice shiver, as if her words were needles pricking his neck. Perhaps her comment had triggered other memories as well.

Cam picked up the toy dragon and held it as if recalling a time when it was his constant companion. "Do you think I am remembering a place I thought I'd never been to? Or do you suppose it's simply a mean trick of my weak magic?"

"No, this cannot be magic. Weak nor strong. I believe your memories are true. I think you once lived in the other world and that is what you are remembering."

Quinn's discovery thrilled her. Did Cam have a connection with the other world as she did? Could he possibly have come from there?

"What did Melikar say about these items?" she asked.

Cam sighed. "He said nothing. He wants me to figure it out for myself." Pausing to remember, Cam repeated the wizard's cryptic words: "'You are free to leave this world if that's where your searching takes you.'"

The princess watched Cam's eyes brighten, as if the wizard's words, blended with her own, suddenly made sense.

"Ay, so *that* is what's supposed to come of my pondering!" he exclaimed. "My searching must begin in the other world."

"Yes," Quinn agreed. "And Melikar can send you there."

Cam locked gazes with her, as if realizing for the

first time what a gift Melikar had given him. "Will you come?" he blurted. "The way we once planned?"

His question stabbed her heart with envy. A lad could go off to seek his fortune, yet a maiden could not. Unfair!

"Cam, we are no longer childmates, plotting a forbidden adventure. I must tend to my royal duties, and you have a quest before you. But oh, I shall await your return with much eagerness. Hurry back to tell me every detail."

"A quest," Cam repeated, as if liking the notion. He leaped to his feet, almost knocking the stool over with his urgency to act. "I must be off at once."

"Oh, but tomorrow's wedding—" The eagerness in Cam's actions stopped the princess from finishing. He was clearly taken with the whole idea of an adventure on Outer Earth—not forbidden this time, but with the wizard's blessing.

Trying not to show her disappointment, Quinn kept a smile on her face. She wished he would delay his trip a few days. How much more enjoyable Ameka's wedding would be with him there. But that was selfish of her, and she knew she mustn't insist. Nothing should postpone his departure, now that he knew what he must do to find the answers he'd been seeking all his life.

Cam started to speak, but the princess stopped him. "No need to say anything. I can tell that your heart has already flown to the other world."

The princess's words made her realize that she'd been sitting there speaking of Outer Earth without feeling the familiar anguish. Immediately, she knew why. Her story with Adam was finished. She had not thought of him once with longing since they had made their peace and said good-bye.

"Go in safety, with the blessings of the High Spirit," she told Cam. Raising two fingers to her cheek, she traced a backward seven, giving him the Sign of the Lorik. It was a sacred Mandrian sign of trust and honor that could not be broken. "Till again we meet."

Raising his hand to his cheek, he returned the sign. "Till again we meet."

The princess dearly wanted to say more. She wanted to say how empty the Kingdom of Mandria would feel without the wizard's former apprentice in the castle to entertain and amuse her.

But imps had suddenly stolen her tongue and turned her coy. She could say no more except farewell.

8

Searching for a Future: Cam

෴

Cam awoke multiple times during the night. His mind was a galloping steed, refusing to be quieted or convinced to sleep.

How amazing for the princess to decipher his childhood memories. Of *course* she would recognize his recollections as snippets of the outer world. She knew what it looked like.

"Ay," Cam whispered in the dark. "I have been to Outer Earth." Turning over, he gazed at the weak flames, kept burning through the night by the magic of pipeflower seeds. He wished he could see what Melikar saw when he studied flames and read the fire. "Was I taken to the other world as a child? Or born there?"

His desire to know was as strong as midsummer thunder-rumblings in the earthen walls of the kingdom.

"Quest," Cam stated to the dark chamber in a bold voice. "The princess called this my quest." Excitement bubbled in his veins like spring water in the grotto.

Then a pang of guilt threatened to squelch his excitement. *If I leave today, I'll miss the joining of Ameka and Dagon in marriage. I'll miss the celebration and a final chance to dance with the princess.*

Cam's hesitation lasted but a moment. *Ay, but would a knight delay a quest?*

Flinging the blanket aside, he scrambled from the cot. Taking what was left of the candle, he stepped to the hearth to light the wick so he could see to dress.

As his gaze fell upon the trunk, still open upon the table he thought of the princess and the way she'd looked at him mere hours ago with those impossibly green eyes.

He would miss the way she tugged her braid while considering difficult questions. He would miss her endearing giggle—especially when he did something doltish, and she was giggling at him.

By the time I return, she might already be betrothed. Or worse, married.

Cam started to sink back onto the cot in dismay, but something told him if he did, he would remain there forever.

No.

He must not stay. In truth, it might be better if he were not in Mandria at all during this time of marriage celebrations. Watching the princess wed another would be more painful than hearing of it from afar.

He must leave at once.

Quickly, he finished dressing and smoothed his hair. The knapsack was already packed with his few possessions, so there was no need to prepare for the journey—except for one thing.

Opening the sack, Cam added the ball, blanket, and scraggly dragon because he could not bear to leave his newly found possessions behind. As he started to close the knapsack something caught his attention. Curious, he drew out a leather pouch that did not belong to him. What had Melikar added to his belongings?

Opening the pouch, he found a set of herb vials, neatly packed: maidenhair for alertness without sleeping, faery glove for a strong heart, and powdered kemble fish for healing.

The wizard's kind gesture touched Cam deeply. Folding the vials back into the pouch, he tied the knapsack and shoved the empty trunk beneath his cot.

Cam blew out the candle, doused the meager flames in the hearth, and stepped bravely from the chamber, eager to depart from the dreary south wing. His heart felt so light as he flung the knapsack over one shoulder, he began to whistle a tune from one of his favorite ballads:

> *They live their lives without a care,*
> *the lasses who never cut their hair.*
> *The bonny maidens of Mandria fair—*
> *Beware! They'll steal your heart.*

When he reached Melikar's portal, Cam felt compelled to knock. After all, he no longer resided there.

In spite of the early hour, the door swung open immediately. Baywin looked at him without any sign of recognition. "May I assist you?" he asked.

Cam had to laugh at the irony of reversed roles. All in a day's time. Not feeling the need to explain himself to his successor, Cam stepped around the lad and found Melikar writing at his desk.

"Sire," he began.

"I know why you have come, and I'm pleased you made this choice so quickly. I feared you might hesitate until it was too late."

Too late for what? Cam wondered, but Melikar rarely explained his words or actions, so it was futile to ask.

"You know what to do," Melikar said. "You witnessed the beginning of the princess's journey to the other world."

Yes, he knew. The moment Quinn left Mandria without him was painfully scorched into his memory. Moving toward the circle of light, Cam stood beneath the wishing pool, clutching his knapsack.

He waited, hoping the wizard would give him some sort of instruction before sending him into the unknown.

"Remember these three things," Melikar said, as if hearing Cam's unasked question.

The former apprentice leaned forward, eager for any advice, yet he hated the way Baywin leaned in as well, hanging on every word from the wizard.

"You must keep the secret of Mandria's existence and watch over its interests. Be careful what you say and to whom. My magic will go ahead and prepare the way. Trust your instincts."

Cam remembered how Melikar's magic assisted Quinn's arrival in the other world. How Mondo, Adam, and Sarah had found the princess at the wishing pool and taken her home with them.

"Second," Melikar said. "Remember where you belong."

These words surprised Cam. How could he remember if he did not know?

"Finally, always uphold the Mandrian truths."

Finally? Was that all?

"Sire? You once told me enchanted beings weaken in the other world and cannot remain long or they will die. Will I—"

Melikar stopped him. "I told you that before to discourage your desire to explore the outer world. But in truth, your magic is not strong enough for it to matter. Your powers existed only because you lived in an enchanted chamber, alive with magic."

Cam was stunned. What was Melikar saying? That he never had wizard's blood to begin with? All these years he'd worried about his weak magic when, in fact, he had *no* magic at all?

He felt as tiny as a flea on a Marnie cat's mouse. And he hated the pleased smirk spreading across Baywin's face.

*Why couldn't the lad have arrived on the morrow—
after my quest had begun?* Cam clutched the knapsack
until his shoulder ached. He hated having Bay here to
witness his anxiety and the beginning of such an important journey. Something so personal should be shared
only with Melikar.

Shaking thoughts of Baywin from his mind, Cam
stood straight, gazing up through the quiet wishing
pool, wondering what the sensation would feel like. He
knew how to return: Reverse the spell Melikar was now
beginning. He would never forget the times he tried to
plant those instructions in the princess's mind while
she was above the river and he was below.

With Baywin watching, transfixed, from the shadows,
the wizard moved to the hearth and lifted a ladle. Dipping
into the magic brew bubbling in the cauldron, he began
to stir. As the liquid swirled in a circular pattern, the
water above Cam's head began to move, flowing with the
motion of the ladle.

Melikar began to chant. Cam focused on the words
swirling around him in the circle of light as the spell
sprang to life:

"*Anger, fear, love, and mirth.
Send Cam of Mandria to Outer Earth.*"

A tugging sensation drew Cam upward. He felt as
weightless as a fish swimming through water.

Seconds later, darkness blanked his mind.

9

The Wedding

 ulcimer music sweetened the air in Albans Chapel. Quinn stepped through the vestibule at the back of the sanctuary and began a slow walk to the altar, feeling honored to be asked to stand with Ameka as she became Dagon's wife. Joining her midway was a knight from the kingdom of Twickingham to stand with Dagon. A child-mate and brother in battle.

For a fleeting moment, the princess wished Cam was the one escorting her down the chapel aisle, but she felt quite certain that, by now, he had passed through the wishing pool and was already finding his way in the other world.

Bother, she thought. *I should have defied the ancient customs and slipped away to travel with him. He asked me to go; I should not have been so quick to say no. What will be left for me here in Mandria with Cam gone and Ameka leaving in three days?*

She hated the feeling that her life was changing and she was powerless to stop it. Fate was an evil knight, charging on a steed, and she, without a shield to deflect his lance. But then, she always knew what her life would be. If born a peasant, fate might have offered more interesting turns than the royal life she was born into. The protocol of being a princess was a book set in stone—a volume filled with the most ancient Mandrian truths.

Quinn stepped slowly down the aisle, returning smiles and trying not to move too fast for fear the young lass carrying the train of her lacy lavender gown might stumble.

She recalled the scene in Ameka's cottage last evening. Ameka was as jittery as a caged squirrel as she waited for Jalla. Quinn kept offering sips of lemon balm to calm her. Finally Jalla arrived, prepared to fulfill one of the age-old customs. Ameka sat quietly on a stool, weeping softly, while Jalla cut off her lengths of chestnut hair.

The tears concerned Quinn, but Ameka assured her they were tears of joy over the prospect of stepping into a new life, mixed with tears of sadness for leaving the cottage—her home since birth—and for leaving the only life and companions she had ever known.

Ameka looked stunningly different after the haircutting. Tears turned to laughter as she tousled her short locks, exclaiming how weightless they felt. Jalla

fastened tiny star blossoms on one side, and the adorn-
ments pleased Ameka very much.

Step, pause. Step, pause. Step, pause.

As Quinn approached the altar, her heart quivered
at the sight of the cousin she adored. Dagon looked so
handsome in his white, caped tunic with golden trim.
His fair hair hung long, like Cam's, and when he smiled
at her, the dimple she knew so well curved endearingly.
She loved the miracle of Dagon and Ameka together.

The princess smiled back at her cousin as she
stepped to one side of the altar and turned to face the
wedding guests.

King Marit and Queen Leah entered the sanctuary.
Guests immediately came to their feet, bowing slightly
with gazes lowered as the king and queen moved ele-
gantly down the aisle. The queen wore a russet gown,
perfectly matching the king's robe, as well as the stone
walls of the chapel.

As they approached the altar, Dagon's father, Lord
Ryswick, entered from a side door and moved to greet
his royal relatives. Quinn's father and Dagon's mother
were brother and sister, although Lady Ryswick had
died years ago.

Music swelled. Quinn's gaze was drawn to the
vestibule. Ameka, in a shimmery gown the color of sweet
cream, began her walk down the aisle. Quinn could not
see her veiled face but knew with certainty her former
tutor was smiling.

So many emotions filled the princess's heart as she

watched Lord Derry conduct the ceremony, she began to feel faint. Finally, the music swelled again as the groom lifted the bride's veil to kiss her.

In a few months' time the princess herself would be standing at the altar of the royal chapel in the castle, ready to marry her betrothed.

Who might it be? What will he look like? Will he gaze at me the way Dagon is gazing at Ameka?

The thought of it made the princess's hands tremble until petals began to rain from her meadowsweet bouquet.

10

The Outer World

Cam opened his eyes, blinking in the unusually bright light of day. He was sitting on the footbridge that curved over the Mandrian River—a river known by a different name in this world, although Cam could not recall it at the moment.

How long had he been here? Moments? Hours? He wasn't certain. He marveled at the fact that his garments were dry after passing through the water. And he marveled at the warmth and brightness of the sun—a brightness that pained his eyes.

As he started to get up, a maiden bounded onto the footbridge, startling him. Quickly, Cam tried to think of an excuse for who he was and why he was there, but the smiling maiden stopped in front of him and set down a knapsack as purple as the tapestries in the Great Hall. Offering a hand, she helped him to his feet.

Holding an arm to block the sun, Cam squinted at her. She was almost as tall as he, with hair not unlike a young Marnie's—gold in color and a bit shaggy. She wore blue leggings, which shocked him since he'd never seen a maiden wear men's garments. And her tunic appeared far too small since he could see her skin where the material did not meet the top of the leggings.

She made him nervous. He looked away, unsure what to say.

"I'm Sarah," the maiden said. "Melikar sent me to find you and bring a change of clothes so I can take you into the city without attracting attention."

He gaped at her, fighting the urge to keep his eyes closed against the brightness. "You know of Melikar?"

"Yes, I'm the Sarah you probably heard your princess speak of. My brother, grandfather, and I know about your kingdom and about the wizard."

"How did he . . . Melikar . . . tell you to come here?"

She ran a hand through her hair, as if to tousle it more, which seemed odd to Cam. He presumed she would attempt to smooth all the pieces that were sticking out.

"He didn't actually tell me, but he *did* restore my memory of Quinn's time with us. I had forgotten all of it after it happened. I mean, I think the wizard somehow caused me to forget."

Cam knew what she meant. He had witnessed Melikar erasing the maiden's knowledge of Mandria. Quinn had begged the wizard to allow Adam to keep his memories of her—and Melikar had granted her wish.

"My brother, Adam, knew you were coming," Sarah continued. "I don't know how he got the message, and I don't think Mondo even knows about it, but . . ."

Her voice trailed off. Cam knew who Mondo was, yet the man's connection to Mandria was a mystery. "I know Mondo is your grandfather," Cam ventured, urging her to continue.

Sarah hesitated, hoisting the purple knapsack over one shoulder. "Adam and I don't think Mondo is going to be with us much longer."

"Ay, I'm so sorry," Cam told her, and truly meant it. Meeting the one who knew of Mandria seemed vital. He hoped he was not too late.

"What I *meant* to say," Sarah explained, "is that *Adam* told me to come and find you, but I *assume* the message came from Melikar. Adam was supposed to come, but he just arrived home on emergency leave from the Army because of our grandfather's health, and he's been acting . . . well . . . weird ever since he got home. He refused to come to the footbridge. I don't know why."

Cam knew. Adam did not want to come because he'd been here earlier—to say a final good-bye to the princess.

Cam also knew how Melikar had communicated the arrival of his former apprentice to Adam. A mental message, planted by the wizard, is so strong that one's mind eventually realizes the thought is not his own, but an important message that requires one's attention.

Sarah leaned over the railing and gazed into the

wishing pool. Could she see the world below? Curious, Cam stepped beside her to have a look of his own. All he saw was a blue-green pool, reflecting two images: a maiden, dressed in garments strange to him; and a lad, wearing garments strange to this world.

Wistfully, he thought of the gentle one who lived below and wondered if he would ever see her again.

"Let's head home," Sarah said. "And, by the way, welcome to the twenty-first century."

Cam wasn't sure what she meant, but he followed her down the path into the forest. His initial thrill at being in the outer world melted into a foreboding sense of vulnerability. For all of his life, he believed his magic would guide and protect him—especially in situations such as this. The power was always there, waiting to be called upon when and if he needed it.

Alas, believing one is an enchanter is useless if no magical powers actually exist.

What a horrible time to discover this.

11

In the Queen's Garden

The princess wandered along a stone path through the castle garden. She wanted to be away from the marriage celebration, away from the festive music of the harp and lyre, and away from the dancing.

Taking a deep breath, she inhaled the heavy scent of turtle bloom, goose grass, and moon flowers. The sweetness of the garden air overruled the earthy aroma permeating most of the underground chambers.

The queen's garden was Quinn's favorite place on the castle grounds. Many afternoons, she'd played tag among the fragrant bushes and along the stepping stones with Cam and Dagon when they were young. Jalla would bring tea cakes and peach nectar for a treat beneath the lime trees.

Quinn felt pleased that her parents had offered the garden to Dagon and Ameka. What a perfect place to serve the wedding feast and to celebrate long into the night.

But Quinn was weary of music and dancing after all the galas in her honor. And, in truth, it was difficult to watch Ameka, glowing with happiness next to her new husband. Difficult because Ameka would be gone on the morrow—not in three days' time, as had been planned.

Earlier, a courier from Twickingham had delivered ominous war news, cutting short the celebration. Dagon and Lord Ryswick, both Knights of the First Order, were needed at home.

Quinn hated the changed plans, yet she knew wars did not stop for weddings or births or funerals.

Beneath a buttonball tree, she found her favorite bench for sitting and pondering life. Being alone was such bliss. Rarely was solitude allowed the Princess of Mandria. Hopefully, she had not yet been missed.

Arranging the lacy gown around her, Quinn realized how impossible was her wish to be alone. Surely one of her ladies was searching for her this very moment.

Keeping her mind in Mandria was difficult. Her thoughts kept drifting to Outer Earth. Where was Cam at present? What was he doing? What did he think of the other world?

She wondered if Mondo's apartment looked the same. Padded benches with stuffed cushions for sitting. Katze, the kitten, who certainly had grown bigger by now. Instant light whenever someone walked into a chamber. It had taken her a while to realize that people made the light come on as they entered a room. Apparently, they did not have candles in the other world. Quite odd.

Squaaaaawwwwwk!

The princess leaped to her feet and spun around. There stood a tousled Baywin, equally surprised by the unexpected sight of her. In his hand was a bow, and on his back, a quiver of arrows.

Flapping to the top of the buttonball tree was a red-feathered trega, a common bird beneath the river.

"Toads and mugwort!" Quinn exclaimed, her heart flapping as vigorously as the bird's wings.

Baywin appeared vexed. "I almost got him, but you scared me, and he flew away."

"Bats, lad! If guards see you hunting in the queen's garden, *you* will be flying to the top of a tree to save your own neck."

He drew back in surprise. "I did not know princesses were allowed to swear." His voice sounded breathy with fear. Her warning obviously unnerved him.

"A princess can swear if a careless imp sneaks up behind her with a pointed weapon." She ended her comment with a wink, so he'd know it was not a Mandrian truth.

Looking relieved at the jest, Baywin apologized. Then, with a mumbled word and a flick of his arm, the bow disappeared and the arrows in his quiver turned into a bouquet of lady's mantle. Whisking them out of the quiver, he bowed and presented them to the princess.

Quinn was truly impressed. Cam never entertained her with his magic in such a delightful way. The minute the thought struck her, she recalled how keen Melikar was about not using magic lightly. Of *course* Cam had never done such a thing. He obeyed his master. The lad before her had much to learn.

Quinn started to chide him again but stopped. He had been under the wizard's tutelage a mere two days. Soon enough, he'd learn the seriousness of Mandrian truths and a wizard's warnings.

Returning to the bench, she scooted over. "Come sit, Bay, and tell me stories to make me feel better."

He did what she asked, gazing up at her as if he wanted *her* to be the teller of stories. "What is it like out there?" he asked. "In the other world?"

Ay, he was just as curious as she and Cam had been at his tender age. "For one thing," she began, "if we were sitting in an Outer-Earth garden, we could look up into an endless sky lit by sunshine instead of by an enchanted glow cast by Melikar."

Baywin furrowed his brow and peered upward, as if trying to imagine it. "Mum used to tell me there were monsters in the other world. Is it true?"

Quinn cocked her head, thinking of one unscrupulous knave who had threatened her. Picturing him was enough to send shivers across her shoulders. "Yes, I believe monsters do exist there," she told him.

His eyes grew as round as the sweet cicely blossoms along the path.

"Tell me about you," she urged, wanting to change the course of the conversation. "When did you first know you had wizard's blood?"

"Once, when I was three-years-old, I wanted sweets, and Mum did not have any. I began to think about candied ginger and how good it tasted on my tongue, then . . . a dish of sweets simply appeared."

"Why, that type of enchantment could be put to

good use. Can you still conjure up food?"

He shrugged. "I was not allowed to make magic at home after the first few times. My mum brought me to Mandria to meet Melikar. She told him other things I'd done—like imagining us a milking goat for cheese and talking to birds who talked back."

Quinn glanced away to hide her amusement. Baywin was being very serious, and she did not want him to think she was laughing at him. "What did Melikar do?"

"He cast a spell to stop my use of magic until I was old enough to return to Mandria as his apprentice. He said it was important to learn how to use magic properly—so here I am."

"Do you miss your mum?"

The lad's lip quivered and tears sprang into his eyes. Quinn put her arm around him and mumbled soothing words, sorry the question had upset him.

"Princess!"

Quinn turned at the sound of a voice. Up the path, running as best she could in full skirts, huffed Gwynell.

"Lass, what is it?"

"Come, m'lady," Gwynell sputtered, out of breath. She fanned herself with the bell-sleeve of her amber gown. "The Twicks must leave at once. Ameka needs you."

"Leave *now*? But the celebration has barely—"

Before Quinn could finish, the sprite of a maiden— as well as Baywin—were off down the path, leaving her talking to herself.

Quinn had to laugh. Gwynell was always beside herself over one thing or another. "You were sent to fetch me," the princess grumbled, even though she knew the lass was out of earshot. "And you shall arrive back at the castle without me. Jalla shall scold you roundly for not looking after me. Will you ever learn?"

Gathering her skirts about her, the princess followed, worried at the sudden change of plans and protocol. But even more, she felt stricken by the thought of losing both of her dearest companions—one to another world and the other to a faraway kingdom.

12

Leaving WonderLand

~

Cam followed the maiden through the forest—an unkempt forest, in his opinion. Mandria's cavernous woods resembled the forests of Outer Earth—only more organized. Aqua ponds dotted green hills. Fruit trees grew in neat orchards. Planted in straight rows were hardwood oak and nut trees for carving. Underbrush was cleared away by Marnies.

Forests beneath the river had two things Outer Earth's did not: morning mist that did not fall from the sky, and the wizard's enchanted sunlight. Both nurtured the vegetation.

"First things first," Sarah began. "You can't go into the city dressed as a medieval wizard's apprentice. You'll draw too much attention."

Cam did not know what "medieval" meant, but hearing Sarah call him a wizard's apprentice startled him. *She knows more about me than I know about her.*

Stopping at a small hut by the side of the path, she slipped the purple knapsack off her shoulder and handed it to him. "Take this into the men's room and switch clothes."

"The men's room?" Cam repeated.

Sarah looked at him as though he'd said something thick-witted, then nodded toward the hut. "See the door on the right? Go in there and change into these jeans and shirt. I'll wait here."

Cam followed her orders. It did not take long to figure out what a "men's room" was intended for. He quickly exchanged his garments for what Sarah called jeans and a shirt. The shoes were odd. Unsure what to do with the lacing, he knotted it.

The grin on Sarah's face when he emerged from the hut told him he'd put everything on correctly. He felt pleased to have done something right. If only the rest of the journey could be this simple.

"Oh, look," she exclaimed, grabbing his hand. "The ring. Is this the same ring Quinn wore when she was here?"

Cam nodded, amazed Sarah would notice.

"Isn't it . . . a magic ring?"

Her question made him sigh. Constant reminders of his failure as an enchanter were bruising his confidence. "No," he told her. "Not magic. Just a ring I made."

She cocked her head as if she didn't quite believe him.

As they walked down the path, people appeared, strolling, riding two-wheeled devices, or running.

Seeing bare legs startled Cam, but he tried not to react. He wondered what these folk were running away from and why others casually moved out of their way. Sarah did not appear alarmed, so he did not ask about it.

Cam knew he was in WonderLand Park. Quinn had described the place too many times for him not to recognize it. He was eager to see the contraptions she'd first believed were torture devices. Later, she learned WonderLand was an "amusement park" where folk came to enjoy themselves—not to be willingly tortured.

The contraptions came into view. Cam was captivated by the sight of people lined up to climb onto various sorts of mechanisms that spun them around or turned them upside-down. He stopped to watch people laughing and screaming at the same time. How exceedingly odd!

Sarah urged him on until they came to the rows of carriages Quinn had told him about. The maiden aimed something in her hand at a red carriage. It beeped and flashed in answer.

Magic! Cam thought, feeling amazed.

"Wait here for me," she said. "My daughter is being looked after by the park's babysitters. I have to go get her."

"Baby*sitters*?"

Cam was appalled. "Is that how they take care of lads and lasses here?"

Sarah laughed. "It's just an expression, Cam."

An expression. *Think, before you speak*, he said to himself, although the voice inside his head sounded more like Melikar's.

Sarah returned, carrying a small child with bright

eyes and a hint of reddish hair curling around a bow stuck on top of her head. "This is Hannah," she said. "Named after Mondo's wife."

"Your grandmother?" Cam asked, trying to remember what Quinn had told him about the other Hannah.

"Yes. She died many years ago. I never knew her."

Baby Hannah grinned at him, showing white stubs of teeth. Cam's heart rolled over. He smiled back, smitten.

Sarah strapped Hannah into a special seat in the back of the carriage. Cam was curious about it but decided not to ask. Better to be thought quiet than dim.

The maiden climbed into the carriage, pulled a strap across her body, and snapped it into place. Next, she showed Cam how to do the same. As they started off, he braced himself, relieved that Quinn had foretold these things. Who knew he'd be given a chance to see it all for himself?

Although he'd raced the tunnels of Mandria on the princess's Paleo ponies, he'd never gone as fast as the carriage was moving. It took him a few minutes to realize Sarah was in control. How relieved he felt to know she could make the machine move according to her will.

There was so much to look at! The endless sky made him feel light and airy. Vastly different from the dim, dank tunnels of his world. Soon the forest gave way to tall castles shooting straight up into the sky. Other carriages flew past them in both directions.

Cam was breathless, trying to take it all in. How could this entire world—so incredibly different from his own—exist this close?

"Is this all one kingdom?" he asked, astounded at

the expanse of the countryside as they passed dwelling after dwelling—some small, others gigantic. Many were built with sharp angles brightly reflecting the sun. They were so unlike the clunky earthen huts, stone-walled manors, and round-turreted castles beneath the river.

Sarah covered her mouth to politely hide a chuckle. "I forgot about all the questions Quinn asked when she first arrived. Let me explain. We're entering a city, which is part of a state, and part of a country. Kingdoms exist in other parts of the world."

Cam hated being laughed at. He vowed to watch what he said.

"How is Quinn?" Sarah added, softening her voice. "Is she okay? Tell me about her."

The question caught Cam off guard. So odd that this "stranger" knew the princess. "She is fine," he answered, saying no more as two thoughts collided in his mind: First, the princess was not fine at all, but the explanation seemed too personal to share with someone he'd just met.

And second, he'd promised Melikar not to reveal too much. True, Sarah already knew of Mandria's existence, but perhaps it would be best to leave it at that.

The princess.

Cam recalled the last time they spoke and how he boldly asked her to come with him. How his mind did not caution his heart before speaking. The words simply leaped out of his mouth like a river frog. Afterward, he'd trembled at his own courage for saying them.

The princess had responded: "Cam, we are no longer childmates," duly reminding him of the Mandrian truth.

Still, he was not sorry his eager heart had asked a

question his mind could not. At least the princess knew he desired her company.

After many twists and turns, Sarah stopped in front of a long row of cottages, stacked one on top of another. "Mondo's apartment is up those stairs," she said, pointing.

Cam stepped out of the carriage and waited for Sarah to unstrap Hannah, who was now fast asleep. Although he'd braced himself for the ride into the city, the former wizard's apprentice felt the need to brace himself even more before climbing the steps to face the mysterious Mondo.

And to face Adam, his rival for the princess's affection.

13

An Unexpected Departure

The princess ran down the path in the queen's garden as quickly as she could in her lavender lace gown and jeweled Mandrian slippers. When she reached the trellis gate, she saw knights on eager horses where wedding guests should have been weaving the customary Clandeau line around the wedding couple.

The sight quickened her heart. Was she too late?

Jalla was waiting. "Where have yah been? Everyone is dashing about, looking for the princess. Yah got your poor mother scared halfway to the grave."

Turning, Jalla nabbed a passing squire. "Lad, go at once to the queen and tell her the princess has been found and is safe. Tell her that her daughter will be in directly to speak with her."

The squire dashed off with his important message while Quinn cringed at the "will be in directly to speak with her" part. A reprimand surely awaited her in the royal tower.

"Come," Jalla said, urging her along.

The nanny led her to a private alcove in the garden where the queen took her afternoon tea. Ameka waited, now wearing traveling garments instead of a wedding gown. The look on her tear-streaked face broke Quinn's heart.

"Dear one," Ameka said, opening her arms to Quinn. Abruptly she drew back, as if remembering royal protocol.

"Yah two are safe here from prying eyes," Jalla assured them. With that, she slipped out of the alcove, yet Quinn knew her trustworthy nanny was standing guard to ensure their privacy.

The princess was not concerned in the least with protocol as she hugged her beloved tutor. "I heard the news" was all she said.

"I am so sorry," Ameka told her. "I know we planned to spend the morrow together, overseeing the packing up of my cottage. And tomorrow night's celebration would surely—"

"Shh–shh," Quinn whispered. "I know you have to depart at once, and it is not your doing. True, I'm terribly disappointed, but your safety and Twickingham's victory are more important than following tradition."

Stepping back, she stood tall to hide her sorrow so Ameka would not feel worse than she already did. "I shall make sure your cottage things are packed and sent off to Pendrog Manor as soon as possible."

"Thank you," Ameka said, blotting her eyes.

"Travel safe," Quinn told her.

"Your father ordered ten of his best knights to escort us, so I am certain we will be safe. I will send word when we arrive. And you must come visit as soon as passageways are safe again."

"Certainly." The princess tried to feel cheerful about the promise of a journey to see the "new" Pendrog Manor. After Dagon's mother died, the house fell into disrepair, but Lord Ryswick commissioned it to be completely redone in honor of Ameka, the new Lady Ryswick.

How could happiness for her tutor feel both joyful and sorrowful at the same time?

A door leading from the castle opened. Out stepped Dagon, who'd also exchanged his wedding garments for traveling clothes. "It is time to depart, my love," he said softly to his bride.

Quinn took his hand and held it in both of hers, yet could not speak for the sadness tugging at her heart.

Startled by her action, Dagon glanced about the alcove for guards, then realized they were out of sight.

He cupped her hands inside of his. "I know my wife will miss her dearest companion," he said with great fondness. "Fate's blessings and an end to this loathsome war is what I wish. And that soon we shall all reunite."

He did not mention the fact that his uncle, King Marit, held the power to hasten the end of the war and for that, Quinn loved him.

Dagon kept hold of her hand and reached for Ameka's. The three stood in a circle, capturing the moment—a moment that would have been more complete had Cam been present.

The princess looked from one to the other, wondering if they felt what she was feeling. At this very instant, the simple and carefree childhood they had known together was ending—fading into history. Now, a new road stretched before them—one they were bound to tread as adults.

And what she feared most about that future road were all the twists, bends, mysterious loops, and perilous crossings that surely awaited them.

14

Meeting the Mysterious Mandrian

~

Cam followed Sarah up the stairs to what she called "Mondo's apartment." He noticed that the steps were made of wood. Stairs in Mandria were always carved from stone, yet the Marnies built furniture out of oak and pine and walnut. *Why not stairs?* he wondered. *Tradition?*

The daydream kept him distracted from the moment at hand as Sarah tapped on a door marked "12-A." Was he more nervous to meet the grandfather or the grandson? He wasn't sure.

A woman opened the door, confusing Cam. She reminded him of Jalla with her ample frame and stern stare. If Mondo lived alone, now that Sarah was married and Adam was in the Army, then who—?

"Hi, Elsy," Sarah said. "How is he today?"

The woman, Elsy, shook her head. "Not good, darlin'. Come in. Sweet tea is brewing. Your brother went to the grocery for me. He'll be back shortly."

The woman was addressing Sarah, but her sideways glances were aimed at Cam.

"This is, um, a friend of the family," Sarah told her.

"Nice to meet you," Elsy said, offering her hand to Cam. "I'm Mondo's homecare nurse."

Cam took hold of the woman's hand and bowed to kiss it.

"Mercy!" she exclaimed, snatching her hand away. "Fair to say it's been a few decades since any young man greeted me in such a splendid manner."

Embarrassed, Cam followed Sarah inside. Why had the woman offered her hand if she did not know what he would do with it? What does one do here with outstretched hands?

"I'll see if your grandad's awake," Elsy said, leaving them alone in an softly lit room with strange furnishings. Cam was glad for the muted light because his eyes were beginning to ache from the brightness outside.

Suddenly an animal streaked across the room, as if wanting to find out who had arrived before hurrying on its way. To Cam's surprise, it looked like a Marnie cat, only much larger.

"Hey, Katze," Sarah said, turning so that Hannah, now awake, could see the animal before he disappeared behind a drape. "Come back and say hello to our guest."

But the cat remained hidden, which was fine with Cam. Marnie cats made him nervous because they did what they pleased and never obeyed their masters the way dogs did.

Sarah placed Hannah in a strange contraption that held her captive on all four sides so she could not crawl more than a few knee-lengths in any direction. Hannah immediately wailed, wanting out. Cam did not blame her.

"Shhh, you'll wake Grandpa," Sarah cooed, sitting next to the baby dungeon to calm her daughter by shaking some sort of a gourd with rattling seeds inside.

"Cam," Sarah said in a hushed voice. "When someone extends a hand to you, take it and give it a firm shake. Let's practice."

She held out her hand. Cam grasped hold of it and shook it side to side.

Sarah laughed. "No—not what I meant. Shake it up and down, like this." She demonstrated. "I'll try to run interference for you while you're here."

Cam had no idea what she meant.

Elsy returned. "He's awake and wants to see you, Sarah. I told him someone else was here, but . . . young man, did you tell me your name?

"Oh, sorry," he said. "I'm Cam of—"

"Cam Mandria," Sarah blurted, interrupting him. "I'll tell Mondo he's here." Shushing Hannah, she came to her feet and left the chamber. Elsy gave Cam a suspicious eyebrow raise, then followed Sarah.

"Cam Mandria?" he muttered to himself. Of course, the nurse knew nothing of his homeland, so the name was meaningless to her. He knew Mondo's second name was Dover, which must mean this was the land of Dover.

Hannah began to fuss. Cam sat on the floor and watched her through the loops of thread separating them. Rarely was he in the presence of babies in

Mandria. How did one talk to them?

Looking about for a toy to distract her, Cam opened his knapsack and drew out the tattered dragon from his own babyhood. Reaching over the top of the prison, he handed the toy to Hannah.

Instantly, she stopped fussing, grabbed hold of the dragon with both hands, and began talking to it in delighted gibberish.

Cam felt pleased that his tactic distracted the baby. "The dragon's name is Mop," he told her, wondering if she understood.

"Mop," Hannah said, making Cam rear back in surprise.

Sarah returned.

As he came to his feet, Cam's heart began to jump around inside his chest like a bucketful of toads.

"I told Mondo he had a visitor from Mandria, and you should have seen his face. He was shocked and delighted. I think your visit will really perk him up. Come with me."

Cam's mind had been trying to stitch together the tapestry that told of his past, that explained who he was and where he came from. *Had Mondo known my parents? Perhaps he can weave that part of the tapestry for me.*

Cam followed Sarah down a narrow passageway, trying to recall a time his knees had knocked together as badly as they were knocking now. The first time he danced with the princess when he was thirteen? The time Lord Blakely cornered him and warned him never again to seek out the company of the royal daughter? Or the time he had fatefully mumbled the spell he thought would send Quinn and himself to Outer Earth?

Ay, his knees probably knocked even more the moment he realized his spell had sent the princess into the other world while he remained behind.

Cam stepped into a small chamber with drawn drapes. Light glowed from some sort of muted moon on the ceiling. An old man lay in the kind of bed only the wealthy owned in Mandria—oak, with four intricately carved posts. An extra blanket lay rumpled on the bed. Elsy picked it up and began to fold it.

Mondo lifted his head from the pillow and focused on Cam. The man's expression was a blend of sadness and disbelief over seeing someone from his homeland. "Cam, is it? From Mandria?"

"Yes, Sire," Cam answered, noting that Sarah flinched and glanced at Elsy when he spoke.

The nurse kept one eye on him as she took away the dishes, then busied herself about the chamber. Cam suspected that curiosity was keeping her there.

Mondo lifted an arm with great effort and held it out to Cam. Stepping close, he took the man's hand and shook it firmly, the way Sarah had just shown him.

Mondo smiled. "I was rather hoping for an embrace. When did you learn how to shake hands the way they do here?"

Before Cam could respond, Sarah blurted in a hushed voice, "Three minutes ago. In the living room."

Mondo looked amused.

"Elsy," he said. "Please crank up the bed so I can sit and talk to my visitor. Then you may leave until dinnertime."

Cam noted the kindness in Mondo's voice. He

watched the nurse turn a handle at the end of the bed, making the other end raise Mondo into a sitting position. Cam had never seen anything like it.

She straightened the bedcovers and poured a goblet of tea. No one spoke while she went about her chores. Finally, Mondo reached to stop her, nodding toward the portal to remind her to leave.

She complied, although made it clear with backward glances that she was dying to stay.

Sarah kissed Mondo on the cheek. "I will leave you two alone to talk while I go entertain Hannah."

Cam stood quietly in the room, staring at the man before him, searching for a clue that he was truly Mandrian. His hair was as white as the queen's pearls, and his eyes were a deep blue-green. Where before had Cam seen that color? *Ay, the wishing pool.*

"Sit," the man commanded, motioning toward a wooden chair, not unlike a Marnie creation.

Cam sat.

Mondo cocked his head to study him. "Why have you come?"

Cam sat up straight, wanting to answer questions as best he could in hopes Mondo would likewise be truthful with him. "I—"

"Pardon me," came a stranger's voice from the doorway.

Cam turned to see who was interrupting his visit with Mondo at the worst possible moment. A man strode into the room, looking from Cam to Mondo and back again.

Was it Adam? Cam had expected someone much

younger. He was dressed in clothes similar to those Sarah had lent to Cam, but while his own hair touched his shoulders, this man's hair was as short as the hair of tunnel donkeys.

"I'm Adam," he said, "and you must be Cam." The man peered at Cam's face as if searching for a clue that Mondo's visitor was not of this world. "You are older than I expected."

This revelation seemed to disturb him, Cam noted, evidenced by the glower on his face.

"I think your presence here will distress my grandfather more than he can handle in his fragile condition. Please leave."

"Adam, don't—"

"Mondo, you know what the doctor said about your weak heart. You don't need someone coming in here, upsetting you like this."

As he spoke, he stepped in front of Cam, blocking his view of Mondo. Glaring, Adam pointed firmly toward the portal.

Cam did not like being scuttled out the door as if he were a bothersome puppy, yet he did not understand the rules of this world. Until he did, it seemed best to obey.

The words "weak heart" echoed in his ears.

Ay, is it true? he asked himself. *The one Mandrian who might know of my beginnings is about to die? And I am being banished from his presence.*

15

The King's Command

Quinn followed a squire up a winding stairway to the royal chamber. The lad, called Witten, was lanky and quick. She could barely keep up with him. He was the squire who seemed quite taken with her lady, Cydlin, who was fifteen. The princess noticed the sideways glances the two gave each other when they thought the object of their intrigue wasn't looking.

Oh, the simplicity of meeting one who so fascinates you at such a young age.

In a few years, Quinn surmised, the squire would become a knight. He and Cydlin would marry and build a cottage, happy to find another soul who filled their hearts with love.

At the top of the stairs, Quinn shook off the dream-image. Such fantasies happened to common folk—never to her.

Stopping outside the portal to her parent's private tower, she waited for the squire to enter and return. What a bother having to be announced to one's own parents. The older she became, the more royal protocol seemed as rigid as a stonewood tree in the courtyard. Or was it simply because her eyes had seen how folk in the other world lived? How freely they spoke and touched and laughed. How few restrictions bound them.

The squire returned and bowed, keeping his eyes lowered, as was the law. "You may enter," he said.

Quinn hesitated. "Witten, look at me."

Startled, the squire kept his head bowed, shyly peeking up at her through his lashes, as if unsure whether or not to look directly into her eyes. "Yes, Your Highness?"

"If you love her," the princess said, "tell her. Tell her before it's too late."

Befuddled and shocked by her words, the squire backed down the stairway, bowing and giving her curious side-glances at the same time. "Yes, Your Highness. Yes, I certainly will."

Quinn listened to his footsteps on the stones and the "whoop!" he gave when he thought he was out of earshot.

"I have no idea why I said that," she muttered as she stepped into the most elaborate chamber in the castle. Walls were covered with colorful tapestries, telling the story of her ancestors' conquest of the kingdom before this one. A kingdom that once sprawled across the green hills of Outer Earth in the time when the outside world was safe for magical beings.

The woven story told of increasing danger for anyone

who possessed the gift. It told how Melikar had saved enchanted beings by leading them to a safe place, and how he had taken them, kingdoms and all, to the underground world he created.

Quinn loved the tapestries and never tired of studying them.

The queen was at her writing desk, and the king was across the chamber, staring thoughtfully out the tower window.

"Mother, Father," Quinn said, bowing to show respect.

The queen rose and approached her. She had changed from the russet gown to a less fancy one of teal, which matched her eyes. Quinn could tell by the disapproving look on her mother's face that she was not pleased with her daughter.

"You ran off from the celebration," her mum began. "Why, child?"

"I wanted to be alone."

"It is dangerous for you to be alone. Never do that."

Quinn was grateful her mother knew nothing of the other times she'd slipped about the kingdom unattended. What might her parents do if they found out? Lock her in the trophy hall with their jeweled crowns for safe-keeping?

"I am sorry I upset you."

The princess lowered her eyes, knowing the best course was to make amends and not attempt to defend herself, which was against the rules anyway.

Her mother nodded, accepting the apology, but not touching her, even though Quinn longed for her to do so. "Your father wants to speak with you, so I shall leave you two alone."

Quinn did not want her mum to leave. She liked having an ally whenever she faced her father. Now she had to face him alone.

As her mother departed, the king turned from the window and strode toward her, resting one hand on his dagger sheath. Quinn never understood why he wore a dagger inside castle walls. It all had to do with earlier times when one never knew if an enemy was hiding in a corridor, ready to leap out in a surprise attack.

"I think you know why I have summoned you here," he began.

Quinn knew. She could stall no longer on the choosing of a husband.

"It is time," said her father.

She looked into his eyes. Sympathy softened his gaze, yet it did not soften his voice.

"You are placing me in a dismaying situation," he continued. "Noblemen and kings, far and wide, are questioning why my daughter does not find their sons suitable. They are beginning to wonder if something is amiss with the princess of Mandria."

"I am sorry, Father, for causing you dismay."

"Tomorrow night," he said, "we shall hold the final gala. The biggest and most lavish ball of all. And you shall make your choice."

Quinn's heart beat like a rabbit's caught in a snare. She had not expected this. Her spirit rebelled, but she knew her tongue could not.

"In addition to those invited for tomorrow's festivities," her father added, "we shall include all the lads you've earlier shunned. They are welcome to return and spend another evening experiencing Mandrian hospitality."

The princess winced. All those dreadful lads who'd stepped on her toes, bragged in her face, drunk too much mead, or said the wrong things would be returning with their clammy hands and haughty airs. *Devil dust!* she swore to herself, borrowing Melikar's favorite curse.

The king paced the chamber, as if making up the plans as he went along. "The Great Hall shall be filled to capacity. I will command the doors be opened so the crowd may spill out into the courtyard as well."

He kept glancing at Quinn for her nod of approval, but she felt like crying instead, and she did not wish to cry in front of her father.

"I have requested the best entertainment. Jesters from Maywich, jugglers from Ivory, dancers from Bertem. Marged has been ordered to prepare the finest meats and the most lavish desserts ever attempted. All for my daughter's final betrothal ball."

Pausing, he playfully lifted her hand to dance a stately triboux across the chamber to the music of an imaginary harp. "Only the best for the future queen of Mandria—my lovely daughter and heir."

Quinn followed his dance steps and returned his smile. She was not angry with him. No, her anger was aimed at the set-in-stone laws that bound the royal family tighter than a robber's knot.

"In return for the biggest event Mandria has witnessed in years, my daughter will choose a husband whose name I shall announce to the crowd at midnight."

Stopping the dance, he held her gaze with a combination of endearment and frustration she knew she was causing him.

"I shall make the announcement at midnight, love, whether or not you have decided. Either your choice of a husband—or my choice for you."

So be it, she answered silently, knowing she must obey.

16

A Mildly Enchanted Dragon

Cam hurried from Mondo's chamber, feeling duly chastised by Adam and hating himself for not arguing for his right to be there with the old man. But what *was* his right to be there?

Hence, there was nothing to argue.

Returning to the living chamber, he found Sarah reading. Hannah was sprawled on top of the dragon, sleeping. The sight of the wee one lifted the gloom that had settled over Cam's head.

Sarah looked up. "How did it go?"

"Your brother banished me from Mondo's chamber."

"Oh, I didn't hear Adam come in. Don't worry. I'll go talk to him."

Cam sank onto one of the padded benches, realizing how tired and hungry he was. He could not recall the last time he'd eaten.

"Do you know where this toy dragon came from?" Sarah asked.

"I gave it to Hannah. Was that okay?"

"Oh, it's fine. Obviously, it did the trick and calmed her down. It's just that . . . well, you'll think I'm crazy, but the strangest thing happened while you were out of the room."

She lowered her voice even though no one was there. "I put Hannah's pacifier on the end table when I was setting up the playpen and forgot to give it to her. When I went to get it, it wasn't there. I turned around and . . . and saw it *floating* toward the playpen. I thought I was seeing things, but it floated right into Hannah's mouth."

Even though the story amazed him, Cam knew the explanation. It was the same one Melikar had given him for the reason he possessed magic—weak though it was. "I will try to explain," he said. "Magic has a tendency to affect its surroundings. A bit must have rubbed off on the dragon, which rubbed off on Hannah, so when she wanted her . . . what did you call it? A pacifier?"

Sarah nodded.

"All Hannah had to do was want it. Her desire was enough to make it happen."

"You mean, the dragon is magic?"

"No, not at all. But it has been stored in a wizard's chamber for fourteen years, so it's *mildly* enchanted."

"It's not dangerous, is it?"

"No," Cam assured her. "I am certain the magic will quickly wear off."

He glanced at the ring on his finger. When its magic

was strong, it had been dangerous for the princess. But now it was nothing more than a piece of metal, forged with the help of Grizzle. The magic had not lasted because he was not a true enchanter.

Cam realized the same truth applied to him. Now that he no longer lived in the wizard's chamber, whatever weak spells he conjured in the past would be impossible now.

Sighing, he turned his attention back to Sarah. "I will take the dragon away if you'd like."

"No. Hannah loves it. Leave it be."

Cam had employed the toy only to temporarily distract the child. Seeing her latch onto it gave him a strange mix of emotions. It pleased him to see the exuberant way she'd claimed his childhood toy, yet he felt something else as well—a deeply confusing urge to cry, "It's mine!" and snatch it back.

Perhaps the latter had happened to his much-younger self, but he could not recall any details or who may have tried to take his beloved Mop.

"You must be hungry," Sarah said. "I'll fix you something and get you settled into your room. Elsy will be back to cook supper for Mondo."

Cam agreed since he certainly had no other plans.

He followed Sarah down another narrow passageway and into a small chamber. There were two beds, a dresser, and a small desk with a chair. Much nicer than the cold, dark chamber in the castle that had almost become his permanent home.

Where will I live once I return to Mandria?

Ay, he had not thought of that. He would have to

find an occupation to pay for lodging and food. Perhaps Grizzle would take him in until he could decide what he wanted to do, although living in the Marnie village with hundreds of cats did not appeal to him.

"Make yourself at home," Sarah told him. "I snitched some of Adam's old clothes he left behind. They're in the closet. You'll find other things you can wear in the dresser."

She set down the backpack containing his Mandrian garments. "The bath is across the hall. Help yourself to soap and towels and toiletries. Stay here for now. I'll talk to Adam while I'm rounding up food for you, but it would probably better if you weren't there."

After closing the door, Cam sank onto the bed. Now what? For a quest, this seemed pretty tame. Calming agitated babies was not what he had in mind. He thought of Adam and scoffed. *The first challenge I face in my quest, and I run away like a frightened squirrel. What a great knight I would make.*

Perhaps he should find out what Mondo did to earn his keep in this world and do the same. Stay here and become a merchant. Sell pigs or cloth or spices.

Sighing, Cam realized that becoming a merchant was not his heart's desire—not any more than the desire to be an enchanter with weak magic.

The door opened. Sarah set a tray on the desk. "I hope a sandwich and soda are okay."

She waited for him to try a taste. The sandwich, as she called it, was nothing more than meat and bread. Not too different from feasts below the river. The beverage was fizzing, which alarmed him, but when he took a sip, he was pleased by its sweet taste.

"This used to be my room," Sarah said. "Quinn stayed here, too. She slept in the bed near the window."

Cam took it all in, feeling serene to know he was in a room the princess had once slept in. He would also choose the bed near the window.

"Did you talk to your brother?" he asked.

Sarah glanced away, as if hoping he wouldn't ask. "Give him time, Cam. He's very protective of our grandfather and seems unduly suspicious of you. My guess is that he thinks you and Quinn go out."

"Go out where?"

She tried not to laugh. "I mean, go out *together*. As a couple. Like boyfriend and girlfriend."

Cam was unfamiliar with the words, but he knew what she was implying. "You mean, do I court the princess?"

"Exactly."

He groaned to himself, hating to explain a truth that pained his heart. "A proper suitor must come from nobility and, alas, I come from . . . ay, I do not even know, so I cannot—"

"Be a proper suitor?" Sarah finished. "That sounds so weird." Tilting her head in curiosity, she added, "Would you if you could? Court the princess?"

The question caught him off-guard. Cam felt his face flush and realized his eyes were looking everywhere but at Sarah. *Bother!* He knew he'd given himself away. No need to answer. Sarah knew.

"Ahhhh" was all she said.

Cam began to inspect a pot of dried lilacs on the

dresser as though it suddenly demanded his full attention.

"Well," Sarah said. "I'll make sure Adam knows you do not *court* the princess. I won't tell him more than that." She winked to show she was aware of his secret. "Maybe my brother will lighten up if he knows you and Quinn are just acquaintances."

"Mere childmates," Cam reluctantly assured her.

"Oh, one more thing."

Her hesitation drew his full attention as the playful glint in her eyes faded. "I don't know how Adam got this message, but I could tell it upset him. Somehow he thinks that the wizard wants Mondo to know he can go home to . . . um, to die." Sarah's voice wavered. She looked as if she were about to cry.

"Go home to Mandria?" Cam asked, not sure if he understood what she was saying.

Sarah nodded.

"Does Mondo *desire* to return?"

"I don't know. Right or wrong, Adam decided not to tell him. He wants our grandfather to stay here with us—his family."

Adam's defiance of Melikar made Cam uneasy. No one ignored a request from the wizard—at least no one below the river. "Do you agree with your brother's decision?"

"No. I think he should tell Mondo. I mean, I would hate to see him leave, but I've always felt bad that he left his homeland with every intention of returning. He stayed in this world when he really wanted to go home. I'll bet he'd love to see Mandria one last time."

Sarah's words pleased Cam. But how could he convince Adam?

"I can't figure out how my brother got this message from Melikar in the first place," Sarah said. "He wouldn't tell me."

Cam had already figured it out. Melikar must have told Adam in person during his brief visit to Mandria. True, Adam was not bound to obey the wizard, but it certainly seemed fair to let Mondo decide for himself.

Sarah departed. Cam sat at the desk to eat his feast. He could not get the meat and bread down fast enough. It tasted quite good—especially the strange yellow crisps that crunched when bitten into.

Afterward, curiosity drew him to the "bath across the hall," as Sarah had called it. A bath might ease the tension of this incredible day.

Stepping into the small room, Cam found a tub but no bucket for carrying water. Recalling how Quinn had told him that water "comes out of the walls," Cam took hold of something that resembled a door latch and turned it. He expected the wall to spring open, but instead, water poured out of a spigot and began to fill the tub.

Cam grinned, marveling at the ease of it all. *Magic.*

Sinking into the warm water felt as healing as any bath in a Mandrian grotto. Closing his eyes, he relaxed until the light coming through a window faded and the room began to grow dark.

Cam was grateful Sarah had set out soap and towels for him. He washed quickly before the light disappeared, then dressed again in Adam's garments.

Back in the room, he lay down on the bed in which Quinn had once slept and promptly fell asleep. A while later, a bright light burst into his dreams, bringing him hastily to his feet.

Sarah entered, apologizing for waking him. She set a bowl of soup and a slice of cake on the desk and cleared away the other dishes.

"Elsy made this for Mondo's dinner, so I brought you some. She's not needed tonight since Adam is here to sleep on the sofa in Mondo's room. I have to get home and put Hannah to bed. Do you need anything before I leave?"

"I can think of nothing you have not already provided," Cam told her. He wanted to ask about the morrow but knew he would find out soon enough for himself.

"Do you mind if Hannah takes the dragon home for the night?" Sarah asked. "I cannot pry it out of her little hands."

Cam laughed. "It is fine."

"She's given it a name. 'Mop,' she's calling it. Don't know where the name came from. I hope you don't mind."

Cam felt pleased Hannah had latched onto the dragon *and* its name. "No, I don't mind. Mop is a good name for a dragon," he said, repeating the same comment Quinn had made earlier.

"Goodnight then," Sarah said. "When you're ready to sleep, just flick this switch." She showed him how to turn the light on and off. "I remember when Quinn was here, she did not know how to make the light go away."

Cam bid Sarah goodnight, then opened the window drape to look out over the dark city, dotted with lights he now knew did not come from candles.

He thought about the princess. How could he *stop* thinking about her when Sarah kept bringing up her name?

Cam moved to the desk for his evening feast. The beef soup was familiar, but the cake did not taste as delicious as Marged's creations—which assured him that some things were better in the world beneath the river.

Taking off his Outer-Earth clothes, he laid them neatly on the end of his bed, then fetched his Mandrian garments from Sarah's knapsack. Putting on the more-familiar tunic and leggings, he decided to sleep in them so he could feel a little closer to home.

After a moment's hesitation, he also pulled out the frayed blanket of his babyhood, placed it over the pillow, and set the worn ball on the small table next to the bed.

Curiosity made him open the closet to take a look at what was inside. As Sarah promised, he found extra clothes and shoes. On a high shelf were boxes. Reaching up, Cam drew one down and opened it. Inside were piles of parchment with likenesses of people captured on them. What a surprise. How did they do that?

Sitting on the bed, he looked at images of Sarah and Adam, caught in time when they were young and as they grew through the years. Amazing.

As he started to put the lid back, something caught his eye. The princess. There she was, dressed in Outer-Earth garments, standing with a younger version of Sarah and a boy with red hair. Scribbled on the back

108

were the words: *Quinn, Sarah, Scott.*

What a shock to find a likeness of Quinn here. He was tempted to take it, but he could not. If all Adam had left of the princess was this image of her, then the honorable thing to do was let him keep it.

Feeling guilty for snooping, Cam closed the box and started to return it to the top shelf when an object shoved further back attracted his attention. Drawing it out so he could see it better, Cam's heart began to gallop.

It was a small trunk. On the curved lid was a faded image of a blue horse with peeling paint. It was a perfect match to the trunk Melikar had given him with his childhood belongings inside.

17

Preparing for the Final Gala

"Toads and mugwort!" yelped the princess as the comb caught a snarl.

"Sorry, m'lady," mumbled Cydlin. "The queen ordered us to do our best since tonight is the banquet and ball to top all others."

"Yes," chirped Gwynell. "Tonight is the night you shall choose a husband!" She twirled in a circle to make her point and almost swooned onto the dressing table.

The princess dipped her head to hide her amusement. If only *she* could be as excited tonight as her ladies. Shouldn't the one doing the choosing be the most keen of all?

Quinn couldn't let Gwynell know how entertaining she found her tonight. If she did not remain stern with her ladies, they would spend the entire evening dressing and fussing with her, and she would miss the ball entirely.

On second thought, perhaps that was not such a dreadful idea.

"Cydlin, please do not yank so hard," Quinn begged. A head pain was beginning to tingle between her eyes. "Gwynell, be a love and go find Melikar. Ask him to send something to dull the ache right here." She pointed at her brow.

"Yes, m'lady."

"And do be quick. I must not anger my father any further by being late to the evening feast."

The lass raced out of the chamber, giving the princess some reprieve. Gwynell was the chatty one. Cydlin was quiet and barely spoke unless addressed.

As she pouted at herself in the looking glass, Quinn's thoughts drifted to Cam. *Why can't he be here tonight to tell me amusing stories and make me laugh? We could stand on the balcony and poke fun at the suitors below who are so filled with their own wonderment.*

She could almost hear Cam whispering in jest, "When the knight who wears a ring on every finger says, 'You are beautiful, and I am falling in love with you,' he will most likely be gazing at his own reflection in the fountain and not looking at you at all."

Quinn shivered, drawing a curious glance in the looking glass from Cydlin. She played Cam's teasing voice through her head once more, repeating the words she invented: "You are beautiful, and I am falling in love with you." Something about imagining those words, spoken by Cam, brought unexpected tears to her eyes.

Standing abruptly, she ignored Cydlin's cry of dismay and began to pace, circling Scrabit, who had laid claim to the middle of the floor, snoring loud dragon snores as tiny puffs of smoke drifted above his head.

All evening, Quinn had been catching glimpses in her mind's eye of the Outer-Earth chamber she had once shared with Sarah. Why? Might Cam be there at this present moment? Was he aware that she had slept in Sarah's room? Could he be sleeping in the very same bed?

Suddenly she missed him as much as she already missed Ameka. All her life, Cam had been nearby, and now he was far away. The realization sparked a feeling of panic, which surprised and disturbed her.

She recalled the time her pony, Trinka, had become contrary and stumbled in the grotto, dumping her into one of the pools.

Cam had saved her. Leaped into the water, boots and all, and wrapped his arms around her, frantically apologizing for touching her. They had laughed about it later. How does one save a drowning princess without touching her?

She remembered how the tone of his voice had calmed her and how she had stopped struggling to let him carry her to safety. He'd set her down gently and hovered over her adoringly.

"I've never felt so safe and protected before," she whispered.

"Pardon?" said Cydlin.

The maiden's voice jerked her back to the present. "Nothing, lass." Composing herself, Quinn returned to the bench so her lady could finish twisting the handful of braids into a pleasing knot.

"You work magic with hair designs," Quinn told her, admiring the maiden's handiwork.

"Why, thank you, m'lady. Alas, this may be the final time."

"Final time? What do you mean?" Quinn heard dismay in her own voice.

"Pardon, I did not mean to upset you. I simply meant that Jalla will be cutting off your hair soon in preparation for your wedding."

The pain in Quinn's head began to throb. Where was Gwynell? "I do not wish to hear about weddings and hair cuttings."

Pinning the final braid in place, Cydlin stepped back, blinking away tears.

Quinn caught Cydlin's eye in the looking glass. "I am on edge tonight, lass. Pay no mind to my temperament. You have done well, taking care of my personal needs and sewing my gowns."

The maiden, blushing at the praise, busied herself at the dressing table.

"Go now and be with your mum," Quinn told her.

"Ay, but I need to finish with your jewels."

"I can see to it. And Gwynell will be back in a bit. Go."

"Thank you, m'lady." Cydlin flew out of the chamber as if wanting to get away before the princess changed her mind.

Quinn stood before the looking glass and appraised the finished work of her ladies. They had done a fine job. She looked like herself—only better. *The queen will be pleased.*

Her hair was divided into four braids, coiled and intertwined, falling just below her shoulders. Periwinkle buds peeked from the twists of the braids. They made her think of the blue rose Adam had tucked into her braid the last time she saw him in the other world. Thinking of him now gave her peace instead of pain, as though she were recalling a dear friend from long ago.

The periwinkle buds matched the deep blue of her gown, newly sewn, and, in Quinn's opinion, a bit too revealing. She gave the bodice a firm upward tug.

Cam floated into her mind, light as a feather, and she felt herself reddening. What would he think of his childmate if he saw her tonight?

"Princess!"

Quinn flinched, as though caught in the act of doing something inappropriate. She hoped her discomfiting thoughts were not readable on her face.

"Yes, Gwynell, did you find Melikar?" The maiden was not out of breath, which told Quinn the lass had taken her time with the errand in spite of the request to hasten.

"Yes, m'lady. The wizard told me to speak your name as I stepped into your chamber, and the pain would flee."

In a heartbeat, Quinn realized it was true. The pain had dissolved the moment the lass stepped through the portal and greeted her.

"Where is Cydlin?" Gwynell asked.

"I let her go early." Before the lass could complain, Quinn added, "And you may go, too."

Gwynell hopped up and down three times in pure

joy, then dashed out of the chamber.

Quinn fetched the sapphire-and-diamond tiara her mum had asked her to wear tonight and slipped it on. Around her neck, she fastened her grandmum's diamond choker.

Gazing at herself in the looking glass one last time, she failed to see Mandria's princess on the cusp of her sixteenth year. All she saw was a melancholy face, shadowed in sadness.

"If only Melikar could give me something to stop the pain in my heart as quickly as he stopped the pain in my head."

Lifting her crinkly blue skirts, she went off to the final gala to choose the one with whom she would share her throne and her future.

But never, ever her heart.

18

Visitor
in the Night

"You are beautiful, and I am falling in love with you."

Cam whispered the words aloud in the dark chamber in Mondo's home. They had drifted into his mind, interrupting his sleep as if some mysterious breeze had blown them in his direction. He did not understand where the words had come from, but he did not need an enchanter to tell him for whom the words were intended.

Raising onto his elbows, he came fully awake. He had never allowed himself to even *think* those words about the princess, yet no truer words had ever bloomed inside his mind.

A familiar image formed in his memory—one he'd thought about often: the time Quinn's pony stumbled in the grotto and he had to dive into the pool to save her. He remembered the feel of his arms around her and how she had clung to him, trusting him completely.

"My heart embraces you," he whispered into the darkness.

The words surged strength through his veins.

And anger.

Flinging back the coverlet, he perched on the edge of the bed and dropped his head into his hands. He had not cried in years. Not since he'd burned himself the time he muffed a fire spell at Melikar's hearth. Those were tears of pain and humiliation. These, spilling from his eyes, were tears of grief.

Here I am on the wrong side of the wishing pool, seeking my future, when the only future I desire is in the world below, about to choose a life without me.

Why did fate have to be so merciless?

A creak told him the door was opening. He knew Sarah had departed. Was Adam coming to banish him totally from Mondo's home?

Outlined in the doorway, backlit with muted light from the corridor, stood a bent figure.

"Sire!" Quickly wiping tears away, Cam sprang to his feet and was across the chamber in two steps to help.

The light came on. Mondo signaled him to be quiet and close the door. Cam obeyed, then started to help the old man toward the second bed.

"No, lad, I spend far too much time bedridden. I prefer to sit at the desk." His gaze took in Cam's garments, putting a delighted smile on his face. "How long it has been since I've seen anyone dressed in Mandrian clothes."

Cam helped him settle in at the desk. "Why have you come?"

Mondo tilted his head to look up at him. "That is the same question I asked you earlier. I still want an answer."

Cam was too tense to sit. He paced as best he could in the small space. "I came to this world on a quest," he began.

Mondo's eyes sparked with interest. "Mandrian lads always love a good quest. What is it you are seeking?"

"I am seeking my past in order to find my future."

Mondo nodded as if the vague answer made perfect sense. "Did Melikar send you or did you come of your own accord?"

Hearing the wizard's name in this world still startled Cam every time someone mentioned it. "Melikar released me from his service to find the answers I was seeking, but it was I who decided to begin my search in this world."

"How did you come to that decision?"

Mondo's voice was weak, but his words seemed well-chosen. Cam had a feeling he knew more than he was letting on.

"Before I departed from Mandria, the wizard gave me a trunk containing all I possessed when I arrived at his chamber the very first time. The princess believed the items in the trunk—and my memories of them—came from this world, so I knew this is where my search must begin."

"And have you found any answers?"

Cam stopped his pacing to think. "Nay, only more questions. For one, I found a trunk which matches the one I left in Mandria. And I found it right here in this very chamber."

Cam watched Mondo's face, waiting for him to react. *Will he chide me for snooping?*

"The trunk! Devil dust, I'd forgotten." Putting a hand to his head, he slumped in the chair.

"Are you well?" Cam asked, concerned by the sudden droop of Mondo's shoulders.

He closed his eyes. "The pain your words give me is deep in the soul—not the body."

Cam dropped to one knee in front of Mondo. "Sire, why do I own a trunk that matches one in this world?"

"Did you open it?"

"No." Cam realized he had not even thought about opening it. Just the sight of it had been distressing enough.

Mondo motioned toward the closet. "Can you fetch it down?"

Anticipation made Cam's hands shake as he reached onto the high shelf and lifted the trunk from its spot. Carefully, he set it on the desk.

"Open it."

Cam unhooked the latch and lifted the lid. Inside were baby clothes. He took them out to see what lay beneath. Toys, tiny shoes, crinkled papers.

"As time passed," Mondo began, "I let go of many possessions I once shared with my wife."

"The other Hannah," Cam stated.

"Yes. *My* Hannah. But this trunk and its possessions I saved in case, after I am gone, anyone needed proof . . ."

119

His voice trailed off. Cam could see Mondo's energy fading and knew he must not tire him out by pressuring him for answers. But he so needed to know what Mondo could tell him.

"Proof of what?" Cam ventured.

Mondo looked at him squarely. "Proof that you come from a family of great nobility."

19

The Princess
Is Announced

Quinn gave her bodice a final tug as she waited with Lord Blakely behind a drape on the balcony overlooking the Great Hall. As the blare of the trumpets faded, Lord Blakely pulled back a corner of the drape so the crowd below could see him. In his grainy voice, he proclaimed, "Lords, ladies, knights, princes—and our one lowly king without a kingdom." He paused for the laughter he knew his jest would bring.

Quinn did not smile when Lord Blakely glanced behind the drape to see if she was laughing. How cruel to make fun of King Millstoke of Banyyan, who just lost his kingdom to the Bromlians and had to flee to Mandria for safety.

Now, a warlord presided over the neighboring kingdom instead of its rightful king—bringing the hostilities one giant step closer to Mandria.

Each time Quinn spoke to King Millstoke, he was charming and kind, albeit terribly shy and nervous. Quinn wondered if his dream was to find a new kingdom to rule, and Mandria was a definite possibility. All he had to do was marry its princess.

Lord Blakely cleared his throat and frowned at her, as if it was against royal protocol not to laugh at his jokes. Stepping in front of the drape, he continued, "It is my esteemed honor to present Her Royal Highness, Princess Quinn of Mandria."

Pulling aside the drape, he motioned her forward. Quinn pretended not to notice the arm he offered. She did not trust him. She suspected he fancied himself with more power than he rightly possessed—simply because he had the king's ear.

The lord gave her a slimy smile and grabbed her hand, kissing it with a flourish for all who were watching. Did he exempt himself from protocol while forcing others to obey the ancient laws? Or was he hoping to be the one chosen? The thought made her ill.

The princess started to yank her hand away in disgust, then thought better of offending him. Moving to the railing of the balcony, she waved at the crowd, giving her best parade smile.

Applause and shouts of approval exploded from the floor below.

The cheerfulness on her face did not penetrate her heart. This behavior was expected of her; she was simply playing her role.

Quinn's first impulse was to scan the countless upturned faces for Ameka and Cam, but that, of course, was pointless since her closest allies were not there—ay, were not even in the kingdom.

Lifting the skirt of her gown, she stepped down a winding stairway ahead of Lord Blakely instead of by his side. Knowing everyone's eyes were upon her made her heart flutter with nerves. She hoped she would not stumble.

Below, a line of suitors quickly formed, each hoping to dance long enough with the heir to the Mandrian throne to make a good enough impression that she might seek him out for further conversation.

Quinn made a point to catch the eye of King Millstoke and give him a sympathetic smile. He returned her acknowledgement with a pleased nod.

Then, taking a deep breath, the princess held her head high to greet her guests. She pretended this was the very first ball of the lot and she was seeing everyone for the first time. Blotting out previous memories, she vowed to be open to the charms of every lad.

With the jaded veil removed from her eyes, Quinn turned her gaze upon each hopeful suitor, knowing she must choose the best—or rather, the best for her. A lad she might, in time, grow fond of.

Someone warm and kind who made her laugh. Someone witty, attentive, and fiercely loyal to her.

Someone like Cam.

20

Cam's Truth

Mondo's comment played over and over inside Cam's head: *"You come from a family of great nobility."*

The words made him weak. He sank onto the bed, stunned.

"I—I . . ." He could not decide which important question to ask first.

All Cam knew was that his hunch was accurate. Mondo *did* know. *He will be able to tell me who I am.*

"I must return to my bed," Mondo said abruptly. "This has taken all of my energy. We can talk later."

Cam wished he possessed real magic so he could help Mondo. *Fie* on thinking all his life he was an enchanter when he was not. And *fie* on believing he did not come from nobility when he did.

He did! Toads and mugwort! Mondo said quite clearly he had proof.

The news was so huge Cam could barely hold it in his mind.

"Please stay a bit longer so you can explain," he urged, trying not to sound as though he were begging, when, in fact, he was.

Mondo's hands began to shake, and Cam knew he needed to heed the old man's wishes.

"I am sorry for pressing you, Sire. I shall take you back to your chamber as you requested." Helping Mondo to his feet, Cam tried to mask his disappointment.

"Sorry, lad," the old man said. "I want to tell you the whole story. Every last word. But it's not in me right now to do so. If only Elsy could fix me a bowl of kemble fish stew for strength, but no such thing exists in this world."

Cam faltered. "B–but I brought some with me. Powdered kemble fish. I have it in my knapsack. Ay, why did I not think of it earlier?"

Hope leaped into Mondo's eyes. "Do you know how to administer it?"

"Of course. I was Melikar's apprentice for all of my life."

Cam knew his brave words did not match his inner courage, because he was not confident about the dosage at all. Yet his prideful words came out before he could stop them.

Helping Mondo to the other bed, Cam drew back the coverlet and settled him in. Then he fetched the herb vials from his knapsack.

Mumbling a silent plea to Melikar for assistance, he carefully sprinkled three shakes of kemble fish powder into the old man's hand. After a moment's hesitation, he added two shakes of faery glove to strengthen the heart.

"Here," he said. "Hold this beneath your tongue."

Mondo did as Cam instructed, then lay back on the pillow.

Cam wished he could dim the bright light overhead, but he needed to watch Mondo carefully to make sure the dosage was correct. Too little would be useless. Too much could stall the heart.

Mondo lay very still as if he were sleeping. His skin was a worrisome shade of gray. Cam began to fret over the dose he'd given. Was it correct? Had Mondo's breathing waned? Was it a poor decision to combine the faery glove with the kemble fish?

Panic flushed Cam's neck. He put his hand on Mondo's. "Can you hear me, Sire? What are you feeling?"

Before Cam's eyes, color began to flow into the old man's face. With a great intake of air, Mondo began to breathe deeply. His eyes blinked open. Turning his head, he gave Cam a bright-eyed wink and smiled. "I can feel my strength returning in waves. Each wave seems stronger than the last. Thank you. Thank you enormously, my son."

Mondo's improvement stunned Cam—but not nearly as much as his comment. "What . . . ay . . . what did you call me?"

Mondo easily pulled himself into a sitting position, which astounded both of them. "I called you 'son,'" he explained, "because you are my firstborn."

Cam stared at Mondo's steady gaze, searching for

words with which to answer. His heart seemed to have forgotten how to beat. All he could think was that he might need to administer faery glove to himself.

"And the trunk you found?" Mondo added. "It belonged to your brother."

21

The Banquet

At the bottom of the stairway, several handsome knights vied for the right to escort the princess to the banquet. Quinn did not feel flattered. They were not begging attention from her, but rather, from who she was, who she would become, and how gaining her favor could change their lives.

Before she had a chance to choose which arm to take, Lord Blakely haughtily cut in and offered his. Ignoring him in front of everyone would be a mistake. Angering him would set him against her, and she did not want that. Not when her father listened to him as though the man's wisdom was higher than His Royal Highness's.

Reluctantly, Quinn took Lord Blakely's arm. Disappointed groans rippled down the line of hopefuls as he escorted her to the royal table. The king and queen were present in the Great Hall. Normally, they observed festivities from their private balcony, but tonight, they were part of the gala.

Around the room sat oak tables, built by Marnies, and spread with such elegance and lavishness, it was difficult for Quinn not to absorb the gaiety of the occasion.

Huge platters of roasted venison and pheasant graced each table. Centerpieces were trees fashioned from oranges, plums, apples, and pomegranates, decorated with ribbons and walnuts. Loaves of bread were baked into shapes: birds, fish, and rabbits.

Marged had certainly outdone herself. Quinn could only imagine the fancy desserts to come.

Glancing about the Great Hall, she counted thirty tables of guests. This was indeed the largest gathering held in the castle that she could remember.

After boisterous entertainment by jesters and a dancing bear, the room hushed as each suitor stood to introduce himself and say something profound, humorous, or in some way memorable enough for the princess to recall his wit after the tables were cleared and minstrels began to play.

Quinn nibbled a bit of bread, but two things kept her from enjoying the feast. One, the anticipatory knot in her stomach, knowing she'd best pay attention to each young man since mere hours remained until she'd be forced to make a choice that would affect the rest of her life.

And two, since each suitor was addressing her, it felt disrespectful to respond while biting the doughy ears off a rabbit.

"I am Risibly of Bally, son of Lord Timmal," said one young lad who'd caught Quinn's eye earlier. She liked his wavy auburn hair and the way he smiled at her in sympathy, as if concerned for her predicament. Perhaps he was a possible choice?

"I have come to Mandria," Risibly continued, "to claim a bride and my place in history."

Raising a tankard of mead, he saluted Quinn and joined in the surrounding laughter at his impudence.

The princess was not laughing. Never could she choose someone who spoke words meant to impress her but sickened her instead. *Perhaps I am a poor judge of character.*

"I am not used to announcing myself," began the next lad, "but in this circumstance, I shall proceed. I am Prince Roth of McDuffie. My father, the king, has given me my own castle, so I have little desire to live in Mandria. However, I have need of a wife worthy of my station; hence, I have come to marry the most influential of those who qualify."

A smattering of applause told Quinn she was not the only one who found Prince Roth a bit too full of his own wonderfulness.

Giving up on her meal, the princess sat back and listened to one lad after another stand and brag to the crowd. Soon it became apparent that they were competing with each other to be the brightest and funniest, with nary a care about the kind of impression they were making on the princess.

Glancing at her mum, Quinn was rewarded with a look of empathy from one who had been in a similar predicament—albeit her mum was one of many maidens hoping to be chosen by the king when he was a youthful prince.

The difference was that her parents had been childmates and already shared a bond that had nothing to do with royalty. She knew they loved each other long before the choosing began.

The king avoided her eyes as he tapped his toe to the music. She knew why he would not look at her. None of the noble knights and princes were what his daughter desired.

Curling her hands into fists below the table, the princess sat resigned to her fate, willing the night to be over. *Does no one desire to know me because I am just Quinn? And not because I am the future queen of the most powerful kingdom?*

22

A Bit Much for One Heart

"**I** am your son?" Cam stammered. "You are my father?"

His mind whirled with the incredible news for a full minute while Mondo, leaning back against the pillow, smiled at him in such a tender way, the former wizard's apprentice felt a joy he'd never before experienced.

"True," Mondo confirmed. "A Mandrian truth."

"And I have a brother?" Cam did not think his heart could bear any more startling news tonight.

"Yes, your brother, Daniel, was born when you were two."

Cam had always wondered about himself alone, yet now he had to widen his mind to take in the realization of having a brother. "Where is he?" Cam asked, moving the chair from the desk closer to the bed so he could settle in and listen.

Mondo's expression shifted as he absently adjusted the coverlet around himself. "Sadly, your brother is no longer with us. I promise to tell all in due time, but for now, look in the bottom of the trunk. You will find papers about Lord and Lady Dover of Kilmory Manor, and their son, Mondo, who was all set to become a Knight of the First Order when he . . . he suddenly disappeared."

"Kilmory Manor?" Cam repeated. "You come from *those* Dovers?" He knew of the family; how could he not? They were the wealthiest landowners in Mandria.

"Lord and Lady Dover were my parents. Alas, they are no longer living either. Melikar was good about keeping me informed over the years. I was heir to Kilmory Manor, but was so wrapped up in my life in this world, I did not wish to go back. The inheritance fell to my aunt, who took over in my absence. When she died, the manor passed to her son, Blakely."

Cam balked at the name. Lord Blakely was the *last* person with whom he wanted a family connection. Shaking off the dismal news, he tried to lock the puzzle pieces together in his mind. One thing still concerned him. "If you left Mandria suddenly and never returned, how did you get papers proving who you are?"

"Quick thinking, lad. It's a good question. Melikar was wise enough to know I might need proof of my identity in the future—and proof of yours. He sent the papers to me."

"How?" Cam asked, still confused.

Mondo smiled as he remembered. "Hannah and I were sitting by a lake one Sunday afternoon when a red-feathered trega landed on a tree branch above us. Hannah remarked on how unusual a bird it was. When I realized it was a trega, I quickly stood, and it flew down to land on my arm. The bird was unusual to Hannah because tregas do not exist in the outer world."

"The bird brought the papers from Melikar?"

"Indeed it did. Hannah thought it was holding prey in its beak, but it was a small packet. The trega dropped the packet into my hands, then flew off toward Wonder-Land Park. I never saw it again."

Mondo's face whitened as the weakness seemed to return. Cam tensed. The kemble fish should not yet be losing its effectiveness. Another dose could be taken, yet the healing power could quickly become a deadly one, much the way that summer sun warmed the underground chambers but too much heat without rain parched the earthen walls and dried up the healing streams in the grotto.

"Are you feeling well?" Cam asked.

Mondo put a hand to his head. "Yes, yes, I still feel strong, yet I forgot how painful it is to think of the family I left behind. I would give anything to return to the kingdom of my birth, live in the manor once again, and walk the tunnels of Mandria."

"You can."

Mondo gave him a disbelieving look. "I defied Melikar by staying in this world. I would not dream of asking him to arrange a return."

"But he offered."

Mondo's breathing quickened. "What do you mean?"

Cam knew it was not his news to reveal. Adam

could protect Mondo all he wanted, but in truth, Adam was Mondo's grandson, many times removed—yet Cam, he had the *right* to offer the news because *he* was Mondo's son.

I am Mondo's son.

He had to keep reminding himself. The truth had not fully penetrated his heart.

More importantly, if Mondo was his father, didn't the job of protecting him and doing what was best now rest upon his own shoulders? Not Adam's?

"Mondo," he began.

"I'd be honored if you would call me Father."

Cam felt tears spring into his eyes. "Father," he said, "this is not my news to share, but the message is an important one, and it has been kept from you, so, as your son, I choose to tell you."

Mondo's anticipation was intense. It pleased Cam to see how strong he had become in such a short time.

Begging the High Spirit to forgive his betrayal against Adam, he continued, "Melikar instructed your grandson to tell you that you are welcome to return to Mandria if you so desire." Cam left out the part about going home to die.

"But how did this message come to Adam?"

Cam recalled the wizard's warning to watch what he said, yet why withhold this information from the one who most needed to know it?

Taking a breath, he told Mondo about the meeting between Adam and the princess. "Before your grandson departed from Mandria," Cam finished, "Melikar gave him the message, but Adam has chosen not to tell you."

The news disturbed Mondo. Shoving back the coverlet, he pulled himself from the bed, standing strong without a cane. "Why would my grandson deny me this final joy in life?"

"He felt you were too weak to travel, and he wanted you here with him and Sarah and the baby. Part of his decision was concern for you and part was his unwillingness to let you go. He cannot be condemned for that."

Mondo stood quietly, lost in thought. Cam knew his father was struggling with the decision. He'd left one family to start another. Should he now leave this family to return to a place where the ones most dear to him were gone?

"I don't fault Adam for his loyalty," Mondo said. "He's been very good to me, and he's had his own sorrow to bear. Losing both parents when he was just a lad. I can see why he does not want to lose me as well."

The old man focused on Cam. "But you, you plan to return to Mandria, true?"

"True." The thought made Cam realize the urgency of it all. He had accomplished what he came here to do. He'd found his identity and knew from whence he came. In fact, the news was far better than he ever imagined.

And . . . dare he dream it? The words themselves seemed afraid to form in his mind: He, Cam of Mandria, was really Cam Dover of Kilmory Manor, son of Mondo, grandson of Lord and Lady Dover—which made him officially eligible to declare his love for the one his heart had embraced for always and forever.

If, indeed, it was not too late.

23

A Turn of Events

The feast ended with lavish desserts offered to each guest by a small army of lads and lasses dressed in silver capes, rushing to attend to the tables they'd been assigned.

Quinn appreciated the expense her father had gone to in order to make this a memorable night. Sounds of laughter from the children lifted her spirits. Vowing to shake off her impending sense of doom, she surprised the hall by stepping out to join the lads and lasses, going from table to table to greet her guests.

She knew without looking that the king and queen were pleased to see her take an active part in the evening, yet she hated feeling as though her actions were spurred by an obligation to please. Her unfeeling heart contradicted her warm smile and kind words, but as long as no one could tell . . .

Several suitors vying for her attention offered bites of their desserts. The princess played along, searching for some sort of a connection with each, but they played more to the crowd than to her, which did not endear them to her.

After the feast ended, guests were invited to the courtyard to watch acrobats and fire jugglers while the Great Hall was transformed into a ballroom.

Music drew them back inside. Quinn was immediately escorted into the first triboux by the Prince of Wick. Him, she remembered. He was the one who'd had such an unpleasant scent about him, everyone had scurried away. Quinn was hesitant to step too close, but he did not seem too malodorous tonight.

The knight from Bootle stepped in to take the prince's place. His scheming grated on Quinn's nerves. He seemed to have their lives all planned out, even down to names for their children: Their son would be Alvid-the-Fourth, after himself, Alvid-the-Third, and their daughter would be Onyda, after his grandmum.

Quinn could not get away fast enough.

The music continued. The line of knights, princes, and sons of noblemen seemed to grow longer. Quinn was exhausted—and hungry after barely partaking in the feast. Worse, each minute closer to midnight—and the announcement—twisted her insides until she could barely breathe.

When the knight from Tarry spilled mead on her gown, the princess begged a break. She summoned Gwynell from the shadows where she had spotted her lady watching the festivities.

"Go to the queen, lass, and tell her I have gone to ask Cydlin to clean a spill from my gown. But, please, stall for a few long minutes, walk slowly, then take your time delivering my message."

I am in no hurry to return and do not want guards coming to check on me, she added to herself.

"As you wish," Gywnell said, raising her brows in delight at being let in on a bit of trickery.

Quinn slipped away from the crowd without a backward glance, quickly making her way along the dimly lit castle corridors to her dressing chamber.

"Cydlin!" she called as she arrived. When her lady did not answer, Quinn remembered sending her home for the evening. "Bother," she grumbled. "I'll have to clean it myself."

"May I help?" came a voice from a corner unlit by firelight.

Quinn's heart skittered. What sort of person had stolen into her private chamber uninvited?

"Show yourself at once!" she demanded.

A figure wrapped in a hooded traveling cape stepped into the light.

Quinn tensed, ready to shout for a guard, but the figure quickly revealed herself.

"Ameka!"

In two steps, Quinn was across the chamber, and hugging her friend. "What are you doing here? I thought you—"

"Shh–shh," Ameka said, hushing her. "I haven't much time."

"What happened?"

"We had almost passed out of Mandria and were planning to take the long way around Banyyan since it is overrun by the enemy. Then couriers brought bitter news. Dagon's own king has been taken prisoner by the Bromlians."

"King Plumley?" Quinn exclaimed. "Oh, that is horrid."

Sighing, Ameka continued. "A terrible battle raged in the heart of Twickingham, but it is over now and the enemy has retreated. Still, Dagon felt the danger was too great for his elderly aunts and me to continue on."

Quinn's heart went out to the Twicks. If only her father would send help, but he seemed deaf to pleas from Lord Ryswick or King Millstoke of Banyyan.

"Where are Dagon's aunts?"

"Lord Ryswick sent them to a safe location—Kilmory Manor. They shall be Lord Blakely's guests until the tunnels are safe for travel."

"Why did you not go to Kilmory?"

"If I could not be with my husband, then I chose to return to my cottage. Dagon understood—and convinced his father. Two knights escorted me home, and, as soon as they departed, I came here."

"Poor Ameka," Quinn said, hugging her again. "Married less than two days and already apart from your husband. Fie on the war."

"I am heartbroken, love. Being alone again in my cottage is not where my life and soul reside. They live with Dagon, my heart."

Pulling back, Quinn felt relieved to face a problem other than her own vexing situation. "I am so sorry at this turn of events. Why not come and stay in the castle? We are family now. I would love to have you here with me."

"Thank you, but that is not what I want either. I want to assume my role as Lady Ryswick of Pendrog Manor. I am not weak. I can travel through dangerous territory."

Peeling off her cape, Ameka flung it onto the dressing chair. "Carry the elderly aunts off to safety, absolutely. But not me. I am young and can ride a horse as well as any soldier."

"You are angry."

"Yes—but not at my husband. Lord Ryswick made the final decision. Dagon wanted me to stay."

"Then you have no choice but to remain here and wait."

Ameka paced across the chamber and back. "I have spent my life with very few choices. But I *do* have a choice now. Plumley is not my king, and Lord Ryswick is not my master. Why should anyone expect me to run away from where I belong? I belong with Dagon in Twickingham, and that is where I am going."

Quinn stared at Ameka. Adoration, fear, and excitement surged through her. "You are going on to Twick? Alone?"

Ameka gave her a determined look. "Remember the times we explored the outer tunnels and how we found those hidden short-ways?"

Quinn nodded, feeling breathless as she listened to Ameka's plan.

"That is the route I shall take," Ameka said. "I might even arrive in Twick before the others since they will have to detour around Banyyan to avoid Bromlian soldiers."

Ameka seemed delighted at the notion of beating Knights of the First Order to their destination. "I know Dagon will be happy to see me."

"But you cannot go on foot."

"No, that is why I'm here. I need to borrow one of your ponies."

The princess watched Ameka's face. In the firelight, exhilaration glinted in her eyes. She had never looked so alive.

Quinn place a hand over her heart in mock hurt. "And I thought you returned because you missed me so much, you had to see me one more time."

Even though the princess was jesting, Ameka answered with a tender look. "That, too, love. That, too."

"Of course, I will help you," the princess said. "We can even slip into the kitchen and get a scullery maid to fill a pouch with leftover food from the banquet." Her stomach rumbled with hunger as she said this.

"Oh, thank you, thank you."

"By the way, there are two other things you will need for your secret journey," Quinn told her.

"Yes?"

"A second pony and a traveling companion."

"But who? Cam would make a perfect escort. I have already thought of him and wished desperately he were here. But, alas, he is not, and I fear if I contact one of the king's knights, he may decline and let my plan be known to Lord Blakely."

"No. We shall not ask a knight. Nor Cam. I am thinking of . . . me."

Ameka drew back in shock. "You?"

A wave of despair made the princess grasp Ameka's arms. "My life as I know it comes to an end this evening at midnight. My only salvation is to leave, to escape a fate I do not want. Let me be your traveling companion. Together, we shall flee to Twick!"

24

Questions and Clarifications: Cam

"May I travel with you when you return to Mandria?" Mondo asked as he lowered himself to the edge of the bed to sit.

"Of course," Cam answered, filled with the urgency of the moment. He wanted to leave *now*. This very instant. Take from the trunk the papers that proved his station in life and go directly to the king to ask for his daughter's hand in marriage.

Or should he ask the princess first?

Cam felt his cheeks flush. Would she think he was jesting? The mere thought of her laughing at his declaration of love scared him far more than facing the king.

"I do want to return with you," Mondo said with a firmness in his voice that made him sound much younger. "I want to go home with my son."

The kemble fish had strengthened Mondo's words

as much as his movements. He rose again to his feet without having to pull himself up, and stood tall—not bent as before.

"I shall prepare to leave tomorrow," Mondo told him. "I have accounts to settle, final arrangements to make, and good-byes to bid. I suppose I can tell my curious neighbors I am going home. They do not need to know where *home* is."

The determination on Mondo's face told Cam he'd made the right decision to repeat Melikar's offer. It was a joy to watch his father move into action after making such an important declaration.

"But right now," Mondo continued, "I am certain you must have many unanswered questions to ask of me."

True, Cam had so many questions, he did not know where to begin. His panicked urgency to depart threatened to overrule his need to find out more about his past. Yet Mondo clearly could not depart until he got his affairs in order.

One day should not matter, Cam told himself. In Mandria, today was Ameka and Dagon's wedding celebration. Two more days of festivities lay ahead, during which the princess would be blessedly free from thinking about betrothal balls.

But after a three-day reprieve, Cam was certain the king—or Lord Blakely, whom the king listened to more than he should—would pressure Quinn to make her choice.

Ay, Blakely, the crafty lord of Kilmory Manor, Cam thought. *I am related to this man! He is my father's cousin.*

145

The realization was disconcerting. Cam easily recalled the anger and humiliation of feeling like a trapped animal whenever the man cornered and questioned him.

But the anger ran deeper than that. Cam was furious at the man for asking questions he did not have answers to—and for reminding him that he was bereft of a heritage—royal or otherwise.

Not anymore, Cam thought. *Not anymore.*

He glanced at Mondo, who'd moved to the desk to sit. Cam prayed that his father's renewed strength might last until they reached the other world. Surely, the wizard knew other ways of keeping Mondo comfortable for the rest of his days.

Cam sat on the bed. "Questions and clarifications," he began. "First of all, Hannah is my mother?"

"Yes," Mondo answered.

Cam knew Hannah's story because Quinn had told him how Mondo, as a young lad, had fallen in love with a maiden who came often to the footbridge above the wishing pool. How he convinced Melikar to send him to Outer Earth so he could meet her and persuade her to return to Mandria with him. And how the plan had gone terribly wrong.

Mondo and Hannah had ended up together, but never returned to the underground kingdom.

"I was born in this world?" Cam asked.

"In this very city."

Taking a breath, Cam asked the hardest question he had ever posed: "Why did you give me away?"

Mondo bowed his head as though he'd waited for

Cam to ask and wondered why it'd taken him so long to come around to it.

"Hannah and I were married for many years before being blessed with a child. I named you Cam, after my grandfather, who taught me fencing and riding. He is your namesake—Lord Cam Dover of Kilmory Manor, he was."

Cam felt a great loss. He would never know this man who was his great-grandfather.

"We—Hannah and I—were thrilled when you came along," Mondo continued. "Two years later, Daniel was born. It did not take us long to realize what we both feared. Daniel had taken after his mother, aging in Outer-Earth years, and you had inherited the trait of aging in Mandrian years. I'd suspected from the start that you had more Mandrian blood than Daniel because you looked very much like the Dover side of the family."

Cam could see their dilemma. "Daniel was younger than I, yet grew older?"

"Exactly. By the time he started school, you still appeared to be a toddler. Neighborhood children began asking questions. Folks assumed something was wrong with our firstborn. Of course, there was nothing *wrong* with you, other than the fact that you did not belong in this world any more than I did."

Cam could only imagine how hard it must have been for his mother to answer curious questions.

"Our decision was a difficult one. I went to Melikar to ask his advice. I thought he might take you back to Mandria and give you to my parents to raise at Kilmory. But my parents did not know what had become of me. I'd simply disappeared. They assumed I'd lost my life—perhaps at the hands of the Tristans, because I used to tame wild horses for my father out in the lesser-traveled tunnels.

"My family had already been through the required year of mourning. I did not want to hurt them more by letting them know I was alive yet had chosen a much harder life than the privileged one they offered. Also, I did not want to cause shock and dismay by sending them a child to raise. A child who might not be accepted because his mother was not Mandrian."

Cam had allowed himself a brief fantasy about growing up at Kilmory and becoming its rich and powerful lord. But he had not considered the possibility of being shunned because he was not a true-blooded Mandrian.

Still, how different his life would have been. He certainly would not have become a childmate of Mandria's princess. This made him grateful for the peculiar twist of fate that brought him to the wizard.

"Melikar agreed to keep you and raise you to be his apprentice," Mondo continued. "I hope you've had a decent life with him."

"The wizard has been more than kind, yet the puzzle of my existence has always plagued me."

Mondo reached to clasp Cam's arm. "I'm sorry for any pain I caused. Your mother adored you and was grief-stricken to let you go. Yet, we believed it was best for you. We knew Melikar would shield you from curious questions and give you a future as an enchanter's assistant."

Cam's heart wrenched at the thought of a mother who adored him and of her sadness over letting him go.

He wished he could remember her. "Tell me about Daniel."

"Your brother left this world at the age of sixty-seven. Adam and Sarah are his great-great-grandchildren."

Cam's head felt full of the clouds that puffed up the skies of Outer Earth. He could not take it all in. His younger brother was so much older. He'd married and raised a family, yet Cam himself still stood on the brink of manhood.

And now, Mondo, who'd taken in Adam and Sarah after their parents died, called them his grandchildren only to prevent folk from asking too many questions.

Cam longed to know what his mother and brother looked like. "Sire, if you will forgive me, I found a box in the closet with likenesses of Sarah and Adam. Might you possess any of Hannah and Daniel?"

"Yes. In my room. The photos are old and faded, but at least you'll be able to—"

The door swung open, startling them both. Adam stepped into the room, anger turning his face into a furious scowl. "What are you doing? I woke up and Mondo was gone. I thought something terrible had happened."

Turning his glare toward Cam, Adam continued, "I warned you of my grandfather's weak condition. If you've caused him any . . ."

Adam's voice trailed off as Mondo rose from the desk with ease and stepped toward the door. Putting his arm on his grandson's, he smiled. "I'm fine. Come join our conversation."

Adam had started to grab Mondo to steady him, but

when Mondo clearly didn't need assistance, he gaped at his grandfather. "What's going on? How are you able to stand without your cane?"

Mondo winked at Cam. "A little Mandrian magic can work wonders in this world."

Cam returned Mondo's smile, yet all he could think was how angry Adam would be when he heard the news. Not only had he divulged Adam's secret and invited Mondo to return to Mandria, but the lowly wizard's apprentice was actually the son of this noble lord—a position proper enough to allow him to court Adam's princess.

25

Planning a Departure: Quinn

⌁

Ameka's face grew pale at Quinn's announcement. "You want to go with me?" she repeated. "To Twickingham?"

"Yes!" the princess answered, growing more certain by the second. "We must not waste time. Gwynell was instructed to inform the queen that I returned to my chamber to clean a stain from my gown, but if I do not return in a timely manner, they will send guards to make sure all is well and fetch me back to the Great Hall."

"But—"

"Listen. I know what you are about to say. My father will be furious."

"And the protocol—"

"Fie on royal protocol! What could possibly be wrong with taking time to find my heart's choice? Should protocol rule my happiness and his?"

"Lord Blakely would say yes."

"Fie on Lord Blakely!"

Ameka's hand flew to her mouth to cover a burst of shocked laughter. "Ay, may the High Spirit forgive me," she said in a breathy whisper. "But I am *thrilled* by this turn of events. Still, the enormity! We shall be in terrible trouble, yes?"

Ameka's words were true. The former tutor could easily be thrown into the dungeon for perceivably kidnapping the princess.

"They will not suspect we are together," Quinn told her. "I am the one whose disappearance will cause commotion. All will think you are safe at your cottage—until Dagon tries to contact you. And by then, we shall be riding up the last lane to Pendrog."

Even as she was speaking, Quinn began unfastening the periwinkle gown. "Help, please. Already I have been gone from the gala too long."

Quinn slipped out of the dress as quickly as possible while Ameka searched her dressing chamber for a simple garment.

"You have nothing suitable for inconspicuous travel."

"Look in my ladies' wardrobe then." Opening a trunk at the foot of her bed, Quinn stuffed the fancy gown inside and out of sight.

Ameka returned with a simple gray frock and cape belonging to Cydlin. She attempted to help Quinn dress, but instead slowed the endeavor. "My hands are shaking, so I cannot fasten the buttons."

"Leave them," Quinn said. "I can fasten them." She cocked her head at Ameka. "I thought you said you were not afraid."

"I am not afraid for myself, yet having you along changes everything."

Before Quinn could respond, Ameka rushed on, "But you must come. Yes, yes, I am sure of it. I love Dagon so much, I am risking my life to be with him. And you are doing the same. Risking your life for your beloved, albeit you do not yet know his name."

The princess could not agree more. "Let's be off then."

Quinn wrapped the borrowed traveling cape about her shoulders and dropped coins into the pocket in case they were needed along the way. Glancing about the chamber, she wondered when, if ever, she would look upon it again.

"Will you leave a message for your father?" Ameka asked, "so he will not think renegade knaves whisked you away?"

The princess hesitated—but only for a heartbeat. "Nay," she said. "I shall not leave a note of apology, even though guilt shall follow me to Twickingham. I am not sorry for claiming my own destiny—be it royal protocol or not."

26

Planning a Departure: Cam

In the morning, Cam was awake at first light. He'd never been awakened by the rising sun—at least not during his years in Mandria. But even if the sun's brightness had not poured into the chamber, the anticipation of this day would have yanked him from his dreams.

His dreams.

They had been a mixed brew of life above and below the river. In one, he and Quinn were riding alone in Sarah's carriage, picking out names for their future children. Oddly, the names "Alvid" and "Onyda" kept coming to him, yet these were names he did not know and meant nothing to him.

In another dream, he was in the queen's garden, teaching baby Hannah names of flowers along the path: dragon's tongue, silver slipper, moonflowers.

But upon awakening, the thought that consumed

him was the notion that he could rise and return with haste to WonderLand Park, locate the footbridge, and initiate the spell to return to Mandria.

The possibility of being in his own world before the day ended was better than any dream. And his mission below the river was as clear as the water in the wishing pool.

Flinging back the bedcovers, Cam rose to gather his belongings. Then was no time to waste. Today was the second day of Ameka's wedding celebration.

I must be patient, he told himself. *It is right and good for Mondo to return to Mandria. And I, his son, can escort him.*

Although it wasn't his nature to be self-serving, he realized that having Mondo with him when he visited the king would be to his benefit, since the king probably knew of Mondo and certainly knew the prominent Dover family, who oversaw Kilmory Manor before Lord Blakely.

With the return of Mondo and his son, Lord Blakely, by right, would have to step down as lord of Kilmory Manor. Mondo was the true heir and after him—Cam. It was a Mandrian truth.

This shall not be good news for Lord Blakely. The man will have even more reason to hate me.

An uneasiness settled over him, making him wish his true identity had nothing to do with Lord Blakely or Kilmory Manor.

Cam arrived at the morning feast, clean and combed, dressed like an Outer-Earth lad in Adam's left-behind clothes. Elsy bustled about the scullery, coming in and out of a sunny nook to serve them. She did not seem pleased to be preparing food for three when she'd agreed to care for one.

Adam and Mondo were making a list of details to be attended to before the departure. Elsy hovered, seeming puzzled by Mondo's renewed vigor. She patted Cam on the shoulder and told him how his visit seemed to be working magic on Mr. Dover.

If only she knew the truth of her words, Cam thought, exchanging amused glances with his father.

The hushed conversation at the table made her hover even more. Finally Mondo dismissed her for the day, walking her to the portal to make sure she left without hearing any snippets of the whispered arrangements.

Cam overheard Mondo expressing gratitude to Elsy for her loyal service. He knew his father was saying a final good-bye, even though Elsy was not aware of the significance of his words.

If I had any magic at all, he thought, *I would cast a spell to make Elsy forget ever meeting Mondo.* Odd to know how to cast an enchantment, yet not possess the power to make it happen.

Cam devoured eggs, cheese, and toasted bread with jam. Familiar food above and below the river. This morning, Adam seemed resigned to Mondo's impending disappearance, although Cam could tell by the sighs and annoyed glances in his direction that the lad was not completely won over by the plan.

"Tell me about going into battle in this world," Cam ventured, hoping to distract Adam from the present situation and to learn a bit about war in what Sarah called "the twenty-first century."

"I've never gone into battle," Adam answered.

"But you're a soldier."

"Yes, but being a soldier here means spending years preparing for war, all the while hoping never to be sent off into battle, even though war is raging somewhere most of the time. Sooner or later, I'm sure I'll get my orders to go."

"How do you prepare?" Cam asked, thinking of the hours of swordplay, jousting, and riding skills involved in the training of a Knight of the First Order.

Adam launched into an explanation of something called "boot camp," then talked of apparatus so strange to Cam, all he could think was how much it sounded like magic: stealth bombers, rocket launchers, laser beams.

In the midst of his overview on how to make war, Adam stopped abruptly and held Cam's gaze. "Excuse me for changing the subject, but I need to say this. I have a bad feeling about sending my grandfather away from modern medicine back into the Dark Ages."

Cam did not know what he meant by "Dark Ages," yet he returned Adam's gaze with confidence. "I shall see to it that your grandfather has the best care and the utmost comfort until the end of his days. That is my promise to you." Lifting his fingers to one cheek, Cam gave Adam the Sign of the Lorik.

The lad straightened in surprise. "I—I'd forgotten about the sign." Hesitantly, he lifted one hand to his cheek to seal the agreement.

Before either could say more, they realized Mondo had re-entered the scullery and had heard their conversation. Returning to the table, Mondo affectionately squeezed Adam's shoulder. "Which medicine returned my strength and made me strong enough to travel?" he asked, glancing mischievously at Cam. "Modern medicine? Or my son's healing magic from the so-called Dark Ages?"

Mondo gave a hearty laugh. Cam joined in, but stopped when he realized Adam was not laughing. Instead, the lad sat stone still, staring at Mondo with a mixture of shock and dismay.

"Son?" Adam repeated in an incredulous tone. "The wizard's apprentice is your *son?*"

27

Fleeing the Castle

After a quick hug for luck and safety, the princess and Ameka exchanged the Sign of the Lorik to seal their pact. They would steal away from Mandria and travel the out-of-way tunnels in which they had played as children. Ameka could get on with the life she had chosen, and the princess could get away from a life chosen for her.

Their steps were quick and quiet as they moved into the corridor and made haste toward the servants' stairway, which led away from the royal chambers in the north tower.

Quinn grabbed Ameka's cloak to slow her. "What of the guard?" she whispered. All entries to the royal chambers were guarded—both in times of peace, and especially, when nearby kingdoms were at war. "He will recognize us."

"Guards are used to seeing me on the servants'

stairs from the times I tutored you," Ameka said. "Stay back and let me proceed."

She drew ahead, leaving Quinn to hide behind a pillar. Pulling the hood of the cape over her face in precaution, the princess waited. Her heart thundered at the enormity of their bold plan.

Disobeying the king meant a lifetime spent in the dungeon—or worse—for a commoner. What might the punishment be for the king's own daughter? *Will I be stripped of my inheritance? My title? Never to be a princess again?*

The words "Princess Nevermore" floated into her memory, reminding her of a time on Outer Earth when she feared that title might belong to her.

I should think more of Ameka than myself. I should not put her into such danger.

She wished Melikar would slip a potion into the royal teapot at tonight's gala, like the one he conjured up with doleran seeds. That spell had worked beautifully during her trip to the other world. The king and queen never missed their daughter because, to them, no time had passed at all.

Perhaps I should have held onto Cam's magic ring, Quinn thought. *It might have come in handy on this quest.*

Quest.

That is what she'd called Cam's journey. And now she, herself, was off on a quest of her own.

Toads and mugwort! Is Cam as frightened of his mission as I am mine right now?

"Find her!" came Ameka's firm voice.

Confused, Quinn peeked around the pillar. She heard the sound of booted footsteps clomping down the stairs. Ameka flew around the corner. "Haste!" she whisper-hissed. "We've only a moment."

Quinn followed close behind, quick-stepping down the spiral rock stairs and away from the royal chambers. "How did you get rid of the guard?" she huffed, trying to keep up with Ameka.

"I told him you had sent for Cydlin and that she hadn't come. I said you were upset and needed her this instant, so he must find her at once."

"Brilliant," Quinn said, but the plan troubled her as they hurried along a corridor. She had given Cydlin a night away from her duties. Would the guard scare the lass to death with his urgent warning? Or send her dashing to the royal chamber in tears?

Footsteps forced them to detour down a dark passageway and wait. It was Gwynell, hurried along by the frazzled guard, who either did not know one lass from the other or simply grabbed the first lady-in-waiting he saw.

After the sound of footsteps died away, Quinn and Ameka emerged from their hiding place and ran for the stairs that led to the kitchen.

Quinn worried what Gwynell might do when she arrived at the chamber and found it empty. *Please let her think I took the other stairway to the Great Hall. Do not let her suspect something is amiss.*

Keeping their faces covered, Ameka and Quinn rushed to the lowest level of the castle. In the kitchen, maidens bustled about, clearing up after serving the grandest banquet the castle had ever hosted.

161

Thankfully, Marged was above in the Great Hall, probably taking bows at the brilliance of her culinary talents. The princess pulled aside one of the scullery maids and asked for two bundles of food from the feast. Before the lass could question her, Quinn slipped a gold coin into the maiden's hand and cautioned her to move quickly and not tell anyone later what she had done.

In a blink, the lass was back, handing over two pouches of food and a tumbler of tea. Quinn was so pleased at her efficiency, she slipped the maiden an extra coin.

The lower level of the castle was connected to the stable for the convenience of the king's hunters bringing wild game to the kitchen. This was the path Ameka and Quinn chose since there were no guards.

Arriving at the stable, Quinn motioned to Taba, the stable master. He was busy with a group of pages, tending the many steeds tethered there tonight. All belonged to the lads above, waiting for the princess in the Great Hall.

Taba was a Marnie, almost as old as Grizzle. He had been stable master for both King Marit and, before him, Quinn's grandfather, King Marit-the-First.

Taba was neither a guard nor servant. Quinn could reveal herself to him, and he would not be bound to report her unusual decision to go off on a pony ride in the middle of the night.

Yet the pages assisting him might be questioned, which is why she drew Taba away from them.

"I know you are busy," Quinn began, "but would you please fetch my two best ponies and prepare them for riding?"

The Marnie was taken by surprise, but it was not his place to question her, so he did not.

"Please choose Tyn and Nelyn," Quinn told him. They were the youngest and fastest of her Paleo ponies.

Taba did as she requested while the princess and Ameka waited outside. In a matter of minutes, out he came, leading the ponies.

"You take Tyn," Quinn told Ameka. "He is gentle. Nelyn and I are still getting used to each other."

Quinn started to pay Taba for his help, then remembered Marnies had no use for coins. Everything in their village was shared. Instead, she plucked a pomegranate from the food pouch and gave it to him.

His eyes told her he was pleased. Bowing, he slipped the fruit into his coat pocket. "Quite a good night for a ride, Your Highness. I have seen nothing unusual this evening."

His words made her smile. Every evening in an underground world was the same—never a good night nor a bad one. But she knew what he meant and what he wanted her to know. He would say nothing if soldiers came to question him.

Grateful, the princess patted Taba's hand as she took the reins. It so startled him, he turned and ran inside.

Ameka had already mounted and was taking anxious glances toward the path from the kitchen. Quinn settled onto Nelyn's brocade blanket. Aiming the ponies away from the main courtyard filled with people, they kept close to the outside wall, following a dark pathway. In silence, they searched for a section of the wall where they knew they would find a hidden door. This was the secret exit they took as children to steal away from the castle grounds without passing through the guarded gates.

Cam had found the hidden exit by accident. In the midst of one of their games, he had spotted Lord Blakely coming his way, so he dove behind the dropberry hedge along the castle wall and promptly found a Prim door concealed in the greenery. Prims were much like faeries who lived in the outer world—only not as mischievous. They came in all sizes, from tiny to tall, and some could change their appearance at will.

Quinn's fluttering heart grew calm, matching the steady rhythm of Nelyn's hoofbeats on the path. *Thank you, Cam, for finding a secret route to the outer tunnels all those years ago.*

Thank you for helping me escape a future I do not desire.

Once again, you have saved my life.

28

An Outer-Earth Knight

Alone in the apartment, Cam fidgeted, not knowing what to do with himself until time to depart for Mandria.

When he thought of what awaited him there after his victorious return as the son of a prominent Mandrian family, his breathing almost came to a stop. It was too much to think about.

He walked the length of the apartment, turned, and walked it again. *Stop thinking,* he told himself, *and make it happen.*

If not for Mondo, he could leave at once, yet his heart did not begrudge the situation. He'd gained a father—and a past. How could one begrudge such good fortune?

At present, Mondo was away, making arrangements for the transfer of his home and belongings to Adam and Sarah. Earlier, he'd informed neighbors he was "off to see the world for the rest of his days." He did not clarify *which* world, amusing Cam.

Adam's traveling bags were stacked by the portal. The time had come for him to return to his station as a soldier. Later, he would board one of the silver fish Cam had seen swimming across the sky and would disappear among the clouds.

Cam allowed envy to wash over him. What must it be like to fly the skies of Outer Earth like a bird? *Magic* was the only explanation he could conjure.

Cam's pacing took him closer and closer to the main chamber. He wanted to enter and study the amazing looking glass that displayed moving pictures.

But between the talking glass and himself sat Katze. Granted, it was easier to face one cat than dozens in the Marnie village; however, this one seemed like a tiger compared to tiny Marnie cats. Cam decided it best to leave him be.

Afternoon shadows crept along the walls, darkening the apartment. He kept looking out the window at a park across the avenue until figures became hazy in the dusky light.

Finally, noises at the portal drew his attention. Light filled the chamber as Adam entered with Mondo.

Cam studied his father. He still stood tall and moved without assistance, yet right now his face was pale and drawn from exhaustion. Knowing that today was his last day on Outer Earth must have churned up all sorts of emotions.

Facing Adam, Mondo said, "One last good-bye, then I shall rest until Sarah arrives to take us to the wishing pool."

The two embraced for a long moment, each pulling away with tears in his eyes. Cam wished he was elsewhere so they could share their final moment in private.

Mondo retreated down the corridor to his chamber while Adam regained his composure, checking his pile of traveling bags to make sure they were all tightly fastened.

"Before I leave for the air base," he said to Cam, "I have questions I need you to answer."

"Go on," Cam said, curious.

"First," Adam continued, "did you know you were Mondo's son when you came here?"

"No. Not until he told me."

"And you grew up in the other world because you had more Mandrian blood than your brother?"

"Yes," Cam answered, longing to know more about the brother he would never meet. "Did you know Daniel?"

"No. He died long before I was born. Mondo told Sarah and me that we came from Daniel's line, so he is a distant grandfather—one 'great' less than Mondo. I guess that makes you my distant uncle."

They exchanged incredulous looks over the oddness of it all.

Adam glanced at a timepiece on the wall, as if worried about running out of time before all his questions were answered. "May I ask about Quinn?"

"Certainly," Cam said, although the question made his stomach feel as if he'd swallowed gravel from the floor of a Mandrian tunnel.

"Does she have plans to marry?"

"No, but it must happen soon. It is royal protocol."

Adam nodded as if he understood the workings of underground kingdoms. "I remember how much she hated protocol. Do you think her hesitation means she's not in love with anyone?"

The chamber suddenly felt as warm as the castle kitchen when all four fires blazed at once. "I do not think she is in love with anyone. The betrothal and future marriage are being forced upon her."

"Seems very unfair." Adam said. He gave Cam a sidelong glance. "Are you not interested in becoming one of her choices?"

"Ay, well . . . yes. Yes, I am." Cam was certain his bumbling answer gave him away, yet he was determined to stand for himself in front of Adam. In the end, the princess had *not* chosen the lad from Outer Earth, yet he, Cam Dover of Kilmory Manor, still had a chance.

"Are you in love with her?" Adam asked, as calmly as if he'd asked if Cam wanted a cup of tea.

"Always and forever," Cam answered, surprising himself by his swift and firm reply.

Adam remained quiet as he considered Cam's answer. "I think I'm slowly figuring this out," he finally said. "You weren't in the running as a suitable groom— until you came here and found your true identity."

"Exactly."

"And what will you do when you return?"

"I shall hope I'm not too late."

Adam held his gaze. "Then I wish the same."

"You do? You're not . . . vexed to know my heart's feelings?"

Adam seemed amused by Cam's response. "I would

have been 'vexed,' as you say, if I'd known this when Quinn was here. But now? Years have passed—in our world, at least. Time has left me certain that Quinn and I do not have a future, even though I once believed we did."

The amount of relief Cam felt was immeasurable.

"The Princess of Mandria will always live in my heart," Adam said. "But if I have a choice at all in the matter, I'd rather know she married you than a stranger chosen for her."

"Truly?"

"You've more than proven yourself worthy. You are loyal and caring to a father you've just met. I can only wish the best for you and Quinn."

"Thank you. You have no idea how much your blessing means to me."

"You're welcome—Uncle Cam." Adam's jest made them laugh together at a truth that seemed stranger than stars in an underground sky.

"I have some things to give you," Adam continued.

Cam's curiosity made him assist in unfastening a large bag.

Adam lifted out a cloth book tied with a blue ribbon. "Will you return this to Quinn? She kept a journal when she lived with us, and I don't think she meant to leave it behind."

Surprised and curious, Cam took the journal.

"Tell her that I never opened it," he added. "I hoped to be able to return it someday, so I am glad for the opportunity."

"I shall see that she receives it," Cam assured him.

169

"Also," Adam continued. "You were curious about the way soldiers in this world go to war. I want to give you a few items designed for Outer-Earth knights. I hope they might be of future use."

Cam could barely hide his excitement as he watched Adam pull the strange objects from the knapsack. "What are they?" he asked. "What do they do?"

Adam picked up an odd arrangement of cylinders and straps. "These are called night-vision goggles. They allow you to see in the dark so you can spy on the enemy."

"You're jesting."

"No," he said, putting the straps over Cam's head to demonstrate. "Look out the window at the teenagers hanging out in the park across the street."

Cam adjusted the cylinders in front of his eyes. He did not know what "teenagers" were, but in the park, he could see lads and maidens milling about—even though he had not been able to see them clearly a few minutes earlier.

"Holy bats!" he exclaimed. "A knight might win every battle if he had these." Pulling them off, he looked with awe at Adam, who was grinning.

"That's the whole point," Adam said.

"What else have you got?"

"How about being able to communicate with someone who is far away?"

"Impossible," Cam told him.

"Not in this world." Picking up two black objects, he handed one to Cam, then stepped to the far side of the room. Adam put the other object to his mouth and softly counted to five.

Cam stared in amazement at the device in his hand. Every word Adam spoke came clearly out of the mysterious black box.

Magic!

"They're called walkie-talkies," Adam explained. "Use only when you need them because you won't be able to find replacement batteries where you're going."

"Find what?"

"It's not important," Adam said. "I have one last thing." He pulled out a couple of garments the color of jumbled hues of earth and trees and sand. "This is for camouflage."

"What does that mean?"

"It helps you blend in with your surroundings when you're trying not to be seen."

Cam thought the garments interesting, but refrained from telling Adam that this flimsy cloth would be no match for an arrow or the blade of a sword. Here was one thing Mandrians clearly did better. A suit of armor was far superior to this—but he would take the garments because Adam offered them.

"Thank you," Cam said. "I have nothing to give you in return."

Adam fastened his knapsack and prepared to leave. "You've more than paid me back. Your promise to take care of Mondo and save Quinn from an unhappy future are the best gifts you could offer."

Moved, Cam held out his hand, the way Sarah had taught him.

Smiling, Adam took hold of Cam's hand and gave it

a firm shake. "This, my friend and distant relative, is Outer Earth's version of the Lorik Sign."

29

Stealing Away

Quinn guided Nelyn along the inner castle wall, thankful for the veil of darkness that hid them. They were close enough to the courtyard to hear music, voices, and a bit of off-key singing as Mandrians celebrated while waiting for the stroke of midnight when the king would step out to the balcony and announce the name of the princess's betrothed.

The gala in my honor dances on without me. Who knew it would come to this? Sneaking away in the middle of the night? Oh, please be with us, High Spirit.

The princess's hands shook with trepidation as she clutched the pony's reins. The price she might pay for fleeing did not seem as high as the one she would pay for staying.

Nelyn stepped lightly on the dark path, as if she felt as uncertain as the princess about this cryptic ride in the middle of the night. Quinn patted Nelyn's neck to reassure the pony, then focused her attention, searching for the dropberry hedge that pinpointed the spot where Cam had found the Prim door.

At the time, they had been curious as to what Prims were doing inside castle walls. Quinn remembered wanting to ask Melikar, but then he would know the group had been leaving the safety of castle grounds for the outer tunnels and would have promptly forbade them from future outings.

"Are we close?" Ameka asked in a nervous whisper. She was not as familiar with the secret routes, because she'd joined the group's outings in later years after she became Quinn's tutor.

"Very close," Quinn whispered back.

Tugging Nelyn's reins, the princess slipped off the pony's back and motioned for Ameka to follow. Carefully, she wound through thick bushes and trees along the wall, talking softly to the ponies so they would not balk at the strange pathway.

The Prim door was almost too low and narrow for the ponies, but with a lot of hushed urging and a couple of apples from the food pouch, Tyn and Nelyn scrambled through.

Ameka and Quinn remounted outside the castle wall, then made their way along a winding pathway smaller than a Marnie tunnel. Quinn did not know where the Prim tunnel ultimately led, because the path split in two just out of view of the castle gates. The alternate route was the one they always chose because it merged with the main public avenue.

The oddity of it all was that when she and her child-mates returned to the castle, they never knew where to find the narrow passage leading off the main avenue to the Prim door, yet they always did—almost as if the passage appeared when they were ready to find it. The princess felt certain this foolish notion was born of their youthful imaginations.

Riding out onto the wide avenue made Quinn relax a bit, but not enough to throw back the hood of her cape. Making it this far was a small victory, yet, they did not want to stay on the main road too long. The well-traveled route was too dangerous for those wishing to be invisible.

The ponies could now travel side by side. Breaking into a gallop, they raced away from the castle. Quinn knew to watch for the exact spot along the main route where a certain cutout in the earthen wall appeared.

These tunnel bays were spaced along the main byways for various reasons: out-of-the-way places for travelers to rest, for tunnel merchants to set up carts to entice passersby, or, during times of danger, for soldiers to stand guard for extra security.

What most did not know was that the back wall of one particular bay was actually a door. This was the sort of exciting discovery that thrilled the adventurous group when they went exploring. Beyond the door, to their delight, lay a maze of hidden tunnels.

Dagon had once suggested Prims had built the secret byways to allow them access to the main tunnels so they could play tricks on tired travelers.

Regardless, in all the years they had secretly passed

through the door, the group encountered only a few travelers, never knowing if they were Prims or humans—or perhaps something else—the thought of which always gave them shivers when they spoke of it later.

Tonight the main avenue was not bustling with people and carriages, much to Quinn's relief. Folk of the kingdom were either gathered at the castle or were staying home for fear of running into Bromlian soldiers who might have crept into Mandria from Banyyan.

Still, being out in the open was an enormous risk.

"How are you feeling, love?" Ameka called to her.

"I cannot stop thinking about the gala," Quinn answered. Surely she'd been missed by now. Had the king sent guards to scour the castle? Was he keeping the news from the queen? And from guests gathered in the Great Hall?

A wave of remorse rolled over her. Not remorse about fleeing, but sorrow over putting her parents through the agony of their daughter's disappearance. "I am so, so sorry," she whispered to herself.

Yet when she pictured the look on Lord Blakely's face when he heard the news, it made her laugh, drawing a curious glance from Ameka.

If the guards reported back to the king that his daughter was nowhere *inside* castle walls, would he launch a search of the entire kingdom? Would he even consider that she might be in the outer tunnels?

Thinking of it now, Quinn realized how daring those childhood jaunts had been for the heir to the throne. *I could have been kidnapped by Tristans or murdered by robbers who did not know their victim was royal.*

The realization of how close to danger she had come quickened her breath. *But had we not explored, I would never be able to do what I am doing now— fleeing the bothersome chains of protocol.*

For that, she was grateful.

"I think the next tunnel bay is the one we are looking for," Ameka called, taking the lead.

Excitement made Quinn's skin tingle—as it always did when she and her companions stepped through the hidden door. Nelyn trotted close behind Tyn, as if knowing the importance of making it to the secret route, ensuring them quick and invisible passage out of Mandria.

Thanks to the celebration in the princess's honor, no eyes saw the ponies veer off into a certain tunnel bay and disappear from sight.

No human eyes, at least.

.

30

Things to Take; Things to Leave Behind

❧

After Adam departed, Cam made sure his Mandrian garments were packed in his knapsack, along with Adam's gifts and the important papers that would prove his true identity to the king.

Waiting for Sarah to arrive to take them to Wonder-Land Park was torture. Cam decided to check on Mondo to make sure he was resting well. Stepping down the corridor, he tapped on the door.

"Come in," Mondo said.

Cam entered to find his father at the small table, sorting parchments with images of people similar to the ones he had found in the box on the high shelf in his bed chamber.

"I thought you might want to see these before we depart," Mondo said. Something in his voice told Cam he'd been crying.

Mondo laid out three images. "This is your mother. The baby in her arms is you."

Cam sat at the table. With a shaking hand, he lifted the image of his mother. The paper was faded in shades of gray, yet the maiden's beauty was evident. Cam could see why the young Mondo would have been charmed by her.

He studied his mother's face, searching for a flash of recognition, but there was none. He stared at himself as a baby, but did not feel as if he was looking at his own face. The images could have been any mother and child.

"What's the matter?" Mondo asked. "I thought you wanted to see what she looked like."

"Oh, I do," Cam said. "I merely hoped to see myself in her face—or in mine as an infant. Or even recall the moment. But I do not."

Mondo placed a hand over Cam's. "Son, it was long ago, and you were just a baby. There's no way you could remember this moment in time. The important thing is that it *was* a real moment, and it *did* happen. Your mother loved you very much."

Cam nodded, feeling a great sadness, while at the same time truly happy to see what she looked like. "May I keep it?" he asked, realizing he could not let go of an image of his mother now that he held it in his hand.

"Of course. Keep it always."

"Who is this?" he asked, picking up the next one.

"Daniel—when he was ten years old."

"My brother," Cam said, grinning at the image that *did* look familiar. "He looks much like I did at ten."

Seeing the resemblance calmed his sadness. What a relief to see *something* that connected him to the Dover family besides Mondo's papers.

"I remember how much you resembled each other," his father said. "Before Daniel surpassed you in growth, people thought you were twins."

"Twins," Cam repeated, feeling a connection between himself and a brother he would never know. "And who is this in the color image?"

Mondo chuckled. "It's me—years ago. Have I changed that much?"

On closer scrutiny, Cam could see the familiar blue-green eyes. The hair, now-white, had been dark then, but the image was definitely a much younger Mondo.

"I was forty when the photo was taken. Hannah was in her seventies by then."

"True?" Cam exclaimed. "Toads and mugwort!"

Mondo blinked in surprise. "I haven't heard that expression in years."

"In Mandrian or Outer-Earth years?" Cam jested.

"In one's heart," Mondo answered, "it matters not how you count." Pausing to study the images one last time, he added, "Ironically, I discovered that the longer a Mandrian remains in this world, the quicker he ages. This is why I seem much older than I would be at this age had I lived my life below the river."

"Would you have trod a different path if you could do it over?" Cam asked.

"And give up my years with Hannah?" Mondo adamantly shook his head. "No. I would not have done anything differently." Placing all three images into a folded sheath of paper, he gave them to Cam.

A commotion announced the arrival of Sarah. They left Mondo's chamber to greet her by the portal. Sarah held baby Hannah, clutching Mop.

"I don't think you're going to get this dragon away from Hannah," Sarah told Cam. "At least not without a few tears."

Cam certainly did not want to make the baby cry. He tried not to let the loss of his dragon bother him. *You did not even know about its existence until two days ago,* he reminded himself.

"Hannah is acting just like her Uncle Cam," Mondo said. "Daniel used to snatch the toy away, which made Cam more determined than ever to hang onto it. He carried it everywhere."

In the deepest corner of Cam's mind, Mondo's words triggered a fleeting memory of a younger version of himself hanging onto Mop for all he was worth. No wonder Hannah's possession of his dragon caused him such an emotional response.

Breathing in and out, he cleared the corners of his memory from foolish notions. "Let her keep it," he said. "I am honored. I will be glad to think of the dragon in the future and know Hannah is taking good care of him."

"Did you hear that, sweetie?" Sarah cooed to the baby. "Uncle Cam says you may keep Mop."

"Mop!" Hannah yelped, giving him a dimpled smile.

And Cam knew that a piece of his heart would always remain in this world with his great-great-however-many-greats-it-was niece.

31

Away from the Kingdom

The maze of out-of-way tunnels was not as well lit as the main avenue leading straight through Mandria into the neighboring Kingdom of Banyyan.

King Millstoke's small kingdom lay between Mandria and Twickingham. How lucky that he was able to take refuge in Mandria before the Bromlians could capture and imprison him.

The princess did not understand how her father could listen to King Millstoke's tales of battle in a kingdom so close to his own and not feel compelled to send soldiers to assist the people of Banyyan.

If I were queen, I would have sent my best knights long before the kingdom fell.

Tightening her grip on Nelyn's reins, Quinn wondered why she saw the situation so differently than her father. Yes, he was acting on the truth that Mandria had fought too many wars over the last century, but it did not seem right to allow the Bromlians to slowly gain power by continuing their assaults.

Quinn's pony stumbled in the dim passageway, forcing her to pay attention to the path. If Melikar's magic lit the main tunnels, perhaps magic of a lesser sort lit these.

Melikar.

The princess wondered if he knew of the hidden short-ways. Surely he must. And if he knew of them, did he also know she had fled the banquet and was stealing away with Ameka?

A shiver of fear over angering him almost made her miss a turn in the winding tunnel. Is it possible she feared the wizard more than she feared the king?

"Are you well?" Ameka called from behind.

Quinn yanked on the reins to slow Nelyn, then waited for Ameka to catch up. "I was wondering if Melikar knows what we are doing."

Ameka's expression changed from concern for the princess to surprise at her words. "Love, Melikar does not need guards to tell him when something in the castle is amiss. Surely he knows."

Ameka's quick reply did not ease Quinn's worry over the consequences of their actions.

"I guess, in truth, we are not disobeying the wizard," Quinn added. "We are disobeying the king. If Melikar knows what we have done, then I feel safer on this journey. I want him to know."

Tyn seemed confused about the unexpected stop. Ameka patted his neck to reassure him. "Are you worried

Melikar will tell the king our whereabouts?"

Quinn remembered the wizard's efforts to keep the king and queen from learning about her earlier trip out of Mandria. "I do not think he will tell," she said firmly. "I believe, instead, he will do all he can to ensure our safety."

"Let's be off then," Ameka urged.

A few travelers passed but paid them no mind. Quinn wondered if they were Prims, and if so, how they felt about humans sharing their routes.

The dim pathway seemed to go on forever. The princess did not know how much time had passed since they'd left the castle. Hours, she was certain. Her weariness was making it hard to push on. "Might we not pause for a bite of food?" she called to Ameka. "I did not eat at the banquet. I am famished."

Ameka had not stopped checking for riders behind them and flinching at unexpected noises. "Can you wait until we leave Mandria and are well into Banyyan? We've quite a ways to go, and I would feel better if we were out of reach of the king's soldiers."

"But we should be safe in these tunnels," Quinn reminded her. "Even traveling through Banyyan."

"We are *guessing* that is true. We do not know for certain—and that is the worry."

Ameka's words alarmed Quinn. "You are right, wise tutor."

"Might you have an apple?" Ameka suggested.

"I gave the apples to the ponies." Reaching into the food pouch, Quinn removed bread for both to eat while riding: a loaf shaped like a trega bird for Ameka and one shaped like a kemble fish for herself.

The two started off again. The fact that neither knew how far they were from the border of the two kingdoms, how they would know when they crossed into Banyyan, or even if this series of tunnels *led* through Banyyan grew more worrisome to the princess as the hours passed.

Quinn pushed ahead on instinct, hoping they were not being foolish to believe these tunnels paralleled the main road. Was it also foolish to believe they might travel safely through a kingdom now controlled by the enemy?

My father is ignoring the Bromlians at the peril of our kingdom. Someone needs to stop them and drive them back to Bromlia.

That, of course, was precisely what Dagon and Lord Ryswick had been helping King Plumley to do—before the king was kidnapped.

They rode long into the night. The princess knew by now that the fateful hour of midnight had come and gone. The king had dispersed the waiting crowd with a version of the truth and had dismissed his noble visitors with apologies and vows to solve the mystery of the missing princess.

Quinn could only imagine how angry he must be. It made her shudder to picture his face. She tried not to think of him or the worry she was causing her mother.

Around the next twist in the passageway, Nelyn came to an abrupt stop, rearing up on her hind legs. Hanging on to keep from falling, Quinn could not believe what had caused the horse to spook. In front of them, the tunnel ended against a flat, earthen wall.

"No!" Quinn cried, startled and dismayed.

She waited for Ameka to catch up, motioning for her to stop as she watched the expression on her friend's face turn from concern to shock.

"Ay, no!" Ameka exclaimed. "I did not know any of the routes ended so unexpectedly."

Panic made Quinn turn Nelyn in a circle to make sure no one was stalking up behind them. "What shall we do? We cannot turn back. They must be searching for us by now."

In answer, a section of the wall shifted. They stared, transfixed by a dark opening, watching it grow larger.

Ameka grabbed Quinn's arm as if wanting to protect her.

Out stepped a tall figure, cloaked in the same color as the earth. "They are coming," a raspy voice said. "Follow me."

"Wh–who are you?" Quinn demanded "And who is coming?"

"The king's soldiers are searching these tunnels. You must disappear, or they will arrest you. Come. *Now.*"

Quinn and Ameka whispered frantically together. "Should we trust this . . . this specter?" the princess asked.

Before Ameka could answer, the tunnel exploded with thundering hooves from a near distance.

With a panicked exchange of glances, the two immediately slid from the ponies and grasped the reins. Frantically, they hurried the frightened animals through the dark opening in the earthen wall.

32

Return to
WonderLand

The Dover family went out the door of the apartment and down the steps as though they were off on an evening jaunt. Neighbors, enjoying the warm spring evening, greeted Mondo, fussed over the baby, and gave curious side-glances toward the long-haired youth who accompanied them.

Sarah started up her carriage, and they sped off along the lighted avenue. Cam sat in the back with Hannah, who was strapped again into the strange contraption that held her tight. Many Outer-Earth customs did not make sense to him. This was one of them.

His anticipation and excitement grew as they drew closer to the only place on Outer Earth where one could travel between the worlds. He was sorry the dark night stole his final view of the vastness of Outer Earth. He would never forget the lightness of a world without walls all around, the feel of the sun on his face, lights that twinkled in the night sky as well as in the dark city, or the curiosity of clouds.

All would be firmly committed to memory. And the sooner it became memory, the sooner his bright future in Mandria could begin.

Sarah parked the carriage, retrieving Hannah and her dragon from the back. Cam lifted Mondo's bag to carry for him. It contained no clothes—only keepsakes from his life in the outer world that he could not bear to leave behind.

The three stopped beneath a glowing arch at the entryway to the park. The words "Welcome to WonderLand Park" curved above them in colored lights. Cam noticed tears in Mondo's eyes. He stepped away to let his father have a quiet good-bye with his granddaughter.

After a few moments, Sarah, with tears streaking her cheeks, motioned him back into the light. She handed the baby and the dragon over to Mondo, then gave Cam a long hug. "You take excellent care of my grandfather," she whispered.

"I promise," Cam assured her.

"And you make sure the princess lives happily ever after."

Happily ever after? This was an expression he'd never heard, but he liked it. "I shall do my best," he said, wondering if Sarah sensed how heartfelt was his promise.

Mondo was speaking softly to Hannah, who listened attentively as if she knew this was an important moment. Cam thought of his own mother, holding him close and whispering her final good-bye all those years ago. His heart ached because she had died before he found his way back to her. And now, Hannah would only remember her Grandfather Mondo in images that would fade with time.

Sarah lifted the baby from Mondo's arms. Hannah began to whimper. They all patted on her until she calmed down.

"I wish there was some way I could receive news about you after you leave," Sarah said. "Just so I know everyone in Mandria who is dear to me is all right."

Mondo and Cam exchanged glances. Cam knew his father was thinking of the red-feathered trega Melikar had sent to deliver the important papers.

"I believe the wizard knows a way," Mondo told her. "With his permission, you shall get your message."

"Wonderful," she exclaimed, then sighed. "Why can't magic exist in this world the way it exists in yours?"

"It does," Cam said, thinking of the fast-moving carriages, people sailing across the sky, and images of life dancing across the front of a simple glass. "I am sure of it."

Mondo's face brightened, as if knowing Cam's thoughts. "I think my son is right, Sarah. You need to keep your heart's eye open to recognize the magic when you see it."

"Well then," Sarah said. "I'm all cried out. I will leave you two here and take Hannah to the toddler rides to play. And I will try not to think about what's happening at the wishing pool." She gave them a teary-eyed smile. "I love you both—my grandfather and my uncle."

Mondo wrapped Sarah and Hannah in a final hug. "My heart embraces both of you," he said in a quiet, trembling voice. "For the rest of my days—and beyond."

Sarah kissed him on the cheek. Hannah baby-waved with a heartfelt, "Bye, bye." Turning, they walked toward the playground. Hannah peeked back over her mother's shoulder. The dragon dangled from the baby's hand, bump-bumping along with each step.

Mondo inhaled a deep breath and faced Cam. "Come, my son. It's time to go home."

The two made their way through the brightly lit amusement park, past rides the princess once thought were torture machines. Past vendors selling delicacies with enticing aromas, past park benches, flower pots, and fancy fountains. Music vibrated the night air, along with shouts, laughter, and screams from some of the more terrifying contraptions.

On the far side of the crowded area, a path led off through the trees. A sign next to the trail read "To the Wishing Pool" in fancy letters.

Mondo and Cam hurried along the path. Tall lamps lit their way. So many people were in the park tonight, Cam worried how he could possibly begin the spell at the wishing pool and not be seen.

As soon as the worry touched his mind, a calmness came over him. Melikar? Could the wizard work his magic from below the pool to surround them with privacy?

Cam remembered the evil knave who had chased the princess when she was trying to return to Mandria. Melikar made sure the lad would never remember what he had witnessed at the pool.

The path broke through the trees into a clearing. The sight of the river, straight ahead, sent chills across Cam's shoulders. Was he more excited about going back—or escorting Mondo to his long-lost home?

The two walked somberly up the curve of the footbridge that arched over the wishing pool and paused in the middle. Couples, scattered about the area, tossed coins into the pool to seal their wishes.

Cam pictured Melikar below, annoyed that his spell allowed coins to slip through the enchantment and *plink* to the rock floor. *Now it is Baywin's job to sweep them up. I have a nobler calling.*

Cam could not help but smile as he realized this truth was no longer the daydream of a young lad of unknown origin.

He *did* have a nobler calling. Good fortune had found the lowly wizard's apprentice. And he was more than ready to claim it.

33

Behind the Door

Quinn and Ameka had barely convinced their ponies that scrambling through a portal in an unexpected wall in a dark tunnel was exactly what they were supposed to do when soldiers on horseback rounded the last corner.

The door *whooshed* shut behind them. At the same instant, strange words Quinn did not know swirled through the blackness inside the wall. A falling sensation left her stomach behind and spooked the ponies. Quinn grasped Nelyn's mane to steady herself, but found she was not thrown off-balance.

Someone cried out. She was certain it was Ameka.

Quinn tried to call to her, but words refused to form on her tongue.

Thunder filled her senses. The soldiers! Galloping horses raced right through them—or where they had been a blink before.

Seconds of breathlessness later, quiet returned. Quinn breathed in the choking smell of dust kicked up by horses' hooves, yet she saw nothing. The princess did not feel frightened, which surprised her. In fact, a gentle calmness patted her brow as if someone was telling her she had nothing to fear. Should she trust it?

A hissing sound drew her attention. Candles were being lit. The princess turned in a circle, taking in her surroundings as objects came into view in the smoky light. Several elfin figures, too dainty to be human, moved about the chamber, lighting dozens of candles until she and Ameka were bathed in a soothing glow.

Ameka stood pale-faced, likewise taking it in. They were in a chamber with rounded walls, similar to Melikar's. The tall figure watched them as she waited for the candles to be lit. Was the one who rescued them an enchantress?

And *were* they rescued? Or captured?

Rising from the confusion of the last few moments came a certain clarity in Quinn's mind. Rescued, yes. Whoever the figure was, she had saved them from being taken by soldiers and returned to the castle to meet their fate. But why?

"Thank you," Quinn whispered into the quiet chamber.

The cloaked figure they'd first thought was a specter emerged from the shadows. Before them stood an unearthly tall woman, with dark, delicate features and spiky hair as red as trega feathers. In the candlelight, she looked young although her raspy voice made her seem older.

"I am Bryok, queen of the Prim clan," she told them.

In all her travels, Quinn had never encountered a Prim—that she knew of—but she certainly never imagined they looked anything like Bryok.

Prims were the clan of Outer-Earth faeries who'd lived in primrose meadows. They'd followed Melikar to the underground world centuries earlier while other faeries chose to remain in the outer world.

"A–are you going to keep us captive then?" Ameka asked.

Exactly what Quinn was thinking, yet she was not brave enough to say it out loud.

"We are not the faeries of childhood tales," Bryok answered, seeming insulted. "There are many sorts of faeries. We are not in the habit of switching babies or luring travelers to their doom in our realm."

The smaller Prims giggled. Their laughter sounded like chimes.

"Why did you rescue us?" Quinn asked.

"Tasks first, then questions." Bryok motioned to the others. "Please take care of the ponies."

Quinn's immediate reaction was to grab hold of both ponies and not let them out of her sight. She could tell by the way Ameka clutched Tyn's reins, her thoughts were the same. Without the ponies, they were trapped, with no hope of traveling further.

As it was, they did not even know their exact location. Were they somewhere in outer Mandria ? Or had they crossed into Banyyan with its deep red soil?

Quinn had been watching for the tunnel walls to turn a richer hue, but perhaps the changing of the earth's color was not as obvious here as it was along the main route. Regardless, they were still too far from Twickingham to travel on foot.

"I'd rather the ponies stay with us," Quinn said firmly.

"Nonsense," Bryok answered. "The ponies have been running for hours and must be fed and rested. And you lasses are hungry and tired. It is dawn, and you have not slept all night."

Hearing the words made Quinn realize what she had been trying to ignore—her hunger and exhaustion. Where had she gotten the strength to keep going all night? Posing the question gave her the answer: *If you know your life is ending, you find the strength to keep it from happening—even if it means leaving everything behind and pushing yourself beyond limits.*

"She is right, love," Ameka said to Quinn. "We must rest, or we shall not be able to finish our journey."

Immediately, tiny hands grasped the reins and led the ponies away. Quinn stifled the urge to demand that the ponies stay. She was royalty, yes, but Prims were not under her command. The fact that Bryok addressed her as "lass" and not "Your Highness" made it evident she was the one in control.

Or perhaps she does not know who I am. If so, Quinn decided, *this is not information I shall offer.*

"I'm not sure how we can finish our journey at all," Ameka continued. "If soldiers have found our escape route, then we shall either have to don a disguise or find another passage." She turned to Bryok. "How do the soldiers know of the secret tunnels?"

Bryok tsked at the question. "These byways are not secret. That was a childish misconception. You were foolish to take this route. When you came through the Prim door from the castle, you were on the *only* hidden path. On that route you should have remained."

"The Prim passage?" Quinn asked, confused. "But it is so near the main tunnel leaving Mandria, how could it be secret?"

"Because, lass, Prim doors leading to hidden tunnels are found only by those whom the Prims want to find them. They are invisible to everyone else. It was not by accident that your companion, Cam, found the door all those years ago."

Hearing Bryok mention Cam by name startled the princess—and confirmed that the Prim queen knew her identity.

Quinn glanced at Ameka, whose brow was furrowed, as if trying to figure it all out. How could they have known they were making a dangerous choice when they left the Prim tunnel for the main avenue? And how awful to learn that their secret tunnels were not secret after all.

"And now you must eat," Bryok said. Stepping across the chamber, she drew back a scarlet curtain, revealing a table spread with the delectable aromas of steaming stew, warm sesame bread, moonberries, and sweet cakes.

"Faery food?" Ameka whispered, sounding hesitant.

Bryok's look of disapproval landed on Ameka. "I am here to assist you in your endeavor. Eating our food will not keep you trapped in my lair. Fear not."

The princess was already at the table, sampling the unusual stew with a flavor she'd never tasted, yet filled her with comfort. Hesitantly, Ameka joined her, clearly unable to resist the heady aroma of hot spiced mead, which she sampled first.

Quinn watched Bryok watching them as they feasted. *She is either our savior, or she is tricking us and we are doomed.*

Right now, I care not which it might be.

34

The Return
of One

As Cam suspected, the instant he and Mondo reached the upper arc of the footbridge, folk in the area began to wander on down the path or back toward the amusement park. He knew the wizard was at work below, gently nudging spectators away from the area.

Mondo leaned over the railing to gaze into the pool. Light from lamps along the path shimmered bright circles in the smooth dark water. "I've done this countless times over the years," he said. "But I never thought the day would come when I could travel through the wishing pool and be home once again."

"It is true," Cam told him, happy to see his father looking so blissful.

"You must instruct me," Mondo said.

Cam replayed the spell in his mind. "You will go

first, then I shall follow. You must turn in a circle to initiate the spell that Melikar is certainly chanting below at this moment."

Cam tried to remember how he felt mere days ago when the spell moved him between worlds. "You will be drawn through the water, but you will not be aware of what is happening. That is part of the enchantment."

"Does it hurt?" Mondo jested, playfully placing a hand over his heart.

Before Cam could answer, Mondo tsked. "Oh, bother." Beneath the hand laid on his heart was a pocket. Mondo pulled out a silver object the size of his palm. "I forgot to return Sarah's cell phone."

"Her what?" Cam asked.

Mondo looked distraught. "Son, she needs this. I cannot take it with me."

Cam was torn between wanting to complete their journey or take care of this final task for his father. Home was so close. He tried not to think about it. "I shall return it to her."

"Are you certain?" Mondo asked, handing the object to Cam.

"Yes. Sarah and Hannah are still in the park. But I cannot be off until I see you safely home."

Mondo's smile was his answer. He embraced his son, then picked up his traveling bag. "Farewell for now," he said. "Please do not tarry. I shall not rest easy until you join me below the river."

"I promise," Cam said. Backing off the footbridge, he glanced about the area. No one was in sight to witness what was about to happen.

Clutching his bag to his chest, Mondo stepped slowly in a tight circle. Cam marveled at how well he looked. Was it still the effects of the powdered kemble fish? Or the knowledge that he was finally on his way home? Both, perhaps.

As Cam watched, a thick mist began to rise from the water in the wishing pool. At the same time, an earthy aroma filled the air, giving Cam a twinge. It smelled like Mandria, like home.

In the night shadows, the mist looked foreboding. Curling around the edges of the footbridge, the mist engulfed Mondo until he could no longer be seen. Below the bridge, the water in the wishing pool was swirling in a wide circle. Now the aura of magic filled the air, making Cam feel wistful.

In moments, the mist cleared, drifting away on the night's breeze. Mondo was gone. The water in the wishing pool calmed and became clear once more.

Cam returned to the crest of the bridge. Joy made him quick-hop a few steps of a Marnie jig. After almost a lifetime on Outer-Earth, his father was now with Melikar. Leaning over the railing, he gave a vigorous wave. "I shall follow as soon as I finish my final task in this world."

"Excuse me?" said a voice. Startled, Cam whirled about, not realizing a woman had come up behind him. Outer-Earth folk swarmed the area once more, oblivious to the magic still floating in the air.

Embarrassed, Cam avoided the woman's eyes as he snatched up his knapsack and made his way off the bridge, clutching what Mondo had called a "cell phone" in one hand. Hurrying back down the path toward the amusement park, he could not refrain from cursing one more stumbling block, keeping him from Mandria and his princess. "Devil dust!"

Was Melikar planting this conflict, or were his own emotions battling inside? All the years he longed to travel to this side of the pool, and now he was here. Why not tarry to study the moving contraptions and figure out how they worked? Perhaps he could describe them to the Marnies, and they could create an amusement park in Mandria. The possibility intrigued him.

Yet time was ticking away below the river. And that is where his heart truly longed to be.

Reaching the gate that led from the footpath into the amusement park, Cam stepped quickly past the activity, staying focused on his task. A commotion around one of the attractions caught his attention. A crowd had gathered, tittering and laughing.

Ignore it, he told himself, resisting the urge to have a peek and see what it was all about. Breaking into a run to hurry up his errand, he came to the brightly lit WonderLand archway then turned up a side path to the toddler playground.

Spotting Sarah was easy with her wild, choppy hair. She perched with Hannah and Mop atop a wooden horse, prancing on a platform strung with lights. The platform circled around and around while jaunty music played.

"Sarah!" he hollered.

Reacting to his shout, Sarah caught sight of him just as the circular platform whirled her from his view. In seconds, she appeared again and waved at him.

Their white-dappled steed lurched up, forward, and down, as if galloping. Did they not have real horses on Outer Earth? They had to create fake ones?

Cam took stock of the situation. *She cannot get off the contraption. I shall go to her.*

Grasping his knapsack, he leaped over a low fence and took a second leap onto the moving platform.

"Hey!" shouted a gruff-looking stranger. "You can't do that!"

Ignoring the man, Cam clutched a gold pole to steady himself, then made his way toward Sarah. Just as he reached her, the galloping horses began to slow and the moving floor glided to a stop.

Immediately, other parents with children riding the horses complained. "Look what you caused," they yelled at him.

"Why did you come back?" Sarah asked, confused.

He held out the silver object. "Mondo wanted to return this."

"Oh, my phone. He borrowed it after he cancelled his own. Thank you for bringing it back to me."

The gruff man ordered Cam off something he called a carousel.

"I am leaving," Cam told him.

"Not without paying for the ride, dude."

"Pardon?" Cam said. "I am not a duke."

"It's okay," Sarah told the stranger. "I'll pay for him."

Lifting Hannah off the horse, Sarah handed her over to Cam, then took coins from a pouch at her waist and gave them to the man. Shrugging, he took the money and left them alone.

Sarah led Cam away from the area. He was happy to have a few more moments with Hannah. The way she was grinning up at him twisted his heart.

Taking the baby from his arms, Sarah asked. "Did Mondo . . . ? Is he . . . ?"

"Yes. He is home in Mandria. I made sure of it before I came to find you."

"Oh, what a relief to know he actually made it home. Thank you. I'll be certain to tell Adam."

Cam bid her farewell once more, touching Hannah's cheek for the last time. "I must follow at once. Spells do not last forever."

With that, he sprinted down the walk and headed back through the amusement park toward the footpath to the wishing pool.

Whatever commotion was happening in the main area was still going on. Cam's curiosity was too great to pass the crowd twice and not see what was drawing their attention.

Bright lights flashing above the attraction read: "Bumper Cars." Cam had no idea what it meant, but he made his way past everyone to have a look.

Before him was a circular arena lit with colored lights. On the smooth floor were carriages like Sarah's, only much smaller. Lads and lasses were driving them, bumping into each other for fun.

What had the crowd so riled up? Cam craned his neck to see better. One child seemed to be putting on a show by making the carriages move the way he wanted—even making empty carriages bump into those with riders.

How could . . . ?

Baffled, Cam moved closer to observe this peculiar child, capable of causing such a sensation.

It was Baywin.

35

A Threat to the Kingdom

"Baywin!" Cam hollered. "What are you doing here?"

People in the crowd immediately focused on Cam.

"You know this kid?" a man asked.

Cam wished he hadn't been so quick to react.

"How does he do that?" shouted a girl. "He made those bumper cars move by themselves."

"Someone tell the park police this guy knows the weird kid in the strange clothes."

"Yeah," came another voice. "What's up with those clothes? He in a play or something?"

Cam's heart lurched up and down like the horse on the carousel. He edged back through the crowd. *I have to get Bay out of here!*

What were "park police"? Maybe they had authority over anyone breaking the law. Were they Outer-Earth lords? Knights? Or perhaps the king's soldiers?

Whoever they were, he did not wish to meet them. Circling the area, Cam realized that the crowd was enjoying the unusual entertainment and did not sense any danger. Climbing over the ropes, he hoped another gruff-voiced stranger did not yell at him and ask for coins.

How did Bay get here? What is he thinking? Why would he use his magic in front of people? Does he not realize the seriousness of his actions?

Surely Melikar knew Baywin was on the wrong side of the pool. Did the wizard have a hand in Mondo's forgetfulness, which had sent Cam back through the park? Perhaps Melikar knew that the only way to retrieve his errant apprentice was to send his older, more loyal one to nab the scoundrel.

Jumping over a low wall into the arena, Cam waited for an opportunity to dart past the bumper cars zipping in all directions. How could he get to Baywin?

The lad spotted him. Instantly, his delighted grin became a scowl. With a flick of his hand, the cars sped up. Lads and lasses stopped laughing and began to scream. Following Cam's lead, alarmed parents leaped over the wall and attempted to snatch their children out of harm's way.

A heartbeat later, the cars ground to a stop. Cam knew at once that one of the workers had shut down the attraction the way the carousel man had stopped the horses.

Children leaped from the bumper cars and raced to their parents. Cam darted across the area to whisk Baywin out of there.

The lad scrambled from his car and aimed both hands at Cam.

"Don't!" Cam shouted. "If you keep breaking Melikar's rules, he will strip you of your power and send you back to Cocklethorn."

Baywin froze, wide-eyed, as Cam's words sunk in. Lowering his hands, he dashed away from his pursuer and scrambled over the back wall of the arena.

"Catch him!" someone cried.

Cam was frantic. He had to nab Bay before anyone else did. How lucky that his threat stopped the lad from doing something horrible—*like turning me into a rat in front of all these people.*

In two steps, Cam was over the wall, chasing Baywin along a path that ran behind other attractions and past a sign that read: "Keep Out." The unlit, forbidden area was filled with machines, large and small, all humming. Ignoring the warning sign, Baywin darted into the area. Cam followed, stumbling in the dark.

A glance behind told him men wearing matching garments were gathering by the warning sign, presumably coming up with a plan for capture. Were these the "park police"? They did not look like knights to Cam, but then, few things in this world looked the same as in Mandria.

Heartened by the fact the men were not pursuing him, Cam bumbled through the maze of machines, lit only by the glow from the park. "Bay, stop! You do not understand the consequences of using your magic unwisely."

Cam meant the consequences for Mandria as well as

for Baywin personally. He did not know whether or not Melikar could indeed strip away the power of another wizard—old or young—yet he was glad he had the good sense to come up with a threat the lad might listen to.

Baywin's escape was blocked by a wall so high, the tallest trees in the forest could barely been seen over the top.

Good. I've got him cornered. He will have to listen to me now.

The lad considered the wall. A string of lights at the top danced in the breeze. He faced Cam. "I've heard amazing stories about this world. The princess even told me there are monsters here. I want to see everything for myself."

Monsters? Cam wasn't certain what the princess had meant.

"If *you* can come here," Baywin added, "then why can't I?"

Cam was not in the mood for explanations. "Fine. You are here; you had an adventure. Now let's go home."

"Did you see all the jolly fun things to do?" Bay exclaimed. "I want to explore a bit, then I'll go back. I promise. You go on without me." The lad paused, then added with a smirk, "Or do you need my magic to get you back?"

Cam ignored the insult, yet Bay had a point. Once Melikar cast the spell for him to return, he had to do so before the enchantment weakened. He did not know how long he would have to wait until another spell could be cast.

Long enough to lose the princess? his mind asked.

The question made him furious enough to narrow his eyes at the one who could always outdo him. "No, I do not need your magic. I need *you* to come with me. *Now.*"

"Later," Bay argued. "After I've had a bit of fun."

Cam stifled the urge to curse at the lad. Of *course*, someone Bay's age would be dazed and dazzled by the lights, music, and attractions. Before Cam could come up with another argument, the lad faced the wall, mumbled a few words, then leaped higher than humanly possible, landing on top. Cam was unable to follow, and he knew he could not trick Baywin into believing he could.

Voices and footsteps sounded in the forbidden area. Baywin jumped off the high wall to the opposite side and was gone.

Flattening himself against the wall, Cam stole along the outer boundary of the area, climbing over pipes and other obstacles. Could he slip away in the dark while his pursuers approached on the main path through the maze of machinery?

His success at escaping was doubtful enough to make him call upon the wizard. *Melikar! Can you help?* Cam hoped the wizard could somehow hear his panicked thoughts. *Get me out of here without being caught and help me find a way to bring Baywin back.*

Just to be safe, he made the same plea to the High Spirit.

Too much was at stake—Baywin's capture, his own future, and, more importantly, the secret of Mandria's existence.

36

Rescuing the Imp

Cam found a back way out of the area marked "Keep Out." It involved scaling a high fence and getting scratched up, but he made it to the other side without being seen.

Figuring it wasn't smart to remain in a deserted area, he circled back to the amusement park, quickly losing himself in the crowd. He felt grateful to be wearing Adam's old clothes. Other lads in the park sported long hair like his, which made blending in easier.

On the other hand, Baywin, in his Mandrian tunic, stuck out like a dragon in a herd of tunnel donkeys.

Knowing that Bay wanted to have "a bit of jolly fun" before going home meant he planned to return to the main area to try one of the other forms of entertainment.

What are the odds of me finding the knave before someone in the crowd recognizes him?

Sighing at the impossibility of his task, Cam figured

he might as well slip back into the forest and try to intercept the lad on his return from behind the wall—then overpower him.

His plan sounded flimsy. *How can I overpower one who has the magic to turn me into any number of harmless animals with a snap of his fingers?*

Frustrated, Cam made his way to the gate that marked the start of the footpath through the forest. Men in matching garments were there, too, guarding the entrance, peering closely at all who passed.

Cam knew who they were looking for: *Baywin and me.*

Nervous, he fell back into the crowd and searched for another way into the area. He wondered if Bay was watching him, waiting for him to give up and return to Mandria.

Not a chance. The thought of Baywin alone in this world made Cam shudder. Too dangerous.

While looking for a way to sneak past the men guarding the path, he worried what Mondo must be thinking—why did his son not follow him home, as promised? Surely, Melikar informed him of the unexpected change in plans.

Hiding behind a vendor's cart, Cam cursed this annoying twist of fate. He should be with Mondo now, on his way to reveal his identity to the king—and receive his blessing to court the princess.

"There he is!"

The shout yanked Cam out of his imaginings. Giving up on a chance to slip past the guards at the gate, he scrambled over a rock wall. A sign warned visitors to stay on designated paths, but Cam ignored it as he raced off into the dark forest, hoping to put as many trees and bushes between himself and his pursuers as he could.

No one came after him. Perhaps the person who shouted needed the assistance of the park soldiers.

Cam did not waste any time. He wound his way through underbrush until he spotted the high string of lights, pointing the way to the wall Bay had leaped from. He headed toward the lights, stumbling in the dark, hoping to find some sort of clue to tell him the direction the lad had gone.

What he found instead was the lad himself, lit by moonlight, sitting on the ground and leaning against the wall.

"There you are!" Cam snapped. "Stop playing foolish games and listen to me. This is serious."

Baywin blinked up at him as if his eyes were not seeing clearly. Cam steeled himself for an insulting jab, but none came. Instead, the lad began to cry.

"Bay, what is it?"

Cam knelt beside him—with caution—in case the lad's tears were a trick, conjured by a baby wizard.

"I feel horrible."

"Why? Did you eat something?"

"No. I was fine, then I . . . got weak and . . . Cam?" he pleaded. "I need to lie down. Can you find me a cot?"

"Lie down? Find a cot? Where do you think you are? Your mum's?" Cam took a closer look at the lad. His face seemed as pale as the moonlight; his brow felt feverish.

The truth ripped into Cam's mind as clearly as if Melikar was shouting it into his ear. "Bay! I know what is wrong with you. Did you not hear Melikar warn about what happens to enchanted beings in this world?"

"Yes, but he said he made up that story to stop you from wanting to come here."

"Ay, no," Cam groaned. "The part he made up was that it would apply to *me*. I am not a wizard. That's why I can be here and not be affected, but you cannot. You are a true enchanter—as you often like to remind me. In this world, you will sicken and—"

Cam stopped abruptly, unable to tell the lad he might die.

Baywin tried to lift a hand to Cam's arm, but it fell back by his side. "Please help me."

Cam could only imagine what might happen if the lad did indeed die here. *I will be held accountable. The park soldiers will arrest me and throw me into the dungeon. I will never get back to Mandria—and if I do, I shall be held accountable there.*

In spite of his annoyance with the wizard's new apprentice, he certainly did not wish him harm—especially a miserable death in another world.

"We have to get you to the wishing pool *now*," Cam said.

Baywin gave a puny yelp of agreement.

"Will you obey me and not fight or run away?"

"Yes."

"Will you listen to me and behave like a good citizen of our kingdom?"

Bay nodded.

"Will you promise never again to use your magic in this world?"

The lad could barely peep a reply.

Cam tried not to enjoy holding power over the scoundrel, but it was difficult. "Let's go then."

He helped the lad to his feet. Bay wobbled after only two steps.

"Too weak," he whined. "Need . . . to stay here till I feel better."

"You won't feel better until you get below the river. Do you not understand?"

With a quivering lip, he nodded. "Carry me?"

Cam had come to the same conclusion. Furthermore, he had a plan to hide the Mandrian garments. Opening his knapsack, he drew out one of the pieces Adam had called camouflage. "Here, put this on."

Baywin was too weak to obey, so Cam put the camouflage top over the lad's head and fished his arms out the sleeves. It hung below his knees. "The bottoms are too big, but this upper piece is long enough to cover your tunic."

Baywin did not like it. "Looks like . . . maiden's . . . gown. . . ."

Cam tried not to laugh. "Hush. It will keep folk from recognizing you—and you will not need to wear it for long."

He hoped the words he spoke were true. Hooking his knapsack over Baywin's thin shoulder, he hoisted the lad onto his back.

Turning in the general direction of the wishing pool, he cut through the shadowed forest to avoid the heavily traveled footpath—and, hopefully, the attention of the park soldiers.

37

Trapped

Huffing to catch his breath, Cam held tight to Baywin's legs as he fought his way through the dark underbrush. Staying far from the lights on the footpath, he kept moving in the direction of the river.

The problem would be the clearing. Trees stopped a good distance from the wishing pool. No way could they avoid crossing the open area.

Melikar, please—

"Stop, kid," came a voice.

A bright light exploded into Cam's eyes. He ducked his head to avoid the beam. Plans crashed together in his mind. Should he run? Or stay and try to bluff his way out?

"Walkers must stay on the path," the man with the torch told him. "This is a forest preserve. Didn't you read the signs? There's a fine for leaving the path."

Cam did not know what a "fine" was, but he knew he needed to obey a voice of authority.

"Bay," he whispered over one shoulder. "Be prepared to use your magic to help us get away from this person."

Baywin was breathing heavily even though he was not the one tearing through the forest. "But you made me promise . . . not to use magic . . ."

Ay, what a horrid time for the lad to start obeying me.

The man trained the light on the ground so Cam could see his way. Dodging bushes and flower beds, he moved to the path as instructed.

The man shut off the beam. "I must ask you to come with me."

"Where?" Cam asked.

"To the ranger station. You and your little brother will probably be evicted from the park."

"Any sign of the kids out there?" came a muted voice.

Cam flinched at the unexpected comment, confused about where the voice had come from. In the brighter lamplight on the path, the man peered at Cam and Baywin, studying them with greater interest.

Lifting something off his belt, he held it to his mouth. "Guess what?" he began.

Cam recognized the contraption. *It's a walkie-talkie, like Adam gave me.*

"I may have the fugitives you're looking for." He gave Cam an expectant look as if wanting confirmation that they were, indeed, the "fugitives."

Cam arranged his face to appear innocent. "Pardon? No, we were just hiking. My, uh, brother, wanted to explore off the path. Then he became tired, so I was carrying him back."

"Back is the *other* direction."

"He wants to see the wishing pool."

"Another time, kids." Into the walkie-talkie, the soldier said, "Got suspects in custody. Am bringing them in."

"Request assistance?" the voice in the box asked.

"Negative. I can handle two punks."

"Sire," Cam said as his mind zinged with a multitude of battle strategies. "What would it hurt if my brother just *looked* at the wishing pool, now that we're this close? He is sick, and he wants to have a drink of the water."

"What did you call me?"

Bats, I have said something foolish. He knows I do not belong here. "I—I do not remember."

"You can't drink from the pool. Are you crazy? You'd get sick."

"Truly?" Cam asked. This was news to him. He always wondered if magic from the world below somehow affected the water. Made it more alive, perhaps. "Please, could he just have a look? We, uh, do not live here. We may never be back again."

"Well, wherever you're from, you need a lesson in following rules." The soldier put away his walkie-talkie and slung the object with the bright light into a holder on his belt.

"Sorry to nip your sightseeing plans in the bud, but I aim to search your backpack, then take you in for questioning. Turn around."

Cam did not react. He was trying to decide if a backpack was the same as a knapsack.

The park soldier shoved Cam, forcing him to turn

around, then opened the knapsack hanging from Baywin's shoulder. "What's this?" he asked, pulling out the night-vision goggles. "How'd you get these? And what were you planning to do in the park with them?"

Cam didn't offer an explanation. He knew the soldier would find the walkie-talkies next.

"Property of the U.S. Army," the man said, reading the words on one of the units. "Okay, kid, this is way too suspicious. You got friends out in the woods, waiting for you?"

"No."

"Then who were you planning to use the walkie-talkies with?"

"No one. They were a gift."

"From whom? The Army? I don't think they hand these things out to civilians." Shoving everything back into the knapsack, he added, "You're in big trouble, guys. Let's go."

"Baywin," Cam said in a steady voice. "Now would be a good time to disregard what I said about . . . you know. Please?"

Bay's breathing sounded ragged. "I feel awful" was the lad's whiny reply. "I want to go home."

The park soldier pulled the silver tube from his belt and shone the light onto Baywin. "Hey, this boy is really sick. Let's get going."

"Not until we go to the wishing pool," Cam insisted.

The man switched the light to Cam's face, making Cam draw back and cover his eyes. "Do you think your kid brother is going to be healed by the water in the pool?"

"Yes, actually I do," Cam said. *By traveling through it, not by drinking it*, he added to himself.

Clicking off the light, the soldier unhooked the walkie-talkie from his belt. "Requesting back-up by the wishing pool," he said. "Suspects are resisting orders."

"Affirmative," came the reply.

Trying to stay calm in spite of the fact that his legs were shaking, Cam turned and walked briskly down the path toward the clearing, trusting that the park soldier did not have a sword with which to stop him.

"I'd rather not use force," the soldier hollered. "But if you keep walking, I will have to."

Cam did not falter in his steps nor turn around. He felt Bay come to life when the man shouted the threat.

The clatter of galloping horses—*real* horses—pounded in the distance, growing louder as more soldiers responded to the call for assistance.

"Bay! They're sending an army to arrest us. Do something!"

The air around him crackled with electricity. Cam turned to see what had happened. Where the soldier had been standing a moment before sat a squirrel, flicking its tail, seeming confused.

Cam grinned. "Excellent use of magic, little wizard!"

Baywin gave a weak snicker at the jest.

Not wanting to waste the opportunity, Cam hollered, "Hang on!" As he raced across the clearing toward the river, horses rounded the last bend. A glance over his shoulder made him falter. Five soldiers on horseback bore down upon them. Outer-Earth folk screamed and scattered from the path.

Cam wanted dearly to dash back into the forest and hide. "Melikar, help!" he shouted as he ran.

"I'm trying!" Bay yelped, even though Cam had not addressed him. "Something is amiss . . . with my power!"

Cam figured the lad's magic was fading as his life force faded. The realization surged panic through him, giving him a bolt of renewed resolve to get the lad back where he belonged.

More electricity crackled as Cam bounded onto the footbridge. People froze to gape at them.

Ignoring the spectators, Cam looked back to see what Bay's magic had done on the second try. Five squirrels?

No!

The soldiers were still there, sprawled on the ground—each one next to a gray rabbit. Bay's spell had worked on the horses, but not on the men.

Not caring who saw what, Cam centered himself in the middle of the bridge and turned in a tight circle to initiate the spell.

"Won't work . . . together," Bay moaned, as if in pain.

Cam had no reason to doubt him. Quickly he set the lad down, leaving his knapsack over Baywin's shoulder. "Do it!" he cried. "Now!"

Bay was so weak, he fell to his knees. The soldiers were getting up, trying to figure out what had happened to their horses.

"Around," Cam ordered, not knowing if he could touch Bay. The lad began to turn on his own, albeit on his hands and knees.

Swirling water met Cam's ears. It was the most wonderful sound in either world. *It's working!* Grinning, he watched the mist rise from the dark water and curl up over the edge of the bridge.

Folk who, seconds before, had been watching in stunned silence or backing away from a scene they did not understand, now ignored the two, wandering away as if nothing unusual was taking place. Cam knew Melikar was helping from below.

He glanced at the soldiers. They were walking toward the footbridge, but seemed bewildered, as if they'd forgotten why they were there.

When he looked back at Baywin, the lad was gone. The mist dissolved into the night air, and the water grew calm.

What now? Do I need to wait? Or can I initiate a new spell while the old one is still playing out?

"Young man, have you seen anything odd around here?" one of the soldiers asked.

"No, Sire," Cam answered.

"Did you just call me *Sire?*"

"Look, there's Officer Moran!" another hollered.

The first soldier emerged from the bushes, dusting leaves from his garments. Bay's squirrel spell had obviously been broken. Even this far away, Cam could tell by the man's movements that he was full of rage at being tricked.

"There he is!" the man shouted, barreling toward the wishing pool. "Grab him!"

Cam leaped to the crest of the footbridge and began to pivot as quickly as he could.

"What's he doing?" were the last words he heard.

The mist chilled his skin as it wrapped around him. Far away, he heard horses stamping and snorting, telling him the horses-to-gray-rabbits spell had broken as well.

He did not care, as long as his own spell—helped along by the wizard below the river—was working.

Before Cam's heart could beat once more, his mind faded to black, the park disappeared, and he remembered no more.

38

In the
Faery's Lair

The princess wrenched awake as if someone had snatched her from a dangerous dream. She squinted into the darkness, bewildered by her surroundings.

Something important had just happened. What would yank her awake, making her know her world had changed?

The only light in the dark chamber came from the glow of one candle, filtering through a thin curtain surrounding her bed and Ameka's. As Quinn focused on the hazy light, the events of the past day and night rushed back to her, swirling inside her heart as the weight of what she had done settled over her.

By now, the entire kingdom knows I fled.

And to where? To be trapped in a faery's lair?

Chilled, Quinn pulled the bedcovers about her. Her body ached from riding Nelyn for never-ending hours.

In the dark, she could hear Ameka breathing, which

223

comforted her. The princess had been so weary, she barely remembered the two of them being escorted by Bryok to this chamber to sleep.

Another unsettling thought tip-toed into her mind. They went to sleep at dawn, yet she sensed that more time had passed than a few hours. She felt as if she'd been sleeping much longer—perhaps an entire day and night.

Are we under a spell?

If it were true, then what tugged her awake so abruptly? A different type of enchantment?

Cam.

The princess sat up. Cam had returned to Mandria.

Joy filtered through the gloom. Circumstances did not seem so bleak knowing that Cam was back in her world.

How do you know for certain? her mind asked.

"I do not," she said. "I just feel it."

"W–what?" came a confused voice. "Did you call me? Are you well?"

Quinn laughed at her tutor, always attempting to take care of her student, even when barely awake.

"I am fine," Quinn said.

The princess could hear bedcovers rustling as Ameka came to life. "How long have we slept? I am not sure what day it is, nor the hour."

Hearing Ameka express the same concern made Quinn certain the feelings were true.

Shoving off the coverlet, the princess stepped onto the cold rock floor and drew back the curtain. The lone candle sat on a table between two baths. Steam rose from the water and disappeared in the flickering light.

Near the baths, fresh traveling gowns hung from an oak stand. Ameka's was purple like wind flowers, and Quinn's was the color of the skies of Outer Earth.

"Come look," Quinn said. "This is lovely."

"Ay, ay, ay!" Ameka answered as she rose. "I am sore from our ride."

"I share your pain," the princess answered in jest.

"Let me undo your braids," Ameka said.

Quinn perched on a stool while Ameka untangled the braids Cydlin had woven for the gala. The periwinkle buds were long lost.

In the soothing, fragrant bath, every bit of soreness and fatigue melted away. The princess had never felt so refreshed.

After they finished bathing and dressing in the new garments, the door opened. Prims paraded into the chamber, bringing pots of food. They arranged everything on the table, then marched out again, carrying the baths.

After they left, Quinn stepped to the portal to try the door latch. She feared it might be locked, but it moved in her hand. So. They were not being held against their will after all. Relief made the knot in her stomach relax enough to enjoy the morning feast of poached trega eggs—rare, but quite a delicacy, fresh peaches, warmed, a basket of honey loaves, and thorn-apple tea in silver goblets.

In the midst of the feast, the princess could not refrain from blurting, "Cam has returned to Mandria."

"Marvelous news!" Ameka exclaimed. "How did you learn this?"

"I do not know. The message leaped into my mind

like a tunnel toad, waking me."

"True?" Ameka watched her face as she sipped tea. "How do you think he will take the news of your disappearance?"

The question caught the princess off-guard. The room seemed to tilt as she considered an answer—or was that unbalanced feeling coming from inside of her?

Would Cam be sad to hear she was not in Mandria? She hoped so. He would be eager to tell her of his time in the other world and would likewise know that she would be eager to hear it.

Would he suspect the reason for her disappearance? How might he feel about her fleeing to keep from giving herself to someone she did not love?

More importantly, would she ever see him again?

"I—I do not know what Cam will think," was all Quinn could reply, yet Ameka's question would haunt her for days to come.

39

Under the River

Cam opened his eyes.

He was lying on the cobbled rock floor in the circle of light from the wishing pool high above. Every muscle in his body was tense from the panic of the past hour.

Once he realized he was home and safe, he relaxed and closed his eyes, willing the pleasant enchanted haze to overtake him once more.

"Cam!" spoke a strong voice.

His eyes flew open. Melikar hovered above him. "Get up, lad. If you stay within the spell, it will draw you back, and you'll never recover completely."

Shaking his head to clear the mist, Cam sat up, ecstatic to be back in Mandria and thrilled that his mission had been a success.

Then worry struck him. He peered up through the pool. "The soldiers—"

"Worry not," Melikar said. "They shall not recall any of it."

Cam's next thought was of his father. "Where is . . . ?"

"Mondo is sitting with Baywin. The lad is quite ill."

Baywin! Cam scrabbled to his feet. Bay was on his cot on the far side of the chamber. Mondo was patting the lad's feverish brow. "Will he be well?"

Melikar did not take his gaze off Cam. "He is young; he will be fine—and wiser, I hope, from his painful exercise in disobedience." The wizard laid a hand on Cam's shoulder. "You did well to bring him back so quickly. I am grateful."

Cam sensed something in Melikar's voice he had never heard before. Contemplating the wizard, he looked deep into the fiery-red eyes. It was so unlike Melikar to express emotion, and it touched Cam deeply. "Thank you, Sire."

"I am more concerned about you than Baywin," Melikar said. "What lies ahead now for Cam Dover of Kilmory Manor?"

Cam could not stop a wide grin from spreading across his face. At first he figured Mondo had told Melikar everything. Then he realized Mondo did not have to speak at all. From the beginning, the wizard knew the true identity of his apprentice. He knew that the lad he agreed to take in and raise did not possess the gift of enchantment. Not one single drop of magic.

But he *did* possess the blood of a nobleman's son. Melikar knew that, too, all these years.

Mondo rose and came to greet him. Years of Outer-Earth's summer sun and winter wind had been erased from Mondo's face. Surprised and puzzled at first, Cam glanced at Melikar, who nodded, as if he knew Cam would figure it out.

Of course. Mondo could not walk the avenues of Mandria with a face weathered by a sun that never rises in the underground kingdom. He would draw unwanted attention when he preferred to be anonymous. Now, dressed in Mandrian garments, he looked exactly the way a nobleman of his age should look.

"Welcome home, Son," Mondo said, embracing him. "You did well."

"I should be welcoming *you* home," Cam told him. "I am surprised you are still here and have not yet left for Kilmory."

"I chose to wait for you. We have business with the king first, yes?"

The wizard turned away at Mondo's words, yet Cam took a breath and boldly asked for his consent. "Sire, is it all right with you if I approach the king?"

Melikar faced Cam. The fond glint in his eyes had been replaced by a somber stare. The cryptic change in his demeanor worried Cam. Did he know something he was not telling?

"You do not need my permission anymore," the wizard said. "Go at once. Mondo has made arrangements. The king is expecting you."

Cam's knees almost gave out. *The king is expecting me!*

Knowing he could not walk through the castle wearing clothes from another world, he grabbed his knapsack—still sitting in the circle of light from its earlier return—and withdrew his Mandrian clothes.

"You mustn't wear those to meet with the king," Melikar said. "You are no longer a wizard's apprentice." He motioned toward the dressing area of the chamber. "You will find appropriate clothing there."

Cam moved to the alcove, where he found a basin of warm water and almond soap. Taking off Adam's belongings, he washed himself, smoothed his hair, then dressed in garments reflecting his nobility. The tunic matched the skies of Outer Earth and was made of the finest cloth woven by Marnies.

Melikar nodded his approval.

"Shall we depart?" asked Mondo.

Cam's conscience would not allow him to leave without checking on Baywin. "Give me a moment," he said, stepping across the chamber to the lad's cot.

Baywin looked small and pale. Cam thought he was sleeping, but the lad reached for his arm. "Yes?"

"Thank you," Baywin whispered. "You saved my life. I—I am sorry . . ."

"Shh–shh. Do not worry yourself about what came before," Cam told him, not knowing any other way to respond. Yet in that moment, with those few sincere words from the true wizard's apprentice, he knew the lad would no longer be his enemy.

Patting Baywin's hand, he said. "Be well. I shall come back to make sure you are up and about and causing trouble once again."

The lad gave a weak smile.

Turning, Cam was suddenly filled with confidence at what lay ahead. He was about to depart the wizard's chamber, yet this time, he did not feel as though he was leaving his only home.

Striding toward the portal, he said, "It is time."

Mondo, looking drawn but proud, followed him out the door and down the spiral rock stairs.

Together, he and his father would face the king.

40

Diggory Gardens

As soon as the breakfast feast ended, Prims returned to clear the table, leaving behind a traveling pouch. Quinn peeked inside. Food for their continuing journey was neatly wrapped, along with a vial of herbs.

Seeing the provisions was an immense relief. Quinn still teetered over the question of whether or not Bryok could be trusted. Why would the faery lavish such kindness and generosity onto her and Ameka? Would she require something of value in return?

The door opened again. This time, it was Bryok. Today, her spiky hair was the color of the moss that thrives in the grotto. Her gown shimmered in the candlelight as if it were woven of flames.

The Prim queen's face had changed as much as her hair. She was still recognizable, yet appeared older. Quinn assumed she was ageless and ancient, as were most enchanted creatures.

"Did you rest well?" Bryok asked.

"Yes, thank you," Ameka replied.

"And our food gave you comfort?"

"Very much so," Quinn said. "Thank you for your hospitality, but I believe it's time for us to continue our journey." The princess held her breath, hoping the Prim would not stall them any longer.

"Certainly," Bryok agreed. "Your ponies have been prepared for another long journey. I will take you to them."

Reassured, Quinn lifted the traveling pouch and followed Ameka and Bryok out of the chamber into the Prim village. The bustling area reminded her of the Marnie village, with its tiny cottages. However, these sported brightly painted doors, which immediately raised Quinn's spirits.

They passed many Prims of various sizes going about their days in enchanted light that seemed more golden than the light in Mandria. Soon they came to a stable with only two stalls. Quinn wondered if it had been conjured because it was needed, hence would disappear once the ponies were led out.

"I shall ride with you to the crossing at Diggory Gardens where you will continue your journey through Banyyan and on to Twickingham," Bryok told them.

"Will we be safe traveling through Banyyan?" Ameka asked.

"As long as you remain in our passageways. Had you foolishly continued the way you began, you would have been met at the border by Bromlians and immediately taken."

Her words made Quinn shudder. How naive they had been.

"The Prim tunnel is the only way to pass through the fallen kingdom without being detected," she told them.

Two Prims led Tyn and Nelyn from the stable. The ponies looked well-cared for, each brushed and bright-eyed.

Down the path came another Prim, leading Bryok's horse—a magnificent steed. The horse was much larger than the ponies, with a coat the rich color of the mahogany favored by Marnie crafters.

The maidens mounted the ponies, then followed Bryok from the village into a tunnel that seemed to open up for them as they rode.

Sitting atop Nelyn once more made the princess feel in control of her journey. How grateful she was, though, for the peculiar reception and kindness from creatures she had heard about only in ballads and tales.

In a short while, the tunnel widened, opening out into a spacious park, with trees, flowers, walking paths, and an enchanted sun much brighter than daylight in the Prim village. Quinn was taken aback when she saw the loveliness of it. The area reminded her of the queen's garden—the thought of which stung her with homesickness.

Bryok reined her horse, so the maidens did likewise.

"This is Diggory Gardens—a crossways and meeting place for our people. The gardens do not change or shift location, the way our passageways do. All tunnels lead here—as long as you wish it so. If evil approaches or danger is on your path, you may take refuge here. No one can do this without my consent, and you, dear lasses, have my permission."

"We are grateful to you," Ameka said.

Quinn nodded her agreement. "May I ask why you have been so generous? And how you knew we were in the path of danger in tunnels we thought were secret?"

Bryok turned to study Diggory Gardens as she considered her response. After a long hesitation, she replied. "Your wizard, Melikar, and I have been companions for a long, long time. I have helped him watch over you, the princess of Mandria, since your birth."

Quinn could not believe what she was hearing. Melikar had a companion? And she was a Prim queen? It made her realize how little she knew about the wizard she had adored and feared all her life.

Bryok turned her gaze upon Quinn. "You are unlike any princess born in the underground kingdoms. No other royal child would dare leave the safety and comfort of her castle to explore the outer tunnels, the grotto, or steal away to the Marnie village.

"Melikar did not want to stifle your spirit, so—with his magic and mine—we created a veil around you for protection. When you and your childmates stole away, you were always safe within our realm—even when passageways mimicked the main avenues and hidden tunnels, which are not as secret as you believed."

Quinn raised up in surprise at Bryok's words. All those times she and her childmates thought they were teasing danger, their surroundings were not what they appeared to be?

"The reason the veil was not around you when you

stole away during the banquet was because you quite caught the wizard by surprise and were gone before he could act. He was not expecting this course of events—especially on the night of the gala. That is why I stepped in to whisk you out of harm's way."

Quinn shook her head in disbelief, never suspecting that the frustration she felt against protocol or the rebelliousness that made her want to experience an unscripted life was clearly being monitored by Melikar—with Bryok's assistance.

"If you and your young companions had ventured outside our realm," Bryok continued, "harm would have found you—especially during times when a full moon shines on Outer Earth. Too many other-worldly beings roam on those nights."

"Ay," Quinn said, not quite knowing how to respond without sounding miffed at the trickery—not *harmful* trickery, of course, yet finding out that most of her childhood adventures had been altered by magic felt terribly disappointing. Still, the memories were true and pleasant, and she would always cherish them.

"I am grateful for your protection, as well as Melikar's," Quinn told the Prim queen, knowing it was fruitless to begrudge what had gone before. And, in truth, the enchanted veil had quite literally kept harm from befalling them, and for that she was relieved and grateful.

Now she *desired* protection. Needed it, in fact. "I wish to remain within the veil this entire journey, yet your mention of future danger makes me believe it is not possible."

"True," Bryok said. "Once you pass through Banyyan into Twickingham, you must leave our safe passageways to reach Pendrog Manor. There you will find Lord Ryswick and his son. As yet, they do not know of Ameka's disappearance. They believe she is safe in her cottage in Mandria. They *have* received news of the missing princess, but have no way of knowing that she is safe and on her way to Pendrog."

"I am so glad to hear this," Ameka said. "I feared our delay in your village may have resulted in my husband hearing of my disappearance and fearing for my life."

Quinn reached to touch Ameka in sympathy.

"One more thing," Bryok said. "The herb vial in your pouch is for your protection after you leave the safety of our tunnels. All you have to do is uncap it. Use it wisely. The enchantment will perform the task you need at the proper time, but can be used only once."

Quinn was bursting with a multitude of questions, yet before she could speak, Bryok tugged the reins of her horse and turned back toward the Prim village.

"Go in peace and safety," she said. "Princess, do not doubt your course. May you find what you seek." With that, she nudged her horse into a gallop and disappeared into the tunnel.

With a solemn sigh, Ameka locked gazes with the princess. "Let's be off then."

Nelyn was prancing in eagerness to continue. Quinn started off along a trail that wove into the heart of Diggory Gardens. Bordering the path grew linden blossoms, donkey ears, and lavender elf buds, peeking open.

The princess was glad to have a few moments surrounded by greenery, which soothed her. May lilies
floated in ponds. A scent not unlike the fresh air of
Outer Earth bathed her senses. The peace she felt as
the ponies trotted the garden pathways seemed like a
haven for her soul.

The pleasantness ended far too soon as thoughts of
what lay ahead twisted her heart. They were riding
toward a land torn apart by war, not knowing how their
sudden appearance might be received. Would Dagon be
angry at her? At Ameka? What about Lord Ryswick?

Peril lies ahead and peril lies behind, the princess
told herself.

Thinking about it only made her heart gallop faster
than Nelyn. She locked the worry and fear deep inside
in a tunnel of their own.

The ponies trotted to the end of the flower-lined path,
leaving the spaciousness of the gardens behind as they
entered a narrow tunnel. A sign by the entrance read:

> *This passage leads through*
> *the Kingdom of Banyyan.*

Quinn noted that it said "through" and not "to,"
which was exactly what Bryok had told them. Inhaling
the wonderfulness of Diggory one last time, she vowed
to keep its magic in her heart—no matter what this day
might bring.

41

The King's Announcement

At the marble entry to the royal tower, Cam and Mondo stopped to wait while a squire named Witten announced them to the king. Cam remembered Quinn mentioning this squire, saying he was smitten with her lady, Cydlin.

Witten returned. "You may enter."

The two stepped into the receiving chamber. King Marit sat at a desk in a massive oak chair, intricately designed. As he rose to greet them, Cam noticed an unreadable look on his face—troubled, and not particularly happy to see them.

Of course, the king was preoccupied by the war in the neighboring kingdoms, as well as the pressure on him to respond by sending an army. Still, the cool reception threw Cam off-kilter.

Feeling uncomfortable and self-conscious, he knelt in front of the king the way he was instructed as a young lad when he took lessons with the sons of noblemen.

Beside him, Mondo bowed low. "Forgive me for not kneeling, Your Highness. I have become an old man."

King Marit studied Mondo's face. "Is it really you? I was only a lad when you shocked the kingdom with your disappearance, yet I have never forgotten the aftermath."

"It is I. Mondo Dover of Kilmory Manor. I suppose Melikar has since told you the facts of my disappearance?"

"Yes, but only recently. I recall the funeral. The year of mourning. And how your father, before his death, reluctantly handed over the ownership of Kilmory to his sister, who passed it to her son, Blakely."

Mondo grimaced at the king's words. "My cousin Blakely may remain lord of the manor. I have no intention of taking away his title—as long as he allows me to live in my home for the rest of my days."

"I'll see to it that he does," the king promised. Turning to Cam, he raised an eyebrow in question.

"Your Highness," Mondo continued. "Please acknowledge Cam, the former wizard's apprentice, as my firstborn son, Cam Dover of Kilmory Manor."

The king stepped back, surprised. "Your *son*?"

Mondo nodded. "It's a Mandrian truth." Quickly, he told the story of why his son was brought to Mandria to grow up, yet could not return to the Dover family at Kilmory.

The king listened attentively, as if the story fascinated him. "I must say this news pleases me since I— and my daughter—have known young Cam all his life."

It is time, Cam told himself. He must not let his father continue to speak for him. He must step out and approach the king on his own. "Your Highness," Cam began, dropping again to one knee. "I have documents to prove everything my father says is true."

"I do not need to see documentation," the king told him. "Mondo's word is enough. However, you might need to convince Lord Blakely that you are the rightful heir to Kilmory Manor."

Cam did not wish to think about that now. He wanted to get to the urgent part of his visit. "Sire, may I continue?"

"You may."

Cam took a deep breath. *This is it,* he told himself. *Choose your words wisely.* "The reason I have come to you, other than to reveal my true identity, is to ask your permission to court the princess."

Both worlds stopped. Or at least that's how Cam's heart felt. Nothing could move or think or feel until he heard the king's reply.

He waited. Waited for the king to say yes. Or no. Waited for the king to say *anything.*

Instead, King Marit turned away, trudging back to the oak chair as though the walk across the chamber aged him twenty years.

Mondo was staring at his son in bewilderment. Cam realized his father had believed the visit with the king was solely to reveal his identity. He had not known his son also planned to declare his heart's intention to the king.

Cam rose to his feet, unsure if his shaking legs would hold him. "Your Highness? Have I overstepped protocol?"

I am too late. The princess is betrothed. The king does not want to tell me she has already chosen a husband.

Finally, King Marit focused on him. "Cam," he said in a melancholy tone. "I would be pleased to view you as a proper suitor for my daughter—you who have been her lifelong companion."

Cam had never heard such delicious words. He felt like shouting, or dancing, or—at the very least—thanking the High Spirit for bestowing such a rich blessing. Yet a foreboding sense told him that the next word on the king's tongue would be "however."

"However," the king continued, "my daughter is not here."

"That is fine," Cam said, actually relieved to have time to prepare himself before facing the princess when such important words needed to be said. "I can speak with her later."

The king's gaze did not waver. "You do not understand. She is not here in the castle—nor in Mandria. She is missing."

"Missing?" Cam and Mondo repeated at the same time.

A deep sadness touched the king's face as he quickly told them about the abrupt end to Dagon and Ameka's wedding celebration and the scheduling of the final gala.

Cam was stunned. He'd thought he had a three-day reprieve from worrying about the princess and the betrothal balls, yet the scroll had been rewritten while he was in the outer world.

"My daughter disappeared during the gala," the king continued. "I do not know if she was kidnapped or if she left on her own accord."

Cam had steeled himself to hear any number of reasons why his dream could not come true—but he had not expected to hear this.

His heart ripped in two. *She is gone!*

"I have sent soldiers into the tunnels. They are searching. No word has come back yet." Pausing, the king put a hand to his head as if he did not want to believe his own words. "This was not supposed to happen."

Cam wanted to leap into action. He could not come this far only to sit still and wait for the outcome. Standing tall, he said, "Your Highness, I shall join the search."

The king looked at Cam as if considering him for the first time. Even Mondo raised a brow at his son's bold comment.

"You will join the search?" the king repeated. "But you are not a soldier, nor have you horse, nor sword, nor shield."

Cam did not care. He wanted to be off this instant. What if the princess was in danger? He had an advantage over the soldiers. He knew about the secret tunnels; they did not.

Yet, the king was right. Without proper trappings, his search would be futile.

"Son," Mondo said, "it has been a full day. Come with me to Kilmory for the night, then we shall outfit you in the morning with steed and sword."

"But there is no time to waste," Cam argued.

Mondo looked to the king for an answer.

"Cam, you were my daughter's childmate. Perhaps you might have more luck than the soldiers. I fear for her life if she has been kidnapped, yet I fear even more that my stubborn daughter has simply run away from me. She may be hiding from my soldiers, not realizing the danger she is in as the enemy draws near to Mandria."

Nodding his head, as though the idea appealed to him more and more, the king continued. "Yes, go. Go search for her. And take this with you."

The king withdrew his sword from its leather scabbard. Cam stepped back, astounded. He had only dabbled in swordplay with his noble lesson mates, yet the king was offering him the finest sword in the kingdom.

"This has seen many battles and come out victorious. May it work the same for you."

Cam took the sword and held it in his hands. The silver blade glinted in the light. The basket hilt, made of pewter, was fashioned to look like a serpent, coiling around one's hand for protection.

Cam felt completely unworthy to receive such a magnificent gift—albeit the mere act of holding it made him stand taller and feel invincible. Speechless, he tied on the scabbard and slid the blade inside.

The king laid a hand on Cam's shoulder, surprising him by the lapse in protocol. "May the High Spirit give you the wisdom you need to find the princess." His voice broke as he added, "Please bring her home to us."

"Your Highness, I shall do my best."

Cam clutched the sword hilt so tightly, his hand began to ache. "I promise I shall not return to the castle until I have found her." Raising two fingers to his cheek, he gave the Sign of the Lorik.

With a trembling hand, the king returned the sign.

42

Questions and Clarifications: Quinn

⟡

The Prim tunnel was barely wide enough to allow two ponies to trot side by side, but that is the way Quinn and Ameka chose to travel because it allowed them to converse along the way.

The walls of the tunnel were the deep red of autumn oak leaves in the Mandrian forest. One could always tell when in Banyyan because of the crimson soil. The earthy scent seemed stronger, too—perhaps red earth was damper. Quinn shivered, noting that the air felt colder as well.

Hours passed. The sameness of their surroundings was tiring as well as boring, making the princess truly grateful for a traveling partner.

Ameka had just asked a question that gave Quinn pause: "When you become queen, will you keep Lord Blakely as a royal advisor?"

Ameka watched the princess with curious expectation, no doubt wondering why she hadn't answered.

"First," Quinn replied, "you're assuming I will become queen. I may have lost that opportunity the moment I walked out of the gala and chose not to return."

"Perhaps . . . but I think not. I'm sure your parents would give anything to know you are safe. They'd be so happy to welcome you back to Mandria, they would never think of stripping away your title."

Quinn hoped Ameka's words were true. Her heart flooded with guilt when she thought of her parents. Guilt and homesickness.

Why can't things go back to the way they were? Lessons with Ameka. Adventures with Cam. No talk of marriage or a future I am bound to by birth. Everything has changed in the past half-year.

"The *worst* that could happen," Ameka continued, "is finding the king's choice waiting to marry you upon your return."

Quinn shuddered, wondering who, in fact, her father had settled upon. Someone she found boorish? Conceited? Heartless?

"If that is the worst that could happen, wise counselor, pray tell, what is the *best*?"

"The best? Why, when you return, the king and queen will be so relieved, they shall forbid any future talk of betrothal balls."

The princess laughed at her ever-hopeful tutor. "I prefer the second scenario. Please arrange it at once."

"As you wish, Your Highness," Ameka jested. "Alas, the future is not mine to declare, but who shall stop me from bestowing it upon you here in this secret passageway?"

"Do keep entertaining me," the princess begged. "If only to stop ourselves from going mad on this perilous journey."

"I am doing my best."

"As for your query about Lord Blakely," Quinn continued. "When—or if—I become queen, he can very well turn his attention to the running of Kilmory Manor and keep his noble nose out of my hopes and wishes for the future of Mandria."

"And what might those hopes and wishes be?"

"I believe the first order of business shall be tossing the despised book of protocol into the deepest pool in the grotto."

"Here, here!" Ameka cheered. "Might I then give you a pat on the shoulder or a hug without being chastised by a guard?"

"Absolutely."

"What else will you do?" Ameka asked.

Possibilities rushed into Quinn's mind, reviving the energy this long trek was draining. "Most of our traditions are wonderful—like our harvest feasts, but many are unnecessary. Do I really need to be announced when I want to speak with my parents?"

Ameka did not answer. Quinn realized she was probably thinking of her own parents, who had been gone for several years—one dying directly after the other.

"Forgive me," the princess said. "I should not speak lightly of my mother and father."

"It is fine, love, and you are right. I was welcome in my parents' presence at any time. It breaks my heart when I witness how reserved the king and queen are with you."

Quinn felt the need to defend her parents' actions, so she added, "The king and queen are only following laws set down long before they were born."

"I understand. Still, I'm happy to know that the future queen shall rewrite the ancient laws."

Ameka's comment caught the princess by surprise, yet made perfect sense. *Yes,* she told herself. *I shall rewrite the dusty old decrees, and Lord Blakely can pack up and move to Bromlia if he does not care for it.*

"More please," Ameka said. "What else shall you change?"

"Stop, you are exhausting my head. Look at me making plans, not knowing if I shall spend my future sitting on Mandria's throne or in its dungeon."

Ameka gave her a look similar to ones she bestowed upon her whenever she had not done her lessons properly. "Well, then, allow me one more. The most important question of all."

"Proceed so we can be done with this frivolous conversation." Quinn spoke in a light tone so as not to offend her companion.

Ameka's demeanor became serious. "What of the rule that the princess must choose her betrothed before her sixteenth birthday?"

"*Off* the books with that one," the princess commanded. "And while we are at it, I shall proclaim that maidens of Mandria may cut their hair whenever they please—not only when their weddings are at hand."

Ameka was grinning at her. "I love this future

queen of Mandria. And who shall this queen choose for a king?"

The jesting mood came crashing down around Quinn's heart.

Ameka noted the change in her countenance. "Forgive me for asking too difficult a question."

"Ay, no. Do not apologize. I have an answer, and here it is. I shall chose a husband when I find him. I may be as old as Jalla, and perhaps as round, but if that is when I find true love, then that is when I shall marry, and not a moment sooner."

Ameka's smile showed how pleased she was with the answer.

As for the princess, she only wished she felt as sure of her words as she made them sound. Some decisions were too painful for her heart to ponder.

43

Home at Kilmory Manor

The king provided a carriage to take Mondo and Cam to Kilmory Manor. A messenger was sent ahead to inform Lord Blakely he had guests who were coming to stay indefinitely, by order of the king.

Cam could not hide his amusement as he sat inside the fancy carriage, listening to the clip-clop of horses' hooves trotting out the castle gate and down Mandria's main avenue. *Look at me. Leaving castle grounds in style and not slipping out in secret through the Prim door.* He loved the irony.

And better yet, the king had ordered Lord Blakely to receive him as a guest. *Me! The one he sneers at because the princess prefers my company to his.*

Kilmory Manor was not far from the castle, yet the winding route was one Cam had never taken. What reason did he have to visit Lord Blakely's home? How was he to know it was his home as well?

A series of tunnels left the main route and wound their way to the open hills of Kilmory. The grand house sat on a hill overlooking gardens and orchards.

The carriage stopped on a gravel path in front of the manor. Cam wondered if Lord Blakely would greet them, but he did not. His non-appearance made it clear how he felt about his uninvited guests.

Cam figured Lord Blakely might not mind Mondo's arrival—as long as he had the king's assurance that Mondo's intentions were not to usurp his lordship. However, Blakely would *not* be pleased to find out the true identity of the wizard's apprentice whom he had endlessly chastised over the years.

Stepping out of the carriage, Mondo paused before the manor house, taking it all in. Tears filled his eyes. "My home," he said, "has not changed since the day I departed for the last time."

A manservant named Lanyan greeted Kilmory's guests, then escorted them into an entry hall lit with dozens of candles. Walls were decorated with paintings of family members. Mondo paused to study them. Dabbing his eyes, he promised to introduce Cam to his ancestors on another day.

They followed Lanyan up a stone stairway to a wing with many guest chambers. Stopping before a portal, Lanyan opened the door and said to Mondo, "Welcome home, Sire. I trust this chamber will be to your liking."

Mondo assured him it would, then faced Cam. "I fear you will be gone before dawn on your quest. Therefore, I shall bid you good-night and farewell. I pray for safety and quick success on your venture."

Cam thanked him. "I shall not be able to sleep, so I may see about getting a horse at once and going on my way. I hope you will be comfortable here. I shall return as soon as possible."

Mondo embraced him. "Go then, Son, with the blessings of the High Spirit. I look forward to your return and to seeing the princess once again."

Whenever Mondo mentioned Quinn, it startled Cam. He had to remind himself that his father knew the princess and had welcomed her into his home in the other world.

Cam followed Lanyan down the corridor. The servant urged him to step quietly past several doors. "Master Ryswick's aunts came to stay with us after his wedding and shall return to Twickingham when passage is safe," he explained.

Upon entering his own chamber, Cam could not refrain from gasping. The room was fit for royalty. An oak bed filled barely a corner of the massive chamber.

"Does it suit you, Sire?" Lanyan asked.

For a moment, Cam did not realize *he* was the one being addressed since no one had ever called him "Sire."

"It is quite acceptable," Cam replied.

"It will be stocked with garments made for you. The tailor will be in tomorrow to find out your preferences. Anything else you need shall be supplied."

"What I need, Lanyan," Cam answered, "is a horse. I must depart at once."

Lanyan looked surprised, as if not believing anyone

could turn down the chance to live in such luxury. A young servant approached and handed a message to Lanyan. He read it, then looked at Cam with renewed interest. "The king has sent one of his knights, Sir Corin, to meet with you in the fencing chamber. I shall escort you there, then assemble what you need for your journey."

Eager to meet the knight, Cam gave one last look at the inviting bed in the quiet chamber, picked up his knapsack, and followed Lanyan to meet Sir Corin.

In the lower level of the manor, the servant left Cam in the fencing chamber. Decorating the walls were swords, shields, and the Dover family crest.

Cam studied the crest. Out of a dragon's mouth flowed the Mandrian River, as if the dragon had created the underground world. The dragon's wings were spread over a house, not unlike Kilmory Manor. He squinted to study the details, but weariness was settling over him like the dragon's wings.

He slumped to a bench below the family crest to wait for the knight—and promptly fell asleep.

44

The Conjured Chamber

$\mathcal{J}$ust as the princess was thinking she could not make Nelyn take one more step, the narrow tunnel opened into a furnished chamber—half curving into the earthen wall on one side of the path and half on the other.

"This looks like a good place to stop for the night," Ameka said.

Quinn wondered if her longing for a rest somehow made the chamber appear. Regardless, the sight of it was a huge relief since it answered the question of where they would stay the night.

Slipping from Nelyn's brocade blanket, the princess stretched her sore muscles, wishing for another bath like the one this morning, which magically eased her aches.

Light in the tunnel brightened, allowing them to see better. One side of the chamber was a makeshift stable with a pile of hay and oats for the ponies. The other side was partially hidden behind a curtain.

Quinn drew back the fabric. In a small area sat two cots with a table in between. On the table sat washing basins. *Amazing.* "Do you think this chamber was conjured for us?"

Ameka took it all in, wide-eyed. "I believe so. Thank you, Bryok," she whispered.

After taking care of the ponies and making sure their reins were wrapped tightly around a wooden post, the maidens freshened up and sat on the cots to share the food in the pouch. Quinn could not believe all that was inside: warm roast hen, ginger tea loaves, oranges, and mead—in just the right amounts to satisfy their hunger.

Ameka checked on the ponies, then withdrew to one of the cots, settling in for the night.

In spite of fatigue, Quinn wandered the area, ears alert, listening. Surely they would be protected here? There was no reason to doubt Bryok's promise of a safe passage, yet a latched door in the chamber would have made Quinn feel more secure. Never seeing anyone else on the path was eerie—especially while feeling as if unseen eyes were watching them.

"Rest, love," Ameka said. "No need to stand guard. I have a strong feeling we are being watched over."

"You are right," the princess said. "I suppose there is a big difference in being watched over and simply being watched."

"Pardon?"

"It is not important. Sleep well."

Quinn settled in beneath a coverlet on her cot.

Immediately, the enchanted glow began to fade until the dark of night—and exhaustion—made the two fall into a deep sleep.

45

Swordcraft

A jab in the chest brought Cam awake and to his feet.

"So this is what I have to work with?" said the man who had poked him with the hilt of a sword. He was shorter than Cam, but solid muscle. Fair hair hung into eyes that were scrutinizing his new student.

The man laughed to show he was jesting. "I am Sir Corin. The king sent me to teach you the skill of swordplay. I have also been instructed to give you these." Pausing, he reached into a pouch and withdrew two vials of herbs. "I do not know their purpose."

Cam did. He took the vials, knowing they had come from Melikar. The first was maidenhair, for alertness without rest, to refresh and restore his strength. Taking it now would ensure his ability to train with Sir Corin throughout the night without sleep.

He still had an unopened vial of maidenhair from

his trip to the other world, but perhaps he should keep it in case another dose was needed.

The second vial contained meadow bog for mental clarity, quick understanding, and instant recall of new information. In the days when he took lessons with the sons of nobles—arranged by Melikar to make sure he learned reading, writing, and social graces—he used to dip his finger into the wizard's supply of meadow bog to have a taste before examinations. The herb helped him recall answers with ease—but only answers he already knew.

Cam opened both vials and swallowed the contents. Immediately, renewed vigor coursed through him. Standing tall, he drew the sword given to him by the king. "Let's begin."

Sir Corin reacted with surprise. "What a magnificent weapon. Where did you acquire it?"

"It was . . . a gift," Cam replied, unsure of how much to say.

The knight proceeded to show him the proper way to wield a sword. He talked of strategy, of reading one's opponent by his actions and his eyes, and he explained the artistry of swordplay. The knight was patient and well-spoken, which helped Cam learn quickly.

They went at it for hours. Thanks to the maidenhair, Cam's muscles adapted without pain or soreness. He felt strong and focused, wielding the sword as though he'd learned the techniques when he was the age of a squire—as noble lads did.

"Well done, lad," Sir Corin finally said. "If you have any designs on becoming a knight, you now possess a necessary skill. And, I might add, you have quite a natural talent for swordplay—which should serve you well in the future."

Cam thanked him, wondering if he had, indeed, found the talent he lacked as an enchanter. Was it in his blood? As a descendant of all the knights of Kilmory?

The sword felt good in his hands—familiar even, as though he was re-learning a skill he had always known.

"Do you need instruction on riding?"

"No. I have ridden the tunnels many times," Cam told him, although he failed to mention that his skill in riding was limited to the princess's Paleo ponies.

"Let's be off to the stables, then. You may choose a steed to your liking and be on your way."

As they left the fencing chamber, enchanted dawn was sending its muted glow across the hills, slowly turning darkness into daylight. Cam had spent the entire night in training, yet felt fresh and eager to begin his journey.

This made him think of his sojourn to the outer world. Already it seemed long ago and far away, yet he'd left that world mere hours ago.

Now, here he was, embarking on another adventure— another quest—perhaps more exciting and dangerous than the last. How dull and dreary he'd imagined his life after leaving Melikar's service. So far, it had been neither.

Sir Corin led him to Kilmory's vast stable. "Some of these horses belong to knights," he said, "so are not for the choosing. Stroll around and find an available one you like."

Cam was a bit unnerved by the size of the steeds

compared to Quinn's ponies, yet he acted as if he knew what he was doing so Sir Corin wouldn't think him an inexperienced commoner.

As he toured the stable, the most magnificent horse kept drawing him back. Her mane and tail were the color of wheat against a chocolate flank. Each time he passed, she stretched her neck to nuzzle his hand.

Some of the stalls were hung with horse blankets displaying family crests, which told Cam those steeds already belonged to a knight. The chocolate beauty was in an unadorned stall, giving him hope that she had not been spoken for. Stroking her neck, he said, "This is the one I want."

"You have chosen well," Sir Corin told him. "Alas, you have also chosen the horse that belongs to Lord Blakely."

Cam yanked his hand away, immediately closing his mind to the idea of this wonderful creature belonging to him. "I shall choose another."

"Not necessary," came a gravelly voice from the portal. Lord Blakely had entered the stable and was watching the proceedings. Walking toward them, he tilted back his head to peer at Cam the way he did when trying to intimidate him.

Cam turned his back, unwilling to allow the man to act superior. By rights, Mondo was lord of Kilmory, and he, himself, was next in line. Lord Blakely had no right to condescend to him.

Cam continued his walk along the line of steeds to show he would do what he wished without the lord's permission.

"The horse's name is Ryanna," Lord Blakely continued. "If she is the one you desire, you may take her."

Cam faced his adversary. "Why? Why would you allow me to claim your horse?"

The lord held up both hands as if not understanding Cam's point. "You are my guest here at Kilmory. I do all I can to make my guests feel welcome. You are facing a long ride, and I know my girl, Ryanna, will be strong for the journey and will see you through."

The man's words sounded kind, yet his piercing eyes did not reflect generosity. Cam did not trust him. Was it a trick? *Does he expect me to defer to him by choosing a lesser steed? If so, I refuse to oblige him.*

"Very well," Cam said in a firm voice. "Please have her readied at once for my departure."

The set expression on Lord Blakely's face slipped at the former apprentice's boldness. After a too-long hesitation, he replied with a coldness in his voice that chilled the air. "As you wish." Turning away, he snapped his fingers at a stable lad.

Cam strode outside to wait as Sir Corin exchanged pleasantries with the lord. *What am I doing?* he asked himself. *Departing on a quest, riding Lord Blakely's steed, with King Marit's sword at my side?* Surely he was living a dream and would awaken on his cot by the wizard's hearth any moment and laugh at his own foolish fantasy.

Sir Corin appeared and grasped Cam's arm. "My work here is finished."

"Thank you for your time and expertise," Cam told him. "I am in your debt."

"My pleasure," the knight replied. "I look forward to hearing tales of your quest in the Great Hall upon your return." With that, he departed.

The stable boy led Ryanna out to him. *Ay, she is grand!* Cam thought, admiring the sleek coat and rippling muscles.

Lord Blakely followed. "I have one question before you depart," he said, no longer tingeing his words with disrespect since Cam had called his bluff. "What exactly are your intentions here at Kilmory?"

Cam knew what he meant. *He wants to know if I plan to insist on my rightful place as the manor lord—after my father is gone.*

Studying the scowl on a face he so despised, Cam knew he could ease the lord's worry with a few words of reassurance.

But why do that?

"Time will tell," is all Cam said. "Time will tell."

Lord Blakely's glower told Cam he clearly did not like the response. Trying not to smile at his own bravado, Cam realized it might be best to depart quickly before the lord changed his mind about Ryanna.

Taking hold of the reins, he led the horse to a mounting block, hooked his knapsack over one shoulder, and attempted to hoist himself up as skillfully as he could. Alas, Ryanna was twice the size of a pony so his effort was more wobbly than regal.

This was not lost on Lord Blakely who scoffed at the inept mount.

Cam did not care what the man thought. Yanking the reins, he coaxed the horse in the direction of the main tunnels, then trotted off to begin the second quest of his life.

A quest that seemed more dangerous and ripe for failure than his first had surely been.

46

The Search Begins

Cam's humble upbringing by the wizard was all that prevented him from filling up with his own wonderfulness as he traveled along a wide Mandrian avenue on his magnificent traveling companion, Ryanna. Cam was thankful to discover that, in spite of her height and girth, she was as easy to ride as one of Quinn's ponies.

The road was almost deserted, thanks to the early hour, offering him the opportunity to ride without having to dodge carriages, horses, and townsfolk.

Part of him worried that passersby might wonder how such a lowly lad had gotten himself a noble steed like Ryanna. Might they point out the oddity to a soldier and whisper that he might be a horse thief?

The thought made him nudge Ryanna into a gallop. Better to make it to the hidden tunnels before the roads filled with people. Besides, that is where his search for the princess would begin and, hopefully, end.

What a perfect place for Quinn to disappear. Who knew of their existence? Did the king's soldiers? Probably not, since he and his childmates certainly would have crossed paths with them, had they been as numerous in the out-of-way tunnels as they were on the main avenues.

Cam always wondered who built the short-ways. Prims? Regardless, he hoped Quinn was thinking the same as he—which often she was—and had chosen the hidden route as her refuge.

If the king's other scenario were true—that the princess had been kidnapped—then that was a whole other matter. Such things were possible and had happened to a Mandrian princess years ago.

Cam recalled how Tristans had snatched her away from her nanny outside castle walls and demanded gold for her return.

Unfortunately, he did not remember how that long-ago story played out—which made him tighten his hold on the reins. What if Quinn was *not* hiding to rebel against her father's strict adherence to protocol? What if she was indeed in danger?

Cam's worry gave renewed urgency to his mission. How would he stand against those who might have the princess under lock and key? The uncertainty was troublesome.

As he rode, Cam watched for the exact tunnel bay that contained the secret portal. He remembered the day he, Dagon, and Quinn had stumbled upon the door at the back of the secluded turn-out.

It'd happened on their very first adventure outside castle walls after he'd accidentally found the Prim door. They'd rushed into the tunnel bay to hide from an approaching carriage carrying the queen. Dagon had leaned against the stone wall in the tunnel bay to rest when it shifted, causing him to leap aside. As they watched, part of the wall swung open, revealing the tunnel beyond.

At first, they were too frightened to enter the unknown passage—yet how could they resist? The route was narrow; its enchanted light, dim. But the further they traveled, the more their cautiousness gave way to intrigue.

How lucky they'd felt that day. Their first adventure off to explore and look what they'd found—a mostly empty tunnel in which they could play a wild game of "Find the Dragon," then sit and talk without guards hovering.

Over the years, they rarely met travelers on the hidden route, and when they did, the strangers paid them no mind. No one ever seemed to notice the three emerging from the tunnel onto the main avenue. And when it was time to sneak back onto castle grounds, they headed down the nondescript side route that took them directly to the Prim door.

Finally, Cam spotted the peculiar tunnel bay. Steering Ryanna toward the turn-out, he passed a few early travelers and tried not to draw suspicion to himself.

Ryanna seemed to sense what he wanted and trotted willingly into the tunnel bay. Cam dismounted, as if he planned to rest—lest anyone be watching. But instead of resting, he led Ryanna deeper into the bay, wondering if other travelers had ever accidentally discovered the hidden door and what lay beyond it.

As he stood considering this, something on the ground caught his eye. A blue periwinkle bud. Odd for it to be here. It reminded him of the princess, who often wore flowers woven into her braid.

Cam pushed against the hidden door in the wall. It opened, spooking Ryanna. After a moment of prancing in place, she let Cam lead her through the portal, which closed by itself behind them.

Mounting, Cam let his eyes adjust to the lesser light, then spurred the horse on, maintaining a steady canter—not too fast—so his eyes could watch for clues along the way. Clues of the princess's whereabouts.

The maidenhair continued to work its magic. He felt alert, even though he had not slept since the previous night on Outer Earth. Matter of fact, his senses were so heightened, he felt as though he was being followed. Faint sounds of a rider behind him tensed his muscles. He hadn't thought much about it on the main avenue, but why was he still hearing the clatter of hooves inside the secret passage?

Pulling gently on Ryanna's reins, he stopped to listen. Whoever was traveling the secret route stopped as well.

What would a knight do? Circle back to face the knave stalking him? What if it brought him face to face with a Bromlian?

He wasn't quite ready to draw the king's sword against someone more experienced. He preferred multiple opportunities to practice before facing an actual challenger.

Cam shook off his worry and pushed ahead. Perhaps, without the benefit of maidenhair, his follower would tire and fall behind.

Hours passed, with nary a change in the scenery and nary a clue for him to gather. As Cam rounded yet another bend, the sight before him made him tug on the horse's reins to slow her.

Was it a solid wall? Or were his eyes deceiving him? How could the tunnel simply end?

Confused, he nudged Ryanna closer. In the dim light, he noticed a new tunnel of fresh earth, twisting sharply off to the left.

Since he had no other option, Cam followed the alternate passage, feeling as though someone meant for him to discover it.

The new route quickly became as drab and monotonous as the old one, making Cam wish for a traveling partner. Mere moments after thinking this, the tunnel opened up into a spacious park with trees, flower-lined paths, and bubbling streams. The sudden burst of color and heady scents surprised and delighted him.

Reigning his horse, he admired the beauty of the place. Its enchanted sun seemed brighter, immediately lifting Cam's spirits.

A sign next to the path read:

Diggory Gardens

"Who built this place?" he asked himself, wondering

about his exact location. He did not think he had come yet to Banyyan. In truth, he hoped the hidden tunnel bypassed the kingdom so he could travel around the danger undetected.

Cam loosened his grip on the reins to let Ryanna make her way to a pond for a drink. May lilies floated on top of the clear water. This would be an excellent place for the princess to hide.

After his horse refreshed herself, he vowed to search every inch of Diggory to see if she was here.

Now would also be a perfect opportunity to find out if he was, indeed, being followed, or if the maidenhair was causing his mind to conjure up his worst fears.

Nudging Ryanna off the path, he steered her into a grove of buttonball trees, slipped off her back, and hid behind the lush branches.

Cam did not have long to wait before sounds of an approaching rider met his ears. When the clopping of hooves stopped, he knew the rider had rounded the corner into Diggory Gardens. Surely he'd reigned his horse to stare in shock at the unexpected beauty, as Cam had done before him.

Quietly mounting Ryanna, Cam readied himself to charge after the knave. What if Lord Blakely had sent a spy? Or perhaps the king, with good intentions, had sent a knight to protect him if need be?

Whatever the stalker's motivation, Cam knew he must face him. Scarcely able to breathe, he waited for the rider to come into view.

And he did.

But it was not a spy on a mighty stallion, ready to

challenge him, nor a Mandrian knight, shadowing his journey. It was a lanky lad, plodding along on a scruffy tunnel donkey.

Cam could not believe his eyes.

The rider was Witten, the lowly squire from Mandria castle.

47

Where the Search Takes Him

∽

Relieved, yet curious (and a bit annoyed), Cam could not resist charging out of the buttonball grove with a shout to scare the lad and teach him a lesson.

Startled, the donkey stopped short, sending an equally startled Witten flying over its head and landing hard in a patch of cocklebur.

Ryanna pranced around the donkey as Cam peered down at the lad. "Why are you following me? And why are you riding a tunnel beast?"

Witten stood up, gingerly picking cockleburs off his tunic and posterior. He looked awful. Mussed hair and disheveled clothes. "I—I'm sorry. I want to join the search for the princess and fight the Bromlians. But I have no horse or sword."

"You are foolish," Cam told him, patting Ryanna's neck to keep her steady.

Witten bowed his head. "I want to earn my place as a Knight of the First Order so I can be worthy of . . ."

His voice trailed off, but Cam knew what he meant to say. *So I can be worthy of Cydlin.*

Cam sighed. He, himself, knew about doing foolish things out of love for a maiden. "How did you find this hidden tunnel?"

Witten looked up, as if eager to tell his story. "I thought I had lost you. You rode into a tunnel bay and did not ride out again. So I ventured in to look, and you had disappeared. I thought you had cast a spell."

Cam did not expect to hear that the lad thought magic was involved. Of course folk would think he had wizard's blood after a lifetime with Melikar. Oh, bother. Eventually, they'd realize he'd been an unwitting imposter all along.

"When I tried to remount the donkey," Witten continued, "he kicked out at me and hit the wall, which turned out not to be a wall at all, but a door."

Cam tried to hide his amusement. Better that Witten clumsily discover the hidden door than a soldier find it.

Adjusting Ryanna's blanket, he considered the dilemma. He did not want to be slowed down, yet how could he leave Witten alone without a horse or sword to protect himself?

"Turn the donkey loose in the garden," Cam told him. "He will be fine here with lots of apples to eat. And you," he added, "will ride with me. I do not know how far along this path I am going, but whatever my destination, it shall be yours as well."

Witten obeyed. Removing the blanket and reins from

the donkey, he slapped its flank. The donkey trotted directly toward an apple grove as if he'd understood Cam's comment.

"Can we not stay here and sleep?" Witten asked, swaying from fatigue. "I stayed awake all night, waiting for you to leave Kilmory so I could follow."

"Ay, you listened outside the king's chamber and knew of my plan?"

Witten looked too exhausted to deny spying.

Cam knew what to do. Opening his knapsack, he withdrew the spare vial of maidenhair. "Drink this. It will allow you to keep traveling without rest."

Witten opened the vial and drank the contents. In a few moments, he stood up straight and inhaled deeply, as if waking up after a long night's sleep.

"Holy toads and mugwort!" Witten exclaimed, making Cam laugh.

Reaching out one arm, he helped Witten swing up behind him onto Ryanna's back—extra blanket and reins in tow.

"We are going to search Diggory Gardens before we continue," Cam explained. "To see if the princess is here." Keeping the reins loose, he let Ryanna trot along the maze-like paths while he looked for any sign that they were not alone.

If Quinn was well-hidden, wouldn't she make herself known when she saw him? Realizing he was there to help? He hoped so.

The lush scenery was soothing. Elf buds, linden blossoms, and donkey ears lined the pathway. The air seemed fresher—not unlike the air of Outer Earth. A part of Cam wanted to stay here and never leave.

Immediately, the notion alarmed him. Was Diggory Gardens an illusion? A trick played upon them by Prims? Causing travelers to linger until they lost the will to leave, then found themselves bound to the gardens forever?

Cam's years as a wizard's apprentice taught him to be cautious about such things. As lovely as the gardens were, he saw no sign that anyone was here—save for the tunnel donkey. Time to travel on.

The flower-lined paths came to an end, narrowing once again into a tunnel. Cam took one last glance behind and noticed Witten was taking a wistful last look as well.

They plunged into the dim tunnel. Cam blinked to adjust to the lesser light. A sign ahead read:

*This passage leads through
the Kingdom of Banyyan.*

Cam hoped "through" meant "out of sight of the Bromlians." If not, they might have to defend themselves.

He sighed. Why couldn't fate have allowed him to find the princess in a timely manner? Preferably, within sight of Mandria and before running into peril—if, in fact, peril waited around the next bend.

Quests were never easy.

Witten was not much for conversation, so even with a traveling companion, Cam wearied of the long ride as day turned into evening. Nowhere along the way did he spot any sort of place the princess might be hiding.

Ryanna showed no sign of slowing down, but Cam

knew she would soon need rest and nourishment. How much farther would they have to travel? His mind reluctantly added, *Until I admit that the princess is not hiding in the secret tunnels, and I have been wrong all along.*

Where could she be? And, more importantly, was she safe?

"What is that?" Witten asked, yanking Cam from his imaginings.

Up ahead, the air in the tunnel shimmered, as if it were alive.

Cam slowed and took a good look. He knew exactly what it meant when the air went shimmery. An enchantment was present.

"Someone has cast a spell in this part of the tunnel," Cam whispered, in case the enchanter was still present.

Ryanna came to a stop without Cam pulling on the reins. She could also sense the magic.

"Is it safe to pass through?" Witten asked.

"It depends. If the spell is intended for us, it might be quite dangerous. If it has nothing to do with us, then we can pass without being affected."

"How do you know which it is?"

Cam was not sure he liked being the one who was supposed to know all the answers. "The spell is probably not intended for us since no one knows we're here." In his mind, he added, *No one human, at least.*

They waited, watching the shimmery light. Cam caught the scent of hay and also thought he heard the whinny of a pony. Yet to the eye, the tunnel was empty. While scrutinizing the area, he noticed for the first time the deep-red color of the earth. "Look at the color of the soil, Witten. We are still in Banyyan."

He could feel the lad shudder. "What if Bromlians are near?"

"I believe we are traveling in tunnels they do not know of," Cam replied.

"I want to *fight* the Bromlians," Witten insisted. "Not hide from them."

"You speak bravely for someone with no sword or shield. Do you think your tunnel donkey can outrun a Bromlian war horse?"

Witten did not answer, yet his courage made Cam wish to be equally bold. "We shall ride through the enchantment," he proclaimed. "Hang on."

Cam nudged Ryanna. She hesitated as if wanting to make sure her rider knew what he was doing. When he nudged her a second time, she plunged ahead, racing through the enchantment as if she believed the faster she ran, the less likely the magic was to affect them.

Cam liked this analogy and applied it to himself as well.

"We did it!" Witten shouted above the pounding hoof beats.

Cam relaxed, pushing ahead, yet his mind lingered over the enchantment. Why was it necessary in the middle of a secret tunnel? Who cast the spell? And for what reason?

He also felt defeated. *I must have guessed wrong. If Quinn came this way, Diggory Gardens would have been the best place to remain out of sight, yet have food and water at hand.*

Perhaps he should admit failure and return to Mandria.

You told the king you would not return without the princess.

Cam fidgeted in the saddle. What had made him so certain?

After a few more hours of riding—and the gradual fading of the red soil to brown—another sign appeared in the distance. Cam slowed so he could read it:

Twickingham

"Ay, we've traveled all the way to Twick!" he exclaimed. The great distance they'd covered surprised him—but, of course, the short-ways did not wind through every village between Mandria and Twick like the main passageways.

An inconsistency troubled his mind. Would the princess have come this far if her only purpose was to hide? If so, why? And if not, then where was she?

"Jolly good," Witten said.

"Why jolly good?"

"Twickingham is my home."

Cam did not know this, yet it was common for lads to leave their own lands and travel to different kingdoms to serve as pages, then squires, then to train as knights. Witten was obviously trying to hurry up the last step so he could become a knight as soon as possible.

The tunnel veered sharply to the left. At first, Cam thought they'd come to a solid wall, but as they approached, a door opened. He steered Ryanna through the door and into a tunnel bay that merged onto a main Twickingham avenue, much brighter than the dim passageway.

Cam glanced about for a landmark. When it was time to return to Mandria, he'd need to know how to find the exact tunnel bay that hid the entry to the secret route.

"Tell me where in Twickingham we are," he said, hoping Witten would mention a location that might stick in his mind.

"We are near Caer Larew."

"What is Caer Larew?" Cam asked.

"My home," Witten told him. "I must leave you here and go pay a visit to my mum. And since we have ended up in my homeland, I shall wish you well on your quest to find the princess, but I must stay behind to help my fellow Twicks rescue King Plumley from the enemy."

"I understand," Cam said, unsure whether he felt more disheartened over losing his traveling companion or because the lad had a home to go to, a mum to welcome him, and a quest that was certain—not clouded with mystery.

"And what about you?" Witten asked. "Where will your quest take you next?"

Cam did not have an answer because he did not have a plan. He had been so certain he would ride off to rescue the princess and be home before the evening feast. *How foolish I have been,* he scolded himself.

"If you do not have a bed for the night," Witten said, "why not come with me to Caer Larew to feast and rest?"

The invitation sounded wonderful—especially since he faced a night alone beneath a tree in somebody's orchard, with an evening feast of nuts and apples, plucked from surrounding branches. "Thank you. It is a kind offer. Which way, then?"

Witten pointed away from Twickingham. "If we take this avenue, I know a back way that will deliver us home without having to pass through the city gates and be questioned by the king's guards. They'll want to know who we are and why we want to enter Twickingham."

"Because of the war?" Cam asked.

"Exactly," Witten said. "The guards make it hard for anyone who wants to enter the city. Once, I was almost turned away even though I have lived here most of my life."

Cam was glad for the out-of-the-way path that led to Caer Larew. The less said to soldiers about who he was or what he was doing here, the better. He nudged Ryanna down the path away from the city gates. "Although you are home now," he began, "promise me you'll return to Mandria someday?" Cam was jesting because he knew the lad's heart remained in the far-away kingdom.

"I shall return," Witten said firmly. "So I can bring my bride home to Twick."

Cam smiled at the lad's well-planned life. Following Witten's directions, he cut up a narrow path off the main avenue. After a few minutes on this route, the tunnel opened out into a wide valley. Caer Larew, a small cottage with a goat in the yard, sat in the middle of a grove of angel trees.

Cam had never been here before, yet when he saw the quaint cottage with smoke curling from the chimney, he felt as if he were coming home, like Witten. He envied the lad's plan for his life. Love and marriage seemed so easily attainable—for the king's squire and the princess's lady.

For others, such as himself, it seemed impossible.

48

Twickingham

Light from enchanted sunbeams gradually brightened the conjured chamber deep in the hidden tunnel until the princess awoke. Rising from the cot, she felt amazingly refreshed. All the aches and pains from a full day of riding had vanished, just like waking from a long, leisurely sleep on her goose-feather bed in the royal chamber.

Again, she felt the same niggling sense they had slept far longer than one night—but perhaps that is how it felt to be truly rested. The only thing the princess remembered was the sound of a single horse galloping past at a furious clip sometime during the night and a lad shouting, "We did it!" But perhaps it was a dream.

Odd, too, not to know whether it was morning, midday, or evening for the rest of the underground world.

The growing brightness woke Ameka. "Morning, love," she said, yawning. "Too bad we do not have a warm feast to enjoy before our journey as we did yesterday. Bryok has spoiled me for life."

Curious to see if any food was left from the night before, Quinn opened the pouch. "Ay!" she exclaimed. "Lady Ryswick, come to your morning feast." Out of the pouch, Quinn drew spiced apples, warm scones with bits of sweetberries, and a flask of hot dragonwell tea. The two did not question their good fortune, but ate every crumb.

The water in the basins was warm, as though invisible Prims had poured it moments before the two awoke. Their gowns were clean and dust-free from yesterday's ride.

Across the way, the ponies were stomping and snuffling, as if eager for another day in the tunnels. Quinn and Ameka dressed quickly and prepared to leave. As they mounted the ponies, the chamber began to narrow into a tunnel once again with enchanted light pointing the way.

Quinn noticed the red-earthen walls and shuddered to think they'd stayed the night in Banyyan with the enemy all around, yet unable to see them. For the latter, she was grateful.

After riding for many hours—and watching the red earth gradually turn to brown—they came upon another sign: "Twickingham" was all it said.

"Thank the High Spirit, we are here!" Ameka exclaimed. "Twick will be my home from now on, so, as of this moment, you are my honored guest."

"Well, then, take me at once to Pendrog Manor," Quinn jested. "With haste, lass."

"I shall," Ameka told her. "I only hope this is the way."

As if in answer to her quip, the route twisted sharply to the left and seemed to end against a solid wall. Before they could react, a door in the wall opened. They steered the ponies through the narrow opening and found themselves deep in a tunnel bay. Another sign read:

> *You are leaving the safety of this route.*
> *Proceed with vigilance and watchfulness.*

Riding out of the tunnel bay, they merged on to a public avenue. Quinn could tell by the fading light that evening was approaching. This confirmed her notion that days and nights in the Prim tunnels did not flow the same as days and nights in the rest of the underground world. Regardless, what a relief to know they would soon be at Pendrog in time for the evening feast—and finished with this dreadful journey.

Ameka adjusted the hood of her traveling cape to hide her face and motioned for the princess to do the same. "We must speak only in hushed voices from here on."

Quinn arranged her own hood to hide her identity. "I agree. We do not know who might be listening." She looked for a landmark so she could locate the tunnel bay that led to the Prim path in case the need arose to turn back—or flee.

Bryok's words came to her. *Only those whom the Prims wish to find their doors and tunnels find them.*

This gave Quinn comfort as she directed Nelyn along the public route.

A few people hurried past, heads down, practically running. Twickingham's roads usually overflowed with activity since it was centermost of the underground kingdoms. Market days were big events. As for faires and jousting tournaments, Twickingham hosted more than any kingdom, even Mandria.

Odd to see the passageway so empty. A foreboding feeling gave Quinn pause. Why were people avoiding the roads?

Ameka urged Tyn close to Nelyn and spoke in a quiet voice. "Who might we say we are if asked?"

Quinn considered the question. Good to have an alternate identity, just in case. "I shall be . . . Lady Onyda," she whispered, saying the first name appearing in her mind. "And you shall be Lady Alvid."

"Alvid? What a dreadful name for a lady. May I not choose my own?"

Several men hurried past. The princess tried not to draw attention to herself by laughing at Ameka's response as she recalled where the awful name had come from: the knight who'd already chosen names for their future children. *Good riddance.*

"Of course, you may choose your own name."

"I shall be Lady Kilmory then."

"Pleased to meet you. Pray tell, Lady Kilmory, which avenue marks the way to Pendrog Manor?"

Ameka did not answer, yet she remained alert, looking at landmarks and trying to remember the route.

"I know you have been here only once, even though

you are the lady of the manor," Quinn said, wishing Ameka's first homecoming had not been interrupted by the war. "I have been here many times and should know the way, but alas, I do not. I never pay attention to the route from inside a royal carriage."

"We shall simply have to ask."

Ameka's words brought instant worry to Quinn. Asking might make them look suspicious.

"Can we not simply ride until we find a landmark to tweak our memory?"

Ameka agreed. "Your plan is the safest. It will have to do."

And it seemed like a good idea until Quinn saw King Plumley's guards ahead at the city gates, stopping travelers to question and identify them.

49

Disguising Identities

"You stay quiet," Ameka advised as they neared the city gate. "I would not want anyone to recognize you."

Quinn figured the guards were searching for anyone with a Bromlian accent who might be trying to slip into the city unnoticed. More worrisome was the possibility that she *could* be recognized since she'd visited Pendrog many times.

If recognized, what would prevent the guards from detaining her while a courier rushed to inform the king's soldiers? Surely reward offers had been posted in the main tunnels for information on the whereabouts of Mandria's princess.

Twisting her hair, Quinn tucked it inside her cape so the guards would see only part of her face beneath the hood and not the lengths of lion-colored hair that might identify her.

"Stop," demanded a young guard, who looked as young as a squire. "Names and destinations in Twick, please."

"Good day," Ameka said, greeting the two lads pleasantly. "I am Kilmory, and this is Onyda."

Quinn wondered why Ameka dropped the title of "Lady" from their invented names. She made them sound like commoners, but perhaps that was her plan.

"We are here to serve Lady Ryswick, the new wife of Master Ryswick of Pendrog Manor."

"I see," the guard said.

Quinn's pounding heart filled the quiet following the guard's skeptical reply. What if the lad knew the wife of Dagon was not even *in* Twick? And what if he noticed the richly brocaded pony blankets? Servants did not possess such finery. Their lie was obvious.

Worried, she watched the lad's eyes as he took in everything and wondered what he was thinking.

His gaze returned to Ameka's face. "Are you saying that the lady of the manor has requested lasses who are not from Twick to serve her?"

"True," Ameka told him. "We were with her before she married."

"In Mandria?"

"Yes. See the gifts she gave us for our journey?"

Quinn watched in amused surprise as Ameka deliberately drew his attention to the pony blankets— precisely what Quinn had hoped he would not notice.

The lad conferred with the other guard, slightly older, who had been watching and listening. The second guard circled them, studying the ponies and riders. "Tell us something about Mandria to prove you have been there."

Ameka started to answer, but the guard stopped her. "I want to hear the other lass speak." Reaching up, he yanked off the princess's hood.

Quinn's apprehension turned to anger. No one would dare treat royalty that way—if, in fact, he knew her identity.

Raising up tall on Nelyn's back, she answered. "In Mandria, avenues are lined with wych elms, the castle is larger than King Plumley's and is built of red stones imported from Banyyan. Marnies are more abundant, due to their loyalty to the wizard, Melikar. And a statue of King Marit-the-First stands in the main courtyard inside the castle gates."

When the guard hesitated, she added, "One ear of the statue is missing because of a rock thrown during the war with the Yannicks a hundred years ago."

The guards whispered together, but still did not seem convinced. "How have you managed to travel through Banyyan when it is overrun with the enemy?" asked the younger one.

"They have no grievance against two maidens traveling to be of service to their lady," Ameka explained. "They let us pass in peace."

Quinn was immensely grateful for Ameka's quick thinking and calmness. Glad also that her tutor was doing the talking. *She sounds so convincing, even I believe her.*

Still, the princess slid one hand toward the pouch given to them by the Prim queen, just in case the guards decided to turn them away. Without drawing attention to her actions, she slipped her hand inside the pouch and clasped the vial Bryok had given them.

As she did so, Bryok's words came back to her: *"Use it wisely. The enchantment will perform the task you need at the proper time. But it can be used only once."* Quinn's decision wavered. *What if a more urgent need for enchantment lay ahead? Yet what could be more urgent than not being allowed to enter Twickingham?*

The guards conferred again. "We do not believe the Bromlians let you pass through Banyyan without detaining you," the elder one said. "Perhaps the real truth is that you have been *sent* from Banyyan by the Bromlians."

Please allow us to enter the Kingdom of Twickingham.

Quinn silently spoke the request as she withdrew her hand from the pouch. She hoped the guard did not notice—or think she was reaching for a dagger.

He noticed.

"Capture them!" he hollered, lunging toward Quinn. The younger lad reached to pull Ameka from her pony.

Quinn barely had time to uncap the vial before being yanked from Nelyn's back. As the vial fell from her hands, the tangy scent of clary sage surrounded them.

Curious to see what would happen, she watched the face of the guard who had just pulled her from Nelyn's back. The alarmed tautness softened into a puzzled smile. "Allow me," he said, holding Nelyn steady so she could mount.

Quinn glanced at Ameka, who was being assisted by the younger guard who had pulled her from Tyn's back seconds before. *She does not know I opened the vial,*

Quinn thought, seeing the bewilderment on Ameka's face.

"Pray, sir," the princess said as if nothing odd had just happened. "Which avenue will lead us to Pendrog Manor?"

The younger guard pointed the way. "I suggest you make haste," he warned in a hushed voice. "We just received dire news and were warned to refuse entry to all travelers."

Quinn started to inquire about the "dire news," but chose to remain quiet, lest her question change their sudden good fortune.

Yet before she could nudge her pony through the city gate, the older lad grasped hold of Nelyn's bridle to draw her attention. "Lass, may I come call upon you while you are serving at Pendrog?"

It took a moment for the princess to realize the guard was asking to court her. The irony of the situation almost made her burst out laughing.

I am fleeing my kingdom to run from those who want to court me, and the first lad I meet in Twickingham wants to do the same.

She was afraid to say "no" since any lass who was truly on her way to become a lady-in-waiting would be honored to receive attention from one of the king's guards.

"That would be lovely," Quinn told him, demurely averting her eyes and pulling the hood back over her hair.

Bidding the guards good-bye, the maidens aimed their ponies toward the path to Pendrog. When they were out of earshot, Quinn confirmed to Ameka what she had done. They thanked the High Spirit—and

Bryok—then shared a good laugh over their dramatic acting.

"Everyone wants to court the princess," Ameka teased. "Even a bold commoner."

"At least he was interested in *me*," Quinn retorted, "and not who I am or how I might fill his future with riches. I admire a lad like that."

Ameka pretended to be shocked. "Do not go and fall in love with a commoner. We are in enough trouble already!"

Quinn laughed at Ameka's reaction, but inside, she added one more future change to royal protocol: A princess—or a regular lass—may receive suitors she fancies, regardless of who he is or his station in life. Someday she would make this a Mandrian truth.

50

Pendrog Manor

As the ponies trotted along the deserted road toward Pendrog Manor, Quinn recalled the soldier's warning of "dire news." Dread made her glance with suspicion at their surroundings. She could tell by Ameka's crinkled brow and hushed comments that she, too, was sensing the eeriness of the almost-empty passageways.

When the next person approached on foot, Quinn reined her pony. "Hello!" she called.

The Twick, caught up in his own thoughts, flinched at the unexpected greeting. Ameka gave a warning look not to reveal herself to strangers, yet Quinn's curiosity was too great.

"Pardon, sir," she asked. "Where are all the people?"

He looked at her as if she had dropped in from another world, which, in a way, she had. "Do you not know?" he huffed as if insulted by her foolish question.

"They are coming."

His answer was more confusing than enlightening. "*Who* is coming?" she asked.

The man gaped at her, as if thinking she must have no sense at all. Looking panicked, he squinted up and down the quiet tunnel, then broke into a run.

"We'd best get to Pendrog at once," Ameka said. "I do not like this at all. Something is about to happen; I can feel it." Nudging Tyn into a gallop, she headed toward the last tunnel to their destination.

Quinn encouraged Nelyn to follow at a brisk clip. The passage wound downward, opening up into a wide valley of rolling hills, orchards, and white cottages. In the midst sat Pendrog, looking more like a small castle than a manor house.

Seeing the familiar setting and the lazy smoke drifting above the kitchen chimneys untied the worried knot in Quinn's stomach. How wonderful to arrive at this welcoming place after the strangeness of the past few days.

At the manor gate, a guard stepped out to greet them.

Quinn waited for Ameka to speak, but she hesitated. Was she not sure how to identify herself?

The guard cocked his head. "Well? Are you going to tell me the purpose of your visit?"

"Pray, sir," Ameka said in a trembly voice. "Is Master Ryswick present?"

The guard studied her suspiciously. "That is information I cannot divulge. What business is it of yours? I am going to have to ask you to leave."

Bats, Quinn swore to herself. To get this far and be

stopped at the portal of their destination was too much.

"Sire," she began, purposely giving him more respect than was usually given to a guard. "We are here to serve the new Lady Ryswick."

Turning her face away, Quinn held her breath, hoping the guard did not recognize her, because she recognized him. He'd served Lord Ryswick for many years.

"The new lady is not at Pendrog," the guard answered. "Therefore, she has no need for maids."

"No, no. You do not understand," Ameka implored. "Dagon, . . . ay, pardon, I mean, Master Ryswick has brought us here in secret to be ready to greet his bride when she arrives."

The princess knew Ameka's approach was a wise one. The guard would never believe her if she revealed her true identity. The thought of Lady Ryswick arriving at Pendrog, travel-worn, on the back of a pony was ludicrous.

The guard hesitated. "If your words are true, then why was I not told to watch for the lady's maids?"

Ameka gave him a thoughtful smile. "With a war looming close and all of your many responsibilities, surely they do not burden you with such details as the arrival of the lady's servants?"

A modest shrug told them he got the point.

"Please," Ameka continued. "If we can send a message inside to Master Ryswick, he will be happy to welcome us. I promise."

Quinn held her breath, waiting for his reply. She wished they still had Bryok's enchantment, even though she felt they'd used it wisely.

The guard hollered for a servant. In seconds, a lad came bounding across the inner courtyard and stepped through the gate. The guard instructed him to find the younger Ryswick, tell him his wife's ladies had arrived, and ask what was he to do with them.

As the lad ran toward the house, Quinn prayed that Dagon would investigate the message before responding that he had not hired anyone and to send them away.

As they waited, the faraway sound of horses' hooves could be heard in the tunnels above the valley. At first, Quinn hoped it might be Dagon or her uncle, but it quickly became apparent the horsemen numbered more than a few.

As the guard froze to listen, his face paled. Grabbing an ox horn, he blew into it three times.

The unexpected noise spooked the ponies. Quinn fought to keep Nelyn steady.

"Be gone with you!" the guard shouted. "I have to seal the gate!"

"Wait!" Ameka yelled back. "You cannot leave us out here. It would be certain death, and you'd have Lord Ryswick to answer to."

The guard wavered, but only for a moment. "In with you then, and take cover if you value your life."

He widened the gate. Tyn leaped through the opening and galloped across the courtyard with Nelyn right behind. Quinn heard the heavy iron portcullis crash down behind the locked gate.

The courtyard came alive as people ran for cover. Lord Ryswick's soldiers poured out of doorways, racing to defend the walls of the manor.

Panic stole Quinn's breath. Never had she been close to real danger—at least not in this world. Blindly, she followed Ameka to the stable and dismounted. The livery master was not there to care for the ponies, so they tied the reins to a post.

Gathering up her skirts, Quinn ran toward the house she knew better than Ameka. "Let's try the servants' entry!" she called, hoping to avoid another stand-off with a guard at the main entrance.

She chanced a glance back toward the guard gate. Arrows were flying over the walls. *I must get Ameka to safety—and reunited with her husband.*

They burst through the servants' entry just as a burly woman came rushing to bolt the door. Startled by the unexpected appearance of strangers, she snatched up a cooking pot and held it like an axe above her head.

"We are not the enemy!" Ameka cried, lunging between the skillet-wielding maid and the princess.

Quinn could tell by the woman's angry face she did not believe Ameka. Through clenched teeth, the woman hissed, "Go out the way you came, and I will not hurt you."

The woman's shaky voice told Quinn she was more scared than menacing. "Please, ma'am," she said, stepping around Ameka. "We are family. Lord Ryswick is my uncle, and Dagon is my cousin. We were coming to surprise them, but obviously arrived at an untimely moment."

The woman lowered the cooking pot halfway, peering at Quinn's face with a glimmer of recognition. "True?"

Beside her, Quinn could see that Ameka was close to tears. Surely this was not the way she had imagined arriving at her new home. And to be this close to Dagon and be stopped by a servant who should know her as lady of the manor was too much.

"True," Quinn answered firmly. "And for your kindness and help, you shall be rewarded." Quickly reaching into her pocket, she drew out a generous handful of coins and gave them to the woman. "Tell me your name," she added.

In spite of her shocked reaction, the woman had the good sense to set the pan down and slip the coins into her apron. "I am Annah," she said.

"Annah," the princess continued. "I know Pendrog because I have been here many times." As she talked, she took hold of Ameka's hand. "If you tell me where the lord and his son are, we shall leave you be."

"They were in the tower with their guest, but now . . . they may have joined the battle. I do not know."

"Thank you."

Quinn steered Ameka through the kitchen and toward the stairway that led to the family tower.

"Thank you," Ameka said.

"Sometimes you save me; sometimes I save you."

The two exchanged smiles as they climbed the rock stairway from one level to the next. Quinn prayed she'd reach her cousin before he dashed out to face the attackers. Running down a narrow corridor that overlooked a banquet hall, they rounded a corner and came face to face with Dagon, emerging from a stairwell. He was dressed for battle, sword and helmet in hand.

All three came to an abrupt stop as the moment froze in their minds. The expression on Dagon's face was a mixture of shock and delight. In two steps he was at Ameka's side, dropping his battle gear and sweeping her into his arms.

No words were spoken. No words were needed.

Quinn's heart felt as if it was filled with fluttery trega birds at the sight. She looked away.

Pulling back, Dagon reached for Quinn, taking her by the shoulders. "I do not know why you are here, my missing cousin, but I am so relieved to find you safe. Safe! And here at Pendrog with my beloved."

Before Quinn could answer, he continued. "We are on our way to help our soldiers defend the manor, but first we must get you two to safety." Dagon retraced his steps and hollered up the narrow stairwell. "Are you coming?"

The princess thought Dagon was calling to his father, so she expected to see Lord Ryswick come flying down the steps.

But the person who came into view was not Lord Ryswick at all.

It was Cam.

51

The Reunion

When the ox horn sounded, Cam had been at Pendrog Manor a mere half hour, sitting in the tower with Dagon and Lord Ryswick, discussing where the princess might be and how to find her.

Before that, he had been resting at Caer Larew, after filling himself with mutton stew prepared by Witten's mum. The lad had casually mentioned nearby Pendrog Manor. The name had brought Cam to his feet.

Pendrog! Of course! Dagon would welcome him and assist in his search. Cam knew without a doubt that he must get to Pendrog at once, so Witten showed him the way.

At the blast of the ox horn, Lord Ryswick had rushed off to confer with his general. Dagon hurried to collect battle armor and hollered at a servant to equip Cam with the same.

Cam waited for the servant to locate the proper attire, but the man was too slow. More important to Cam was not losing track of his host. Grabbing his knapsack and checking to make sure the king's sword was sheathed tightly to his belt, he raced to catch up with Dagon while his mind whirled with the unfairness of it all. This was *not* supposed to be happening.

What is wrong with fate? Isn't it paying attention? I was supposed to ride off on this new quest and rescue the princess—or at least find her perfectly fine and not needing to be rescued at all.

Why had the Bromlians chosen this untimely moment to attack the manor? *Here I am with the king's sword and only one lesson on how to use it.*

Thoughts of impending doom flushed the back of his neck. *Am I to make it this far only to die outside of Mandria without ever laying eyes on the princess?*

As he pounded down a stairway, Cam heard Dagon holler up to him, "Are you coming?"

Dashing out of the stairwell, he almost collided with Dagon, who'd stopped in the corridor to speak with two . . .

The princess! Toads and mugwort and praise the High Spirit!

There she was, gaping at him with the same disbelief and astonishment that was surely painted on his own face as well.

She was dressed in a traveling gown the same outer-sky blue as his tunic. A hooded cape hid her hair, but oh, he would know that face, those eyes anywhere.

"You are here!" he exclaimed, restraining himself

from scooping her into his arms the way Dagon was holding his new wife.

"And you!" she cried, taking a step toward him as if she, too, was unsure how to greet an old friend who was no longer able to hide his true feelings. Could she tell?

"Ay, Cam," cried the princess. "I cannot say how wonderful it is to lay eyes upon you. I knew you had returned to us. I could feel it."

Her words surprised and touched him. "I have been searching for you," he said. "I promised your father I would bring you home."

The delight on her face faded from tenderness to sorrow.

Bats! I should not have said that.

"We must not tarry," Dagon said. "Ameka and Quinn will go at once to Pendrog's hidden chamber for safety while Cam and I face the enemy."

"No!" Ameka cried. "I have already come through much danger to be with you. I shall stay by your side."

The look on Dagon's face as he gazed at his wife almost broke Cam's heart.

"My love," Dagon said. "You are precious to me. I will do all I can to ensure your safety. And now, I am also responsible for the future queen of Mandria. I must insist that you both go to the safe chamber."

Leaning over a parapet, Dagon hollered at a servant in the banquet hall below. The lad immediately bounded upstairs to assist his master.

Ameka drew a trinket from around her neck, kissed it, and placed it over Dagon's head. "For luck, my knight, my husband."

The princess stepped close to speak to Cam. "I have nothing to give you for luck in battle," she told him. "Except this."

Raising upon her toes, she took his face into her hands and kissed his cheek.

Cam could feel everyone's stares and knew they were as stunned as he by the princess's bold break in protocol.

His heart did not care. In spite of his trembling knees and the breaking of Mandrian laws, he wrapped his arms around the princess and whispered into her ear, "I am so glad I found you."

To his surprise, she whispered back, "What took you so long?"

52

The Hidden Chamber

The princess's heart had not recovered from gazing into Cam's eyes or feeling his strong arms around her when Dagon's servant briskly hustled her and Ameka away to Pendrog's hidden chamber.

She felt as if she were floating down the steps. Ameka was talking. The servant was rushing them. Yet she heard nothing but her own mind playing back Cam's words and the look on his face when he saw her in the corridor.

The trio stopped before a cabinet that was really a door, but did not look like one. Although initially curious about the location of a hidden room she had not known existed, Quinn had not been paying attention, hence had no idea where the servant had taken them.

The door-disguised-as-a-cabinet was ajar. The

servant pushed it open and fairly shoved them through the thick-walled portal. Inside, another servant bolted the door.

The glow of candlelight warmed the stark area. A few elderly women and two young nannies were overseeing children and babies. They looked up in surprise at the arrival of strangers.

Ameka was still angry at being whisked away. She remained quiet while Quinn greeted the other women, who did not recognize her.

"I know we should be thankful to be here," Ameka whispered. "To be home at last. But this is not the way I was supposed to arrive at Pendrog—greeted by a skillet-wielding maid and hustled off by a servant to hide."

"I know," Quinn answered in sympathy. She steered Ameka across the chamber to a bench, away from the chatter of the women and children.

"We were to arrive in a decorated carriage for our reception," Ameka continued. "Three days of feasts and celebrations to which King Plumley was invited. And you, of course, and King Marit and Queen Leah."

Quinn settled in on the bench, hoping their stay here would be short. "I'm sorry it did not happen the way you'd hoped. But now you will have an exciting tale to entertain your future grandchildren."

This drew barely a hint of a smile from Ameka.

"You know what the High Spirit says," Quinn told her. "'When a journey begins with upheaval, it will end in peace and contentment.'"

"Thanks for your reassurance." Ameka said. Pulling off her traveling cape, she helped Quinn remove hers as well. "We are home now. No further need to hide our faces."

"*You* are home," Quinn said. "My journey continues."

"True, love. How I wish you could remain here with me."

"Please keep your invitation open. I may be in need of a new home." The princess winked to show she was only half jesting.

Ameka watched her face, yet did not respond.

"What? What are you thinking?" Quinn asked.

Ameka sighed. "He is in love with you."

"Pardon?"

"Cam. Cam loves you. It is impossible not to notice. I am wondering now, after seeing the joy on your face when you looked at him . . . I am wondering if the princess has found in Twickingham what she could not find in Mandria."

Ameka's words scorched her heart. Such thoughts were too new. Her mind was not ready to consider them.

"Do you really . . . ? Is it obvious . . . ? Ay, Ameka! Is what you are saying true? Do you think Cam has feelings for me?"

Ameka laughed.

"It is not a jest."

"I know, love, I am sorry. It has long been obvious to Dagon and me that Cam adores you. We knew protocol would not allow a match, so we said nothing, but we have been watching to see if his feelings were returned—or if perhaps, *he* is the reason the princess of Mandria has remained unbetrothed."

Quinn's insides were all a-tumble. "I do not know. I have never allowed myself. . . . Oh, but it's *Cam* of which we speak. He is my dear childmate and confidant. I care very much for him."

"Have you fallen in love?"

"Stop! These questions are too hard."

The door opened. A servant stepped in and came toward them, carrying a tray of cheese, sweetnut rolls, and fruit from the dragoneye tree, along with a flask of mead. "Annah in the kitchen sent this tray for you. I do not know how she knew you were here."

Ameka took the tray and thanked the servant. "We must eat and rest—however hard it might be to do so while a battle is raging around us."

"And," Quinn added, "when those most dear to us are in the midst of it."

Hearing her own words made the last few days come crashing down around the princess. Dropping her face into her hands, she sobbed—for herself, for Cam and Dagon in danger—and for the future of her kingdom.

53

Going into Battle

Cam could barely tear his thoughts away from the princess—how she looked as she stood there gazing at him, and . . . the kiss. The kiss! Her token of luck.

Stop, his mind told him. *You must pay attention.*

Cam drew his focus back to the fact that he was dashing alongside Dagon, racing toward a battle with the Bromlians.

The unknown terror ahead made him long for his previous quiet existence—sweeping the hearth in Melikar's chamber, fetching herbs from the Marnie gardens, or taking instruction in potions at the wizard's bench.

How was he to fight beside Dagon—a Knight of the First Order? Even with the king's lucky sword?

Dagon led him down a series of stairways to the lowest level of the manor. Unlocking a door at the end of a corridor, they stepped into a small chamber with nothing in it but another door.

"I need to send you on a special mission," he told Cam. "This is a secret entry to the manor. The door leads to a tunnel which exits on the far side of a hill beyond the manor wall."

Cam was surprised to learn of Pendrog's secret entries and hidden chambers.

"I must remain here to help my father command the battle," Dagon continued. "I need you to slip outside the wall to see how many of the enemy surround us and where their ranks are deepest. Keep out of sight and return by the same route."

"I have a better idea," Cam said, feeling bold.

"Pardon?"

Dagon had never acted superior to Cam since they had grown up together, but then, Cam had never offered battle suggestions to Dagon, the knight.

Quickly opening his knapsack, Cam pulled out Adam's walkie-talkies. "Take this," he said, handing one to Dagon. "I will keep the other. When I have something to report, you will hear my voice in the box."

Dagon looked at him as if Prims had snatched away Cam's good sense.

"Watch," Cam said. Turning his back, he moved to the far side of the chamber. Holding the object to his mouth, he pushed a button the way Adam had shown him, then whispered, "Dagon, this is Cam."

Dagon reared back as the voice spoke to him from the object in his hand. "Holy toads!" he exclaimed.

"To answer," Cam instructed, "push this button

and speak into the box, then release the button to hear my answer."

"Where did you . . . ?"

"I'll explain later," Cam said. Hoisting his belongings, he opened the inner door. The secret passage looked like a rabbit burrow, barely large enough for a person to scuttle through.

"Be safe," Dagon told him. "And return as quickly as possible."

"Safety to you as well," Cam answered. "Someone who waits in the hidden chamber is counting on you to stay alive."

As he turned to enter the passage, Dagon said. "I believe the same words could be said about you."

Cam moved quickly through the dank tunnel, feeling his way with his hands. Dagon's words echoed in his ears. He hoped he lived long enough to find out if the sentiment was true.

Fumbling his way to the end of the passage, he finally bumped against a door. Feeling for a latch, he opened it. Leaves and twigs rained down as he stepped outside into the dusky light of nightfall.

Perhaps it would be wise to leave his knapsack inside the door so he could move about less encumbered. But first, he removed the other gifts from Adam. Now he understood the purpose of the camouflage. He was near the enemy, yet he wore no armor. The garments would make him difficult to see in the fading light. Quickly he put them on over his clothes, then started to refasten the king's sword on his belt.

Cam hesitated. Did he really need a sword on a

spying mission? *It's not as if I'm going off into battle,* he reasoned. It would only be in his way, and . . . Cam realized his hesitancy was really due to the belief that the bumbling-wizard's-apprentice part of him would lose or break the sword, then have to face the king and explain his own ineptness.

Carefully removing the belt, he left the magnificent sword inside the door with his knapsack.

Cam slipped the walkie-talkie into a pocket, then quickly decided to take along the third gift Adam had given him. Looping the strap of the contraption around his neck, he was set.

Closing the chunky door, he took a minute to arrange more leaves and branches to hide the entry. Then he scanned the area, committing it to memory so he could find it again. The door was built into a hill in the midst of a grove of dragoneye fruit trees.

Taking a deep breath to calm his galloping heart, Cam moved along the side of the hill, trying to stay hidden in the underbrush. He circled back toward the manor house, walking as softly as possible to keep from rustling fallen leaves. In Mandria, the Marnies kept the underbrush in the orchards cleared, but Twickingham did not have near as many Marnies as Mandria.

As he walked, Cam touched his cheek as if clutching the token Quinn had given him to wear into battle.

You are not exactly going into battle, he told himself.

If his mind was tricking him, then he would claim the trickery. It was easier than believing he was putting his life at stake for the safety of Twickingham.

Yet, something told him this mission was about more

than defending one manor house in one kingdom. It was about fighting for the freedom of all the kingdoms.

What kept King Marit from seeing this? And why had he not sent Mandrian soldiers to aid his departed sister's kingdom? These were questions Cam thought about daily.

As he stepped carefully through the orchard, dire worries about the uncertain future of the kingdoms filled his mind. Enchanted dusk made it difficult to see, yet he could clearly make out torches in the distance and knew their source: Bromlians.

Cam stole as close as he dared, staying behind the soldiers, yet he knew they would have knights in the hills, watching to be sure no one attacked from the rear.

Hiding behind a fat triple berry bush, he adjusted the straps and cylinder contraption around his head. What had Adam called it? Night-vision goggles?

Ay, look at that! In spite of the dark, he could see soldiers pooling around the main gate and climbing ladders leaning against the wall. *Magic!*

Taking the walkie-talkie from his pocket, he called to Dagon. Immediately, the lad answered. "There are not hundreds of soldiers, as you feared. Half a hundred, perhaps, but they appear to be well equipped with scaling ladders, crossbows, and torches. They seem to be putting all their effort on the east wall and the main gate."

"How close are you to see all this?" Dagon's alarmed voice answered. "Fall back at once before they see you."

"I am not close. I am looking through . . . never mind. I will show you later."

"Excellent information," Dagon said. "Just what we need to defend the manor and plan a counter-attack. You have taken on this heroic quest with much bravery Cam. My father and I are indebted to you. I shall pass this along to him and his generals. As for you, please return immediately."

"I am on my way," Cam told him, not feeling heroic at all the way his heart was pounding from fear. He slipped the walkie-talkie into his pocket with shaking hands and removed the goggles. Backtracking, he made his way in the dim light, through the orchard, watching carefully for the exact grove of dragoneye trees.

Darkness made it difficult to walk without stumbling. He feared he was making too much noise. The moon of Outer Earth would come in handy at a time like this. Holding one of the cylinders to his eye helped him find his way without as much faltering.

At the hidden door, he dropped the goggles on the ground so he could pull off the camouflage garments, lest he encounter someone in the manor who thought he was the enemy.

"Stop!" came a loud voice from the darkness.

Before Cam could react, rough hands grabbed him and shoved him to the ground. Rolling onto his back, he looked up into the faces of two knights wearing battle stripes on their faces and the Bromlian crest on their chests.

Something hard and blunt came down on the side of his head.

He remembered no more.

54

The King
Responds

A shake of the shoulder woke the princess.

Opening her eyes, she peered around the candle-lit chamber, confused of her whereabouts.

Ameka shook her again, urging her to rise. "Dagon and Lord Ryswick are here with news."

Clarity drifted back: the arrival at Pendrog, the hidden chamber. Dagon and . . . if Dagon was back, then Cam would be, too.

Cam!

Rising from the bench, she stepped across the now-empty chamber. "Uncle!" she exclaimed, pleased to see Lord Ryswick.

He bowed to his royal niece, as was protocol. "I am happy you are here with us and thankful to know you are safe. We have news from your father."

Quinn stiffened as all sorts of possibilities worried her—the worst of which was the king's command for Twickingham soldiers to escort her back at once.

"How angry is he?" she asked.

"Not angry, love," Ameka answered. "He is relieved to hear of your safe arrival. And there's more." Stopping, she motioned to Dagon to continue.

"Your father has finally broken through his resistance to send Mandrian soldiers to push back the Bromlians. When he heard his own daughter was under attack here at Pendrog, it brought the war to his portal. Finally, he listened to *us*—instead of to Lord Blakely."

"Although I do not understand your decision to leave Mandria and travel here," Lord Ryswick added, "I am glad your action resulted in help coming our way. At this moment, King Millstoke is leading a Mandrian army of a thousand soldiers through Banyyan, reclaiming his kingdom. He will push on to Twickingham until every last Bromlian has fled."

The princess blinked away tears of relief and happiness. Who could have guessed that her act of defiance was, in fact, helping the underground kingdoms?

"Has Cam already departed for Mandria?" she asked, trying to inquire about him without sounding desperate for news. Her feelings were wounded by the notion that he would leave so quickly without first seeking her out to tell her.

Lord Ryswick and Dagon exchanged glances.

Quinn's heart rolled over. "What is it?"

"Love, sit for a minute," Ameka said, leading her to a bench.

Quinn sat as instructed because she could not imagine what sort of news they were about to tell her.

"Cam performed an amazingly brave deed for Pendrog—and for Twickingham," Lord Ryswick began.

"Quite courageous," Dagon added. "Unfortunately, on his return to the manor, he must have met up with Bromlians in the hills."

Quinn's mind refused to acknowledge their words. She could not bring herself to ask further questions.

"Cam is missing," Dagon told her. "We found his possessions and brought them inside." He motioned toward the portal, and there, indeed, sat the familiar knapsack—and a sword, which, to her amazement, she recognized as belonging to her father.

The princess's heart was squeezed so tightly, she could barely breathe in and out. *There is hope. He has been captured. We can rescue him.* She knew she needed to keep telling herself these things because she refused to allow any other ending to play out in her mind.

"Meanwhile," Lord Ryswick said. "You are free to leave this chamber and join us in the banquet hall for the evening feast. All is quiet now. The Bromlians have retreated because of darkness. We hope they will not be back in the morning."

"What a relief," Quinn said, thankful the fighting was over—at least for now. "If only we could figure out how to tell the enemy the Mandrian army is on its way. They would never stay behind to attempt another attack."

Dagon's head jerked up as if the princess's words triggered an idea. "Perhaps we can," he said. "And maybe we can determine Cam's whereabouts at the same time."

All eyes turned to him to hear more, but instead of speaking, he knelt and opened Cam's knapsack, sorting through its contents. "Ay, this is good!" he exclaimed, smiling up at them.

Quinn hurried over, trying to see what had pleased him. "What did you find? Please let me help."

"It's not what I found that's important. It's what I did *not* find." Dagon's explanation only confused the princess more.

He studied her a moment. "I *do* think you might be able to help. Come with me."

Bidding good-bye to Ameka and Lord Ryswick, he promised he and Quinn would join them soon in the banquet hall.

The princess hurried after her cousin, puzzled by his cryptic words and actions. Yet if his idea helped rescue the former wizard's apprentice—who refused to let go of her mind or her heart—then she would do anything Dagon asked.

55

In the Enemy's Lair

The first truth filtering into Cam's mind was the horrible throb in his head, making him moan in pain.

"He is waking," said a voice with an accent that was definitely Bromlian.

The past hours flowed thickly into Cam's consciousness: the attack on Pendrog. His mission to spy on the enemy. The capture.

Opening his eyes, Cam peered at his surroundings. He was in a shallow cave on the side of a hill, lit by a single candle held in place by rocks. He could hear voices outside the cave but could not see anyone. Moments later, a giant of a knight entered the cave. Holding a torch over Cam, he peered down at him.

Splashed across the man's left cheek were swatches of color the same deep purple as goat berries. In the flickering torchlight, the man in battle paint looked menacing.

Scooting away and sitting up, Cam glared at him. He hoped his outdoor dungeon was on a hill near Pendrog. If he'd been moved closer to the Bromlian border, escaping back to Pendrog might be impossible.

As he rubbed his head to ease the pain, he noticed a rope wrapped tightly around his ankle. The other end was tied to a tree outside the rock enclosure.

"Food," the Bromlian knight said. Handing Cam a chunk of bread topped with dried meat, he backed out of the cave and disappeared from sight.

Cam ate the meat at once, then nibbled at the stale bread, which was hardly fit for tunnel birds.

Snatches of conversation caught his attention. He strained to listen. From what he could tell, the Bromlians had buried those who had not survived the attack and were deciding whether to move on across Twickingham to meet up with other bands of fighters or stage a second attack on Pendrog at first light.

If only I could warn Dagon, Cam thought.

Then he realized, he could. Reaching into his pocket, he took out the walkie-talkie. What were the chances that Dagon would still be in earshot of the box?

Facing the back wall to muffle his voice, he started to whisper Dagon's name, but before he could say it, Dagon's voice called to him.

"Yes, I am here," Cam whispered back. "Lower your voice so the enemy does not hear. They are nearby."

"Are you well?" Dagon asked, sounding concerned.

"As well as can be expected, except for a knot the size of a thorn nut on the side of my head."

"What is your location?"

"I have yet to determine it. Somewhere on a hill in a half-cave. I must warn you. They speak of another attack at dawn." Cam was glad the Bromlians were too concerned with noisily eating and drinking to pay him much mind.

"Ay," Dagon said. "You must tell them that the Mandrian army, a thousand strong, is on its way."

Dagon's words made hope leap into Cam's heart. "True? Or is your message intended to scare them?"

"True. King Millstoke sent a message by way of a trega to let us know he had succeeded in securing Banyyan and has taken back his throne."

"Praise the High Spirit," Cam whispered. "Good news, indeed."

"There is more," Dagon said. "They are riding on to Twick without delay and should be here at dawn. The Bromlians do not stand a chance."

"I shall tell them but cannot make them believe me."

"I have an idea," Dagon said. "Can you set the talking box in a secluded place so they can hear a voice, but will not know from whence it came?"

"Of course."

"I shall wait to give you time to tell them the news. Whether or not they believe you, a voice from the dark should convince them."

"Brilliant," Cam said, pleased that Dagon had taken to the device from Outer Earth so quickly. Silently, he thanked Adam.

"And fear not," Dagon added. "We shall rescue you."

"Thank you," Cam said. "Now on to our quest."

Glancing around the dark cave, he wondered where

to plant the walkie-talkie. Outside would be best—and as far from where the Bromlians were gathered as he could place it.

Moving quietly to the rocky edge of the cave, he knelt, positioning what Dagon called the "talking box" in the bushes.

"The prisoner!" came a shout.

"No worry," said another. "He is tethered."

Quickly, Cam moved away from the hidden walkie-talkie and ventured out of the cave as far as the ankle rope would allow him to step. A few torches lit a large group of soldiers. He did not know how many more were within earshot. "Hello," he called. "I have news of importance to tell you."

Laughter was their response.

A torch moved toward him until he could see a man's painted face. "You, the enemy, have news for us?" he asked in a mocking tone. "Speak then."

Cam took a breath to steady his voice and hide his fear. "You might like to know that the Mandrian army is on its way to Twickingham."

"Not true!" the man said. Pivoting to his men, he hollered, "Do not listen to this Twick's lies."

Turning back to Cam, he asked, "Why do you wish to help us? We could end your life in an instant."

Cam's knees buckled, but he steadied himself against a boulder and willed his legs to stop trembling. Facing the knight, he said, "First, I am not a Twick. I am Mandrian."

"Perhaps he is a knight," another suggested. "Riding ahead of the army. We should hear what he has to say."

As the soldiers gathered around, pressing in on him from all sides, Cam thought of the princess waiting inside the manor house, and it emboldened him.

"Do not let him speak," warned another Bromlian, older than the rest. "He is not a Mandrian knight. Look at his odd clothes. He is plotting to deceive us."

"No, Sire," Cam responded, wanting to get his message out before they turned against him. "I am not a knight. I came in peace, and in peace I offer you information that will save your lives and the lives of many Bromlians. If you leave now, you shall not have to face the Mandrian army."

In the flickering torchlight, Cam could read uncertainty on the surrounding faces as they watched him and discussed the news among themselves.

"Listen, my children!" came a sudden voice from the darkness. Everyone, including Cam, flinched. Soldiers around him scuttled away, wide-eyed, then crept back as if trying to determine if a specter was among them.

"I am the High Spirit."

The Bromlians reacted strongly to the words. A few fled, some dropped to their knees, others drew back or locked arms in fear.

Cam was equally bewildered, yet remained close enough to listen since he knew where the voice was coming from. It took a moment to realize what was happening. He had been waiting for Dagon's voice to explode out of the darkness, loud and strong, frightening everyone.

He had not expected to hear the voice of the princess.

56

Voice from the Darkness

Quinn's hand shook so much as she held the odd black contraption to her mouth that Dagon had to hold her arm steady.

The fact that she could speak from Pendrog and her words could be heard far away by Cam—and his captors—was too amazing for her mind to accept. True, she recalled that folk in the outer world possessed similar objects that allowed them to speak with people who were not present.

Pretending to be the High Spirit accounted for the trembling. She begged the Spirit to forgive her for what she was doing, yet she was doing it to save a kingdom and to save a life. Surely, *many* lives.

"My children," she said into the box. "It is my will for you to sow peace, yet you sow destruction. I gave you a kingdom and a home, yet you desire more. You take away land that belongs to others. They are my children, too."

Quinn closed her eyes, trying to remember all she and Dagon had scripted for her to say. She hoped her words were being heard, causing the intended reaction, yet there was no way she could tell.

Dagon nudged her to continue.

"The lad you have captured is a peaceful citizen of Mandria. Release him at once and make this your first step in righting the wrong you have done against me.

"Be content with the gifts I have given you. Return to your land. Be well and happy there. Let others enjoy what I have given them.

"If you do not listen and obey, a great army shall appear with the dawn, and you shall never see your homeland again.

"Listen, my children."

Grinning, Dagon took the talking box from her hand and slipped it into his pocket. "Well done, High Spirit," he said, then gave a hearty laugh.

The princess took a breath, not quite ready to laugh about the trickery. "Do you think the High Spirit will forgive me for what I have done?"

"Ay, you have performed a miracle. If the enemy heard you and heeds your words, you and Cam will have done a great service for Twickingham and for all the kingdoms who fear the Bromlians."

"And if they ignore me?"

"When they see the Mandrian army arriving with the dawn, they will be sorry they did not believe your warning."

Foregoing protocol, Dagon gently took her chin in his

hand. "What is it, dear cousin? You should be happy."

"I shall not be happy until Cam returns safely to Pendrog."

"Dagon!" came a voice.

Dagon hastily retrieved the box from his pocket. "Speak, Cam."

"I have good news. My captors have fled like frightened tunnel rabbits."

"It worked!" Dagon exclaimed.

Grabbing the talking box from her cousin, Quinn spoke into it: "Cam of Mandria, return to Pendrog at once. I command you."

"I would be happy to do exactly that. However, the frightened rabbits took the torches and left me bound to a tree with no knife to cut myself loose. I shall have to stay here until dawn unless the High Spirit can perform another miracle."

Dagon motioned for Quinn to push the button so he could answer. "I will help the Spirit by sending out soldiers with torches to find you."

"Thank you," Cam said. "I shall watch for them."

Dagon winked at the princess. "Feel better?"

Now Quinn felt like returning his smile. In jest, she pushed him toward the door. "Quit stalling and go send off the searchers with their torches."

"Yes, Your Demanding Highness."

Turning serious, she added, "And thank you, m'lord. Thank you with all my heart."

57

Celebration

A thousand torches lit the Great Hall of Twickingham Castle. The air burst with joyful music from dulcimers, lyres, and mandolins. Twicks, Mandrians, and Banyyans danced and feasted well, boisterously celebrating the end of the Bromlian war.

At the blast of three trumpets, the crowd hushed. In strode King Plumley, released from captivity and returned to his castle. Cheers erupted in the hall as the beloved king greeted his guests. Ascending a wide, marble staircase, he sat on an ornately carved throne to watch the festivities.

Cam observed all this from the sidelines on shaking legs. He had not gotten much sleep last night after waiting in the damp cave until torches appeared in the distance. He shouted until he was hoarse, directing them to his outdoor dungeon.

Before the Twicks could reach him, a Bromlian soldier, about his age, slipped back to the cave to cut the rope, uttering apologies on behalf of his kingdom as he melted back into the dark forest.

Cam had rubbed his sore ankle, heartened by the fact that one of the enemy had enough honesty to return and set him free.

He stumbled toward the torches to meet his rescuers. From there, it was a long trek back to Pendrog. In spite of the late hour, half the house was waiting to greet him, but the only one Cam wanted to see was the princess.

When she finally appeared at his side, all he could think to say was, "You saved my life."

She had clasped his hand and answered. "It does not begin to match all the times you have saved mine."

Then she fussed over his bloodied face and thorn nut of a bump until Annah from the kitchen whisked him away to clean and bandage it.

Now, scrubbed and rested and dressed in garments borrowed from Dagon, he shuddered at the fate that could have befallen him if Quinn and Dagon had not intervened.

Another blast of trumpets silenced the rowdy crowd.

"Cam of Mandria," a voice thundered, snapping him back to attention. "Please approach the throne."

Cam adjusted the bandage around his forehead as he moved through the hall, following the same path the king had taken. Dagon and Ameka had joined King Plumley at the top of the steps, standing to his right. On the other side stood Lord Ryswick and the princess.

Cam stopped halfway up the marble steps as instructed and waited for the king to come to him. As the king approached, a page set a velvet pillow on the step in front of Cam. He knelt and bowed his head.

The king drew his sword and held it above Cam's head. "For your bravery in the midst of battle," he said. "For your wisdom and quick thinking. For your part in helping Twickingham rid itself of invaders and restore its rightful ruler, I, King Plumley, with the blessings of the High Spirit, knight you, Sir Cam of Mandria, the newest member of the First Order of Knights."

As he spoke the final decree, the king tapped Cam's head with his sword, then once on each shoulder. "You may rise," he said.

A great cheer filled the hall with as much elation as Cam was feeling in his heart. This had happened so fast, he hadn't had time to consider the meaning. Sir Cam! He could scarcely believe it.

King Plumley had urged him to stay and serve in Twickingham, but Cam declined out of loyalty to King Marit and to Melikar—not that they were the *only* reasons he chose to return to Mandria.

Facing the crowd, Cam punched the air in victory, which started another round of cheering. The irony was that now he did not have to worry what occupation awaited him in Mandria. He was a Knight of the First Order.

He did not need Lord Blakely's permission to live at Kilmory Manor. He would build a manor of his own with his wages.

He did not need the king's sword. He would return

it and craft one of his own with Grizzle's help.

And he did not need Mondo's papers to become worthy of the princess. He, Sir Cam, had become a "proper suitor" on his own merits.

The king invited Cam to circle the Hall, receiving thanks and congratulatory pats on the back, then to join the others at the royal table at the top of the stairs.

Music began to play—a lively estampie. Cam moved through the crowd quickly, modestly accepting thanks and praise. He was eager to make his way to the princess before she tired and departed for her chamber.

Unfortunately, every mother grabbed hold of him, urging him to dance with her daughter—or with *all* of her daughters. He joined one Clandeaux line to be polite, then begged off due to his injury.

Witten appeared, pounding him on the back in congratulations. The lad had decided to remain in Twick to serve King Plumley and earn enough to build a cottage for Cydlin.

"I have a feeling you shall do your kingdom proud," Cam told him. "As long as you never charge into battle on a tunnel donkey."

"Good advice," Witten said, laughing.

Finally making his way back to the marble steps, Cam was officially greeted by King Plumley, Dagon, and Ameka. He clasped arms with Lord Ryswick, then bowed to the princess.

"Are you going to dance with every single maiden in the hall except me?" she asked.

He cocked his head, studying her endearing expression of mock concern. "I would love to dance with you, but first, we have a lot to talk about."

"In that case, I am needing to be rescued from the noise and music. Shall we step outside on the balcony?"

Thrilled, he offered his arm.

The air was cooler on the balcony, which overlooked seven fountains in the courtyard below. In the distance, they could see Pendrog Manor nestled in the valley, aglow in candlelight. Cam had been musing about building a house similar to it, although he hoped he would never have need of a hidden room or a secret exit.

He faced the princess. Tonight she looked stunning in a gown the same rosy shade as bee balm in the queen's garden. A beaded headpiece covered her hair. Her beauty took his breath away.

How long had he dreamed of this moment? Being struck speechless was never part of his dream, yet this moment scared him far more than being at the mercy of the enemy.

"Tell me everything," Quinn said. "But foremost, how is Mondo?"

Cam realized she did not even know yet that Mondo was his father. "Mondo was well when last I saw him in Mandria."

"You saw him in Mandria?"

"Yes, I brought him home."

"Ay, how wonderful. I never thought I would see him again. And how is Sarah?"

"Sarah is fine, as is her baby, Hannah."

Quinn's expression softened when she heard the baby's name. "How perfect," she said.

"I have much to tell you about my quest," Cam

continued, "and something to give you," he added, remembering the journal Adam gave him to bring back for the princess. "But there will be lots of time for those things. At present, there is something important I must ask you."

Curiosity touched her face. He would have felt better if she looked as if she knew what he was about to ask. Should he kneel? Should he take her hand? *Don't be a dolt,* he told himself.

He stood up tall, afraid to touch her, afraid to look into her eyes, yet the latter, he could not resist.

"Princess," Cam began, clasping his hands together to keep them from shaking. "I want to ask permission to court you. To be considered a proper suitor."

In the hall, the music stopped as if all the world wanted to hear the princess's reply. Cam watched her face for a clue of what she was thinking. Her lips twitched in a smile, yet she said nothing.

The music started up again. This time, a spirited trebello. Its dizzyingly fast tempo matched the beating of Cam's heart. Should he repeat the question? Did she not understand?"

"You are too late," she told him.

The dancing in Cam's heart stopped. His throat closed up. What was she saying?

"I do not need any suitors. I have already made my choice."

You have? he said—or meant to say, but the words did not come out. He bowed his head, unable to look at her. "I feared I would be too late," he whispered, more to himself than to her.

"I feared you would be, too," she told him.

He chanced a look into her eyes. "What do you mean?"

She breathed in and out, as if the words were hard for her to say. "I made my choice, and my choice is you."

His heart rejoined the dancing. "You chose me? Even though I was not in the running?"

"It did not matter. My heart knew you were the perfect choice, but my head did not. When I finally stopped listening to what I was *supposed* to do . . . well . . ."

She gave him such an intense look, he swore the balcony tilted, making him reach hold of the railing to keep steady.

"Honestly, Cam, I did not realize what my heart was telling me until I found you here. Then I knew. I absolutely knew." Reaching up with both hands, she lifted off the beaded headpiece.

Cam drew back in surprise. Her lengths of golden locks were gone. "Ameka cut my hair," she told him. "For my betrothal."

Cam could not believe she had cut her hair for him—before he had even declared his love. Feeling bold, he reached for her hands, and she slid them into his grasp. It was a perfect fit. "I have always known," he told her.

"Why did you not tell me?"

"I was not allowed."

"Protocol," they both said at the same time.

"You chose me before I became a knight?"

She nodded. "Your title did not matter to me."

Deeply touched, Cam realized how much it meant to be her choice in spite of any title—or lack of one.

"The irony," he said, "is that I have always been qualified to court you. But I never knew it until mere days ago."

"True?" Her eyes blinked wide in curiosity. "Tell me."

"I will. But right now, there are other words more important to say." Taking a breath for courage, he pulled her into his arms and kissed her gently. She melted into his embrace.

Then he spoke the words he had known in his heart and dreamed of saying to his princess for as long as he could remember: "My heart embraces you."

In his ear, she whispered back, "For always and forever."

And Cam knew this declaration of love would become his favorite Mandrian truth.

Epilogue

One month after the end of the Bromlian War, on Princess Quinn's sixteenth birthday, she and Sir Cam Dover were married in the royal chapel in Mandria Castle.

Ameka stood with Quinn. Mondo stood with his son. Baywin carried the marriage bands—forged by Grizzle from the metal of Cam's magic ring.

Melikar cast a spell that caused the day to be so warm and cheerful, those who had once lived a sunny day on Outer Earth were happy to experience it once again.

The celebration lasted three days, shared with Dagon and Ameka, who had previously been unable to properly celebrate their marriage.

As a wedding gift, the king and queen built a wing onto Mandria castle for their daughter and new son.

Soon it was filled with a young prince and princess, who chased Scrabit, visited Melikar's chamber, explored with Baywin, and played at the kingdom's amusement park, UnderLand, built by Marnies.

Adam's gifts from Outer Earth—along with the princess's journal describing her time there—were placed in a museum to be studied with great curiosity by future generations, although the magic that made the talking boxes work faded with time.

Melikar sent a message to the outer world by red-feathered trega to let those who cared know how the story ended.

As for the princess and the wizard's former apprentice? They lived happily ever under.

Always and forever.

Cam's Quest

What came before . . .

Caught between two worlds and an ancient fear,
a young princess and her adoring Cam, apprentice
to the wizard Melikar, embark on separate journeys—
inward and outward, amazing and terrifying. Between
the secrets and the magic lie love and betrayal.

Will they find their way back to one another?

Discover the beginning of the story of
Princess Quinn and wizard's apprentice in
the updated and expanded edition of:

Princess Nevermore

By Dian Curtis Regan

Available now at your local bookstores and libraries.